MW01147479

A Time To Dance A Time To Run

By

R. H. Miller

1663 Liberty Drive, Suite 200
Bloomington, Indiana 47403
(800) 839-8640
www.authorhouse.com

First published by AuthorHouse 04/29/04

ISBN: 1-4184-2516-8 (sc)
ISBN: 1-4184-2515-X (dj)

Library of Congress Control Number: 2004105315

Printed in the United States of America
Bloomington, Indiana

This book is printed on acid-free paper.

Chapter 1

It was always startling to watch from a distance as the trains would leave the hillside and seem to float through the middle of Wuppertal between the buildings. They were suspended from the trestle built above the Wupper River and followed the river's course through the city. The trains were so punctual that Maria and her mother, Anna, could set their watches by their passing, which were punctuated by the sound of their whistles as they drifted through their open window.

Maria and her mother lived in the suburb of Wuppertal called Eberfeld in an apartment that sat part of the way up a hill. It looked over the city and the valley. Many of the opera singers and ballet dancers from the theater lived in this part of the city - many of them in the same building. The pastoral view appealed to their artistic sensibilities. The houses and other buildings on the hills sparkled like colorful gems on the green velvet meadows. At dusk, the enchanting yet orderly lights of the city gradually dispersed into random specks of light on the hillsides surrounding the valley. It was difficult to discern where the mountains ended and the black bespeckeled sky began.

One warm spring evening after dinner, Maria and her mother were looking out their window at the serene valley. Anna was knitting while Maria was lost in her thoughts about *Spectre de la Rose,* the ballet she was working on. The smell of warm bread from the bakery a few buildings down the street mingled with the sweet fragrance of spring buds that drifted through the windowsill on a light breeze. Through the din of the city, they heard the yelps of playing children. An anonymous trolley clanked along the street urged on by the occasional honk of a horn. The lazy clop of horses' hooves would start and stop as some delivery wagon made its way through the neighborhood. Maria thought it was wonderful to sit and think as the city was putting itself to bed. The familiar sounds of the city rekindled her longing for Frankfurt and her brothers.

Suddenly, the tranquillity was interrupted by the distinct hum of bombers in the distance. Simultaneously, the frightful wail of the air-raid sirens wrapped itself around the city and pierced into the darkness like a dagger made of sound. The bombers had been arriving at about this time in the evening for about a week or so. The people had been informed that they were relatively safe in Wuppertal during many of the routine practice air-raid drills; they were told that the pilots used Wuppertal as a landmark to turn south and head for Cologne.

Maria was immediately snapped out of her daydreaming. She and her mother knew the war was raging, but these flights were a jarring harsh reminder of how lucky they were to live in Wuppertal. For some reason, this city was being spared. It had never been bombed. It was rumored that it was being saved to serve as a center for the occupation troops of the American plutocrats if that time would ever come. In fact, the Germans had a saying about the Americans. "*Wiesbaden und Wuppertal das wollen wir verschonen für die Plutocraten drin zu wohnen.*" Translated, that meant that Wiesbaden and Wuppertal were being spared as a place for the plutocrats to live. Aside from participating in the ever-present air-raid drills, and these disconcerting flights, they felt safe for the time being.

The air-raid sirens continued to menace the night. Traffic screeched to a halt. Traffic lights went out. As had happened many times before, city lights went out. The mountainsides went black. The two of them turned off all their lights in the apartment, as they were accustomed to do. They were rather nonchalant as they sat at the window looking out at a black world drowning in a deafening drone. This was a regular nightly routine for them. Besides, the radio announcer had broadcast that the air-raid was to be on Cologne. They were not concerned about the bombings because these broadcasts were usually accurate.

"There they go again," Maria's mother said. "I'm sure glad we don't live in Cologne. They are really getting hit day after day."

"Yes," Maria agreed. "Poor Cologne is going to get it again. I can't even imagine how bad it must be there."

Abruptly, the night sky turned into bright, terrifying daylight. The entire city jumped out of the black as if it had emerged from hell. They could even see colors.

"My God! It's a Christmas tree!" Maria screamed.

They had heard of, but had never actually seen, the flares that light up the sky so the bomber pilots could see their targets. Then, several more shattered the darkness with harsh, brilliant light.

Maria could not believe the reality of it all. "My God. They're going to bomb Wuppertal!" She yelled, her voice tinged with panic. "Let's get to shelter!"

"Oh my God in Heaven!! What are we going to do!?" Anna yelled, looking up for God.

They had been through hundreds of air-raid drills, so they should have been prepared for this moment. However, nothing can prepare you for the precise moment when death begins to seek you from the sky, and this was the first time they had ever been in a bombing. The bombs began to explode everywhere before the last word left Anna's mouth.

Maria ran to the closet, grabbed her clothes, and threw them on the bed. They had been trained during the air-raid drills to have a bag with valuable papers ready by the door. She grabbed her mother's arm, and the bag with their identification papers and other valuables, and ran for the door. She ran back to the dresser to get their purses. Then she ran back to the bed to grab her clothes. She even took them off the hangers in a flash. In her confusion, she was running in circles. She could not understand why she was doing this.

Try to keep your senses about you, Maria thought to herself. Do what you were taught in the drills.

The two of them ran down the stairs. When they opened the door to the street, Maria felt that they would never make it to the bomb shelter a couple of blocks away without being killed.

It was frightening to hear the explosions. Although most of the bombs hit Barmen, neither of them could tell the difference. The percussion of the explosions and the blinding flashes of light dazed them. The shock and disbelief that they were in a bombing panicked and confused them. Neither had considered the possibility that they might not be able to get to a bomb shelter. There was no basement in their apartment building, so Maria pulled her mother under the staircase next to her. It wasn't good protection from a bomb. The steps were old and creaky; they could barely hold a person's weight. They would therefore, not be able protect them from a bomb that could flatten an entire block.

Some of the other people who lived in the building ran down the stairs. Some ran in through the door from the street. When they saw Maria and Anna huddled under the stairs, they ran over and pressed themselves against them to get under the flimsy stairs. Standing under the stairs was like hiding under a blanket. It gave them comfort of sorts, but unlike the thing outside the childhood blanket, they knew that this monster could really get them.

The sirens wailed, the bombers droned on, and the bombs blasted relentlessly while they clung on to each other in terror under those inadequate stairs. The light of explosions outside punctuated the darkness.

Then, abruptly, an eerie silence fell. It was almost as frightening as the sound of exploding bombs. They all unfolded from the huddle like layers peeling off of an onion. Maria and her mother took the first tentative steps toward the door. Maria looked down at her armful of clothes and realized that she had an armful of empty hangers. In her haste, she had picked them up and left her clothes on the bed.

"My God. Look what I saved." She laughed as she held out her armful of clothes hangers.

Everyone laughed a subdued chuckle even though they were all in shock. This first bombing experience left all of them dazed and numb. None of them wanted to believe that their city had been bombed.

One woman said, "I think it's over. Do you think it's safe to open the door?"

"Go ahead," another woman told her. "But be careful."

Another woman was sobbing hysterically by this time, "Oh my God. We are all going to die. This is the end." She howled as her husband tried to shake some sense and order into her with soothing words.

Trepidation overwhelmed them as they tentatively opened the door to the apartment building. Half of the city, on one side of the river, was in flames, while the other half was mostly untouched. Wuppertal was made up of two suburbs, Barmen on one side of the river and Eberfeld on the other. Only Barmen had been bombed. Eberfeld, where they lived, was untouched

They all started to chatter numbly. The din of their voices reached a crescendo as each talked louder to express their personal anxiety. Every one was concerned about each other's safety. Some were crying, and others just stood in the street in complete disbelief. Franz, the first violinist in the theater who lived on the third floor of their building, walked past them, completely unaware of their presence. He had been in the shelter two blocks away because it was the closest shelter on his walk. He was dazed and stared only at the destruction across the river.

"Where are you going?" his wife asked him.

"My violin! My violin! I left my violin at the theater. I have to save my violin! It is my life. It's my life! It's all I have in the world that matters to me. I have to get to the theater to save it. It is completely irreplaceable. What have they done to my violin?" He sobbed, wiping tears from his face. His wife ran to him. She clung desperately to his arm, trying to hold him back, pleading and crying.

"Franz. No. No. It's too dangerous. Please don't go. Please."

But he would not be stopped in his mission to save his precious violin. He kept walking toward Barmen, dragging her along with him.

"It's too dangerous. You will be killed," the hysterical woman screamed. "You are insane to go into that inferno. What is the matter with you, man!?"

All of them tried to convince him that it was not safe to venture into the center of the city. Their voices mixed in a cacophony of pleas.

Finally, Maria told him, "I will go with you, but if it gets too dangerous, we will turn right back. OK?"

She was a bit hesitant because of his obsession with her, but they were all concerned that he was too distraught to walk alone in the dangerous chaos that had welled up in the city. He was emotionally unstable. They feared that he might intentionally hurt himself.

Maria's mother, Anna, did not want them to go and protested strongly, but everyone was strangely stubborn in their own need to be helpful to each other in this chaos. Maria convinced her that they would be safer as a group, so Anna yielded and stayed behind with Franz's wife. She slid off his sleeve, sobbing.

Three of the other girls in the group decided to help Franz also. They felt that Eberfeld was not too badly hit. Anna and Franz's wife looked on helplessly as he and his group of four stunned ballet dancers went down the hillside toward what used to be Barmen to try to save a violin that was surely destroyed.

The new opera house had recently been opened in Barmen. It was spectacularly modern compared to the old one in Eberfeld on the other side of the river. It was nothing like some of the outdated monstrosities where Maria had performed in the past. It was clean, efficient, state of the art. They all knew that it must have been hit because as they moved through Eberfeld streets on the outskirts of Barmen, thick smoke and fires filled the air. Rescue sirens occupied the air as thickly as the acrid smoke of the flames. Maria wanted to turn back because she was afraid that they would get in the way of the firemen and rescuers. However, the group pressed on closer to Barmen to rescue Franz's violin. On the next block in Barmen, they passed a house that was partially in flames. The back part of it was burning. The crackling sound of the hungry fire shattered the air between the sirens.

They could see the shadowy figure of a man trying to pull something very large through a set of double doors and out onto a terraced courtyard. There were no fire engines there because they were all tied up with destruction elsewhere.

As the tiny group moved closer, the man recognized them and yelled, "Help me! Help me save my piano! It is all I have."

They realized that it was Joseph, the symphony orchestra conductor. He was trying desperately to drag his grand piano out of his burning home. Still dressed in his tuxedo and white gloves, he had made his way home through the destruction from a bomb shelter just to save his piano.

They were all choking from the heavy smoke, but they ran over to help him. All of them pulled, pushed, tilted, and dragged the grand piano through the doors. The flames in the burning house came closer, casting an eerie dancing light through the sheer curtains behind the French window panes of the door. Finally, the instrument jerked free. They quickly dragged it into the courtyard to the opposite side of the terrace, far from the flames.

"Thank you! I don't know how to thank you!" Joseph sobbed as he fell onto the top of the grand piano, weeping as if hugging a family member. At that moment, the wall of the house collapsed behind them, spewing bricks and flaming ashes at them.

"What about my violin. We have to save my violin!" Franz suddenly yelled. They had forgotten about his violin in their effort to help Joseph.

"Oh Franz. Forget it. It is gone - destroyed. Let's go back," one of the girls tried to persuade him.

"Yeah. This is insane. It's not safe here," another dancer yelled.

"You know Franz, they are right. It is too dangerous for us to go on. Please. Please. Let's get out of here. Let's go back," Maria pleaded with Franz.

They all tried to talk him out of his "insane" quest, but they couldn't convince him. He was not reasonable. He could not comprehend that the futility of saving a violin in the basement of a bombed, burning building was not the same thing as pulling a grand piano through a door and onto a sidewalk. However, Franz was so passionate in his pleas that their little group continued on. Maria was alarmed at the smoke and heat, but she conceded to this crusade a while longer. The smoke and heat near the center of the city, by the theater, was too intense. They had to give up and turn back.

Franz was incredibly stubborn. Yet he finally came to his senses and gave up on his violin when he caught a glimpse of the theater through the thick smoke. It was a twisted mass of steel on one side and was burning to the ground on the other side. Barmen was lost; the theater was gone.

It took them all a long time to walk back to their apartments because they had to continuously avoid fire-fighting equipment and ambulances. They kept trying to cheer up Franz.

"It will all work itself out, Franz. At least we have a place to sleep tonight. Think about all of the people who have no home to go to." Maria tried to comfort him.

"My career is totally ruined. The violin gave life to my playing. I was the instrument, and it was the maestro," he stammered.

Except for their chance encounter to help Joseph, they all realized how irrational it had been for them to attempt to go into the center of a burning city.

Anna and Franz's wife were clearly worried to the point of distraction when they saw the returning group.

"I must have been out of my mind to have let you even think about what you did," Anna told Maria.

She and Franz's wife rambled on endlessly at the foolishness of the quest. Maria and the others realized the folly of their actions as they looked back over the flaming city.

Neither Maria nor her mother could sleep that night. The reality that the war had come to the heart of Germany, to them personally was terrifying. All night, their emotions ran from panic, to terror, and to sadness. They cried, laughed, and worried about the future.

"You have got to move to my apartment in the Black Forest," Maria told her mother. "It is away from bomb targets, and you will not have to run for shelter. Your weak knees will be the death of you if you stay here."

"Honey, I hate to leave you alone, but I think you are right. You avoid that nut Franz. He worries me," Anna answered.

"Good. We will get you on a train to Waldrennach tomorrow. Don't worry about Franz. I can handle him."

Maria had established a residence in the tiny village when they vacationed there during the summer. She also had a thought deep in her mind that it would be a refuge if they ever needed it. Anna agreed reluctantly. Since the Black Forest apartment was not near any cities or manufacturing centers, they both figured that it would be a safe place for the time being.

The only communications left in the city were the radio and word-of-mouth. The radio announcer had asked the people to gather in the park in front of the old opera house in Eberfeld. People whose homes had been lost could get directions there for shelter. Injuries could be tended, and food and clothes would be distributed to those who had lost everything.

It was at that chaotic yet orderly assembly where Maria found others from the theater. After the general announcements to the people, the theater officials told them that there would be a meeting at the same park later in the day.

There would, of course, be no ballet performances, but the theater officials and the city officials decided to put on a Beethoven concert the next day as a way to bolster the people's morale.

Later, near the end of the day, Franz did retrieve his violin. The new theater had a special concrete vault in the basement. The stagehands had put all of the instruments in there. His violin was one of the instruments to be put in first because it was a rare, irreplaceable Amati. A friend had taken in Joseph and his grand piano. The piano was safe, and Joseph still had his "family."

The next day, people came from everywhere. Word had spread rapidly. The theater in Eberfeld had been converted to a warehouse and was not useable, so there were no theaters left in the city. As a result, the orchestra had to play in an armory on the side of the hill overlooking Wuppertal. Its broad doors were opened so that the people sitting on the streets and hills could hear the music along with those packed inside.

It was a brilliant, clear day. Only small clouds dotted the deep blue sky. The orchestra was dressed in anything they could salvage from the bombing. Some were dressed in tuxedos, while others were dressed in the only clothes they had left. Franz wore a tuxedo, but he was the exception since many of the other musicians from Barmen had lost everything. Maria and her mother were sitting outside on a street curb, and weeping as this rag-tag, beat up symphony orchestra played Beethoven's Fifth Symphony. It almost seemed like this was the true moment Beethoven had in mind when he wrote this symphony. People sat on the street curbs beside them also sobbing. The music somehow seemed fitting and heroic as they looked over the ruins of Barmen from the hillside. They felt glory and pride in their fear and sadness.

The Present

Maria closed the frayed pages of the old *Tagebuch.* She had found her diary in an old battered trunk she had brought with her from Germany fifty years earlier. It had been stuffed in a recess in the attic for years. Maria had blankly let the pages slip by her thumb from back to front after she found it, and nestled in a threadbare chair by a window for more light. She had randomly stopped somewhere near the middle and began to read.

The war had been a terrible time. She had forged a career as a prima ballerina in a country that did everything to stand in her way. She had been applauded at the top of her profession, a delicate flower of the stage. At the same time, she had survived lost love and the desperation of war and death. She reopened the book to the beginning and began to read.

Chapter 2

It was 1938, and Maria had to make a decision about what to do with the rest of her life. She was almost sixteen, which was the time career decisions were made in Germany. The trades seemed like the only secure future for her, so she and her mother planned to look into seamstress work. She was not too enthusiastic about doing that for the rest of her life, but the reality of living a comfortable life in a Nazi world did not leave her much choice. She was not at the top of her class academically because she had spent most of her days in the Frankfurt girls' Catholic school in trouble, in the hall or at the head master's office. She enjoyed sewing, crochet, and things like that. She was resourceful. If she did not like a class, she created a problem so that she would not have to sit through it. Religion classes drove her crazy so home skills type of classes received most of her attention.

One day, she received a notice from her teacher that a representative from the government wished to interview her about her future plans. This was standard practice at that time, and it was especially important for families who had lost their breadwinner. She had to plan the track she wanted to take in her adult life. Within a couple of weeks, she received an official letter with a swastika and Reich markings on the envelope. A government representative went to their house to interview Maria and her mother. They were both nervous about the visit. Her mother was especially nervous because she did not want the government nosing around in their lives since it was better to stay as "invisible" as possible in the political climate of the times.

A day or two after she received the letter, a woman from the state came to interview and investigate them. There was a heavy knock at their door. Anna opened it and stood momentarily speechless. The woman looked official in her neatly tailored brown uniform, and she was carrying a dark brown leather binder under her arm. Her hair was pulled tightly back, rolled into a bun on the back of her head.

She introduced herself rather tersely. "My name is Freulein Butterbach." She pushed herself past them and showed herself to a seat without being asked. Maria and her mother were nervous before this interrogator arrived, and they shot glances back and forth to each other. Maria sensed that her mother was becoming increasingly more uneasy. Maria was not sure how to react to this woman's demeanor as they followed her to sit down. Maria thought to herself that Fraulein Butterbach was a rather old Freulein, somewhere in her late fifties or early sixties. She thought to herself, Freulein. Freuleins are young women. This is an old bat.

Freulein Butterbach told them that it was time for Maria to make a decision about what career she was going to pursue. She asked a lot of questions about her father and what he did for a living, what her brothers were involved in, and so forth. This was to determine if she would need financial aid. Her mother gave short answers giving only the information requested since it was not a good idea to say any more than necessary because that would lead this stranger into other lines of questioning.

The Freulein lit a cigarette, stood up, walked around the room, brushed the curtains aside, and looked blankly out the window. She then strutted over to the piano, where the family pictures sat picking them up one by one, first looking at each picture, and then looking at the back of the frame as if she could find information there. Maria could see the tension in her mother's face knowing that Anna did not like strangers in the house, especially this one, who was scrutinizing their family treasures. The woman repeatedly turned one picture over in particular.

"Is this you?" She asked.

"Yes," Maria replied.

"Do you dance?"

"Yes," she answered.

"How long?"

"Since I was three years old."

Freulein Butterbach whipped out a note pad and began to write. She asked Maria the names of all the dancing schools she had attended and she seemed impressed that Maria had performed with the Frankfurt ballet as a child. She wrote down all of Maria's theatrical appearances. She thought that Maria might want to pursue a career as a ballet dancer because she had taken dance lessons for so long. She informed Maria that she was going to contact the *Dr. Hochs Conservatory with the Hochschule des Theaters* on her behalf and get back to her. From that response, it seemed like their worries about the interview were exaggerated because this uptight interviewer had considered an option that had never come into Maria's mind.

Freulein Butterbach opened her briefcase, tucked the note pad neatly into it, stood up, and took one last puff on her cigarette. As she crushed it out in the ashtray, she asked with smoke coming out between her lips, "Are you interested in pursuing a career in the theater?"

Maria said, "Well, yes, of course if it is all right with mama."

"I see no problem with that," her mother replied. "We have always loved the theater. See what you can do."

Frauline Butterbach showed herself to the door and with a terse "Heil Hitler" and a quick salute of her right hand, she closed the door behind her.

The instant it was safe, Maria jumped up, squealed, and hugged her mother. If this would come to pass, she would not have to go into a trade; she would be a professional ballet dancer. She practically swooned as she danced around the apartment hugging the curtains, kissing pictures, and humming.

The next three or four weeks seemed to last three or four years. Maria was beside herself with anticipation. Then one day, she received an official letter with swastikas and Reich markings all over it. A government representative was coming to their house again. Within a day or two, the same woman, Freulein Butterbach, showed up at their door. This time, she seemed a little softer; this time, they were not so nervous. She showed an interest in Maria and had developed a genuine interest in providing for her future well-being.

She had made an appointment for Maria to have an interview at the Conservatory. She told Maria that the Conservatory had a foundation that financed students with outstanding talent with scholarships. She told Maria that they would interview her intensely, and then she would have to try out by dancing for them. A panel of Ballet Meisters would judge the candidates. There was some small talk, and then the Freulein let herself out with her usual "Heil Hitler."

Maria was excited and frightened because this was something she truly desired, and she was sure she would get it if she practiced hard. She tried some clever schemes like practicing dance routines that she already knew to different musical scores so that she could be prepared if the judges used their own music. She kept her mind occupied this way until the day of the tryouts.

Maria was a basket case the day of her tryouts. She paced around the apartment and occasionally broke out into a dance while humming a tune. She kept her mind busy going over routines and music on the way to the theater. The tryouts were in the Schauspielhaus, where only Shakespeare, Goethe, and the classics were played. Maria thought it was odd to hold tests there, but her anxiety was more stressful to her than where she was going to dance.

She felt very tiny when she walked into the large hall. The judges sat behind a table along one wall in front of a line of lofty windows with ornate drapery on them. A piano sat against the opposing wall. She felt as if she had entered a giant cave ruled over by lords of the dark world. Her heart pounded as she took a seat in the empty chair that faced the four inquisitors.

The interview went smoothly. It revolved mostly around her training and performances, what dance schools she had attended and where she had performed. She even recounted for them her first role as a tulip at five years old with the Frankfurt ballet. She became a little more at ease at the simplicity of the questions. The interview wasn't nearly as bad as she had expected it to be.

After the interview, she was asked to demonstrate her mastery of dance. The dance tryout was interesting. An instructor would show her some steps, and she would have to do them immediately after being showed without any time to practice. It was almost like having to sight-read music at an audition. Then she was asked to do one of her ballet dances, a toe dance, and a character dance. Character dances were ethnic dances from other countries. This included a mazurka, a tarantella, a Hungarian dance, and a Russian dance. She even had to do a little tap dancing. The purpose of this part of the audition was to demonstrate the scope of her diversity. All the while, she had to be alert and aware that the judges were evaluating the fluidity of her movements, her poise, and her grace. They noted if her foot positions were clean, how her toes were pointed, her arm movements, her hand positions, and all of the elements involved with dance.

When it was over, she felt confident. All of her practice, especially her tactic of doing familiar dances to unfamiliar music, had paid off since she had to dance to music selected by the judges just as she anticipated.

She knew she did fairly well in the interview. She also thought that she could read in the judge's expressions that they were impressed with her dancing. Then it was time to wait. She walked out of the hall full of hope and expectation, not feeling so tiny any more. She had her first sense of a job well prepared for and well done.

A week later Freulein Butterbach, the woman from the government, came to their house again. This time, when Maria's mother opened the door, she waited to be invited in. She seemed to be almost friendly, but she was still extremely stuffy and aloof. Her tailored suit did not have a wrinkle in it.

She walked over to her usual favorite chair, sat down, opened her leather case, pulled out some official looking papers, and as she handed them to Maria, said, "I have good news for you. You got the scholarship. You are a very lucky lady. You are in."

"You must be kidding. I never expected this so soon. Is it really, really true?" Maria started to cry, and so did her mother. They hugged each other while Maria jumped up and down, jostling Anna.

Maria ran over to the woman, grabbed her hand and said, "Oh, thank you. Thank you."

"You can start any time, but if I were you, I would go down there tomorrow. They will order everything you need: toe shoes, ballet shoes, leotards, and tights, plus you will collect thirty-two marks per month spending money so that you will be ready when school starts." A small smile crept across Butterbach's usually stern face as a brief moment of humanity emerged, but was quickly repressed.

"Everything I need and thirty-two marks per month?" she choked. "Oh mama, this is not real. It can't be true."

"It is, my child," Freulein Butterbach said in a monotone before Anna could respond. "We will have your Ahnenspiegel ready in a week or so. I will try to expedite the work on it because classes will be starting soon."

It was an extremely good idea to get an Ahnenspiegel. It was a booklet that proved you had pure Aryan blood vis-à-vis a government analysis of your family background for several generations. German troops were occupying the Sudetenland, and the Czech government had resigned. By this time, synagogues were being burned, big Jewish-owned department stores were being closed, and other businesses had the Jewish Star of David painted on them. Maria and her mother knew that there was something terrible going on with the Jews; therefore, they knew that this Ahnenspiegel was an important document to have and carry.

A week before classes started, Freulein Butterbach returned to their house for another visit. They assumed that it was to give them their Ahnenspiegels and official Reich papers and to finish up all the details for the Conservatory.

Anna opened the door, but this time, Freulein Butterbach pushed it open and strutted over to the coffee table, where she tersely took out a cigarette, lit it, and scowled, "We seem to have a small problem.'" dragging out the word "small." Maria had not noticed before, but she had a swastika medal on her uniform. The woman's whole demeanor was scornful with none of the sympathetic tone of earlier encounters.

"What is it?" Maria asked.

"Well, your mother's mother's mother's name was Rebecca Lysetta. You can't start at the Conservatory until this is checked out," she snapped.

"Why not?" Maria asked. Her heart began to pound.

"Because this is a Jewish name, and your papers must be in order." She spit out the words with a cloud of smoke in a cold, menacing manner. " I will let you know what transpires. Meanwhile, neither of you are to leave the city, and you must report to our office twice a week to verify your location." She crushed the cigarette in an ashtray on the table, showed herself to the door, raised her arm full out in the Nazi salute, and boomed, "Heil Hitler!"

Maria developed a sudden feeling in the pit of her stomach as if she had fallen off a cliff and was going to throw up.

Strangely though, her mother did not panic. She said to Freulein Butterbach in a calm strong voice, "I know there is no Jewish ancestry in our family."

"I hope so, for your sake," she scowled as she abruptly slammed the door behind her.

For days, Maria mulled this catastrophe over in her mind. What if there was Jewish blood in their family. Not only would she not get into the Conservatory, but they might also be in danger because their blood was not "pure." She did not understand what this had to do with whether she was a good dancer. Drifting in and out of panic, she had no idea of the tragedy that was unfolding in her country.

As the first day of classes came and went, and she still had no response, she probed her mother repeatedly concerning the family background. "Why would anybody name their child Rebecca if there were not some tie to the Jews?" she asked hundreds of times.

"I don't know," her mother said. "Maybe her mother and father just liked the name. Don't worry, sweetie. There are no Jews in our family. You'll see. Everything will be all right."

"What about my nose. It looks Jewish. It's that Happersberger nose. Oh God. Maybe it is true."

"Don't worry about your nose. It is beautiful, very German, and totally aristocratic," her mother told her.

About three weeks later, there was a knock at the door. It was Butterbach. She told them that she had been working hard on their case so that Maria could start school. She believed that they were Catholic and not Jewish. She told them that the authorities had traced Rebecca Lysette's origin to a small town through the records of the Catholic Church and the courthouse.

"We could find no explanation for her name, but all of her records were Catholic. For some reason, I knew you weren't Jewish." With that pronouncement, she handed one Ahnenspiegel to Maria, and then one to her mother.

"Guard these papers very carefully. With the blemish of that name following you around, you may have to use these often."

Maria could not restrain herself. She ran over and gave Butterbach a small hug that she stiffly returned with a smile. Maria had finally received her Ahnenspiegel, and started classes three weeks late.

Chapter 3

When Maria arrived at the conservatory on her first day, she was full of excitement and awe. She was nervous, happy, and scared. She was a real curiosity to all the other girls there because no one ever started conservatory studies late. It just wasn't done. However, the government was able to override even the rules of *Dr. Hochs Conservatory*. Maria wandered down some halls studying the room numbers and the names on the doors. She walked past a large practice room and found the dressing room next to it.

As she walked into the room, it was filled with the chatter and giggles of girls getting into their dance clothes. Some were already dressed and stretching their legs on the benches. The moment she entered the room, the girls turned and looked at her, and the room fell into a silent hush.

Maria looked around the room and found the locker that had been assigned to her. She sat on the bench and began to take off her jacket to change her clothes. The silence and the stares were quite unsettling, but she was determined not to let the situation deter her. All kinds of crazy thoughts went through her mind. Do they know about the government investigation? Am I marked in some way? Just act nonchalant, she thought to herself.

One girl in particular, who was on the other side of the room, stood and glared at her, and just, kept staring. Suddenly, she got up, walked over to Maria, and said, "We are three weeks into our studies. What are you doing starting so late? Who do you think you are? You must think you're real good."

Maria just ignored her. She didn't want a fight; she just wanted to dance. She did not look at the obnoxious girl and kept tying her toe shoes.

That must have infuriated the girl. She shouted, "Look at me. I'm the queen here honey and don't you forget it." With that she slapped Maria in the face so hard that she fell against the lockers.

Maria ran out of the dressing room and into the practice room bewildered, not knowing what to do. Fortunately, Maria's classes were in a different part of the building in different rooms from the girl's classes, so she concentrated on making a good impression on her teacher, and that is what sustained her through that first, rough day.

The ballet practice room was stark, lined with mirrors along the full length of one wall with two parallel ballet bars in front of them about waist height. A piano sat on the opposite side of the room where, the musician played classical music for the practice sessions. Maria felt very small and frightened that day in that large room. She had to look at the reflection of her insecurity in the mirrors the whole day. She felt inadequate. All the pride she felt at being selected over hundreds of other applicants for the conservatory faded from her heart.

A few girls would talk to Maria a little and answer her questions about this girl. She also discovered, by eavesdropping on the other girls, that this girl was at the top of her class in her second year, perhaps the best dancer in the conservatory, and she intimidated all the other girls. She was an upper classman, and the upper classmen generally considered the new students to be a low caste. She intimidated the other first year girls as much as she had intimidated Maria, but she had missed all of that during her initial absence.

When she went home she told her mother and her brothers, Karl and Heinrich what had happened. They were furious. She told them, "I am not going back."

They thought that this was just a show put on by a spoiled brat, and that it was over. Karl talked her into trying it for a few more days to see if this girl would eventually leave her alone.

The next day, the same thing happened. Maria could see the outline of the girl's hand in the welts on her face reflected in the mirrors that lined the practice room. They lasted for almost an hour. It was humiliating to her, and she kept trying to hide the welts with the back of her hand, holding back her tears. She knew that she could not let the other girls see her cry because they were all perturbed by her late arrival at the conservatory. To show any emotion would give them the power to drive her out, and she did not want that, but she wasn't sure.

That night, she told her family that she was going to quit.

Karl told her, "As you go through life, you have to fight back. You don't quit just because someone else tells you to. I can't go and beat her up for you. You have to stand up for yourself, or you will end up being a loser. If she comes up to you to slap you again, all you have to do is smack her first as hard as you can right in the middle of her face."

"I can't do that. I don't want to hurt anybody. What if she starts to fight?" Maria replied.

Karl said, "Does it hurt when she slaps you? Does it hurt your face? Does it hurt your soul? Well, you know how to rehearse. Here, practice on me." He put a small pillow up against his cheek, coaxing her to slap it as hard as she could.

So she practiced slapping the pillow on her brother's face that night.

The next day in the dressing room, the girl was there waiting for her like usual. She moved so fast that she knocked Maria in the face, and once again, Maria fell against the wall, dropping her dance cloths on the floor.

Maria composed herself, stood up, and shouted at the other girl as she turned to walk away. "Wait. I have something for you."

When the girl turned around, Maria slapped her in the face so hard that she reeled across the room against the opposite wall. She looked completely stunned as she wiped her face with the back of her hand and glared at Maria. Much to Maria's surprise, she simply turned around, and stomped out of the dressing room, and went to her ballet class.

Later, after school, she was waiting for Maria outside the door. Terror gripped Maria. She was sure she was going to die at the hands of this monster, but to her surprise, the girl just started talking to her. She asked Maria what her name was, and where she lived, and in general she was almost friendly. Maria learned that the girl's name was Heidi. From that day on, they developed a friendship, and Maria earned the respect and admiration of the other girls. If Heidi accepted someone, it was ok for everyone else to associate with her.

When Maria returned home that afternoon, she had a big smile on her face. Her mother seemed to know that everything was all right by the look on her face. When Karl came home, she gave him a big hug and kiss. They were all amazed at how well things had turned out. She did not know it then, but Karl's advice would help her the rest of her life.

Studying at the conservatory was hard work. Maria was always performing at a function somewhere in Frankfurt. In the warm weather, the students performed outdoors sometimes at the *Palmengarten,* on the terrace and the lawn. They were often asked to perform for clubs and fund-raisers. One night, Maria was scheduled to perform with the conservatory as part of a fundraising effort for something at the *Volksbildungsheim,* an organization that raised money to promote fine arts for the people. It was a gala event with a ball. Her mother wore an evening gown, and Karl and Heinrich both wore tuxedoes. She and her family attended increasingly more of these types of events since she started at the conservatory.

At one of the activities there was a raffle. They were raffling off a giant basket filled with food, champagne, cheeses, caviar, and food. The basket was almost a meter long, a half-meter wide, and a meter high. Of course, they bought some tickets.

After the show in which Maria had danced, some official called out the numbers. Her brother Karl had won the first prize. They were all very excited to win this wonderful basket. However, when the man at the microphone held up the first prize, it was a life-sized, bronze bust of Hitler. The basket was the grand prize. When the gentleman brought the bust to their table, they did not react, and there was really no big reaction from the rest of the people, either. A bust of Hitler was not too popular with this crowd. After the event, they all walked home because it was not far from the *Volksbildungsheim.* As they rounded the corner to an area away from other people, Karl and Heinrich began throwing Hitler's head back and forth as they ran down the street in front of Maria and her mother.

Then Karl threw it on the pavement, and they started to kick it back and forth like a soccer ball. If someone would approach, they would pick it up and act very civilized only to throw it back down and kick it again after the stranger passed. Maria kicked it once or twice if it happened to roll in her direction. Her mother even kicked it once from under her evening gown. It was so heavy that she almost broke her toe. All of their feet were sore by the time they arrived home. The wonderful bust then quickly found its way into their storage bin in the basement.

Early during her second year at the conservatory, Maria met a wonderful girl named Mini. She was there to study the classical piano to become a concert pianist. Her minor was ballet. As they talked and walked home with each other after school, their friendship deepened. Once, Mini convinced Maria to take a music theory class with her. Mini said that she would tutor her if she needed any help. Maria thought that she might do OK in that class because she played the piano a little.

However, the class was a disaster from the minute Maria walked in the door. There were some cute guys in the class that she thought would make this fun, and she made sure she had a seat by a handsome blond boy. They kept exchanging glances until the professor walked in. This man was evil. The first thing he did was to assign them seats. He moved Maria away from the cute boy. Then he began quizzing the class on their knowledge of music theory. He was walking around the room calling on different students asking questions that she did not understand. When he came to her, he asked what key had six flats. She looked up at him from her seat, back to the floor, and back to him. She did not know the answer, so he ridiculed her.

"Are you retarded, or being troublesome?" He paused as he looked at his roster. "Fraulein Happersberger?"

"I just don't know the answer."

"Then what are you doing in my presence. If you do not know the answer to a simple little question, how can I expect you to learn the subtle intricacies of the great music that fills the universe with glory? Do not waste my time, child."

After class, Maria cried, and Mini was very supportive. Mini convinced Maria to try one more day. Besides, the cute boy would be there, so Maria tried again the next day with even more disastrous results; she immediately transferred to a different course. Mini was disappointed, but they still danced together a lot at floorshows as part of their work for the conservatory. Mini's relationship with her mother was just like Maria's relationship with her mother. Their mothers met when they both accompanied their daughters to conservatory functions or ballets, so they became friends too. Those two even gave each other nicknames. Maria's mother became Haschen, which means little rabbit, and Mini's mother became Bumpus, which means little fart.

One evening, during her second year at the conservatory, someone began pounding on Maria's apartment door. It was the manager-in-charge-of-extras from the theater. He was a little man, a little taller than a midget, very dark and hairy, out of breath because he had rushed from the theater.

"I need someone to play the part of the lead page in *Tannhauser.* One of the girls has become quite ill, and she cannot make it for the performance tonight. Can you do it?" he huffed at her.

"I would love to. What an opportunity! But why do you ask me?" Maria blurted excitedly.

"I was told that you can improvise and dance so well that you can handle the job," the man told her.

" Wait a minute. Let me get my stuff," Maria said in a flurry of activity. She located her dance bag and hurried to the theater with him.

What an honor, she thought to herself. She had been specifically asked to fill in. She felt like a great dancer, because she was going to dance with the regular thirty-six member Frankfurt Ballet. She discovered later that it was more like just walking around than dancing, but for the time being, she was in seventh heaven. She wasn't scheduled to appear in any performances during Wagner week, so this was great. Wagner week was one of the biggest events of the year for theaters throughout Germany accompanied by outdoor performances, and fireworks in some cities. It was a festival time when even the theater lobbies were transformed with props to resemble scenes from Wagner's works.

There had been an all night rehearsal the previous night. Maria couldn't remember there ever having been such an occurrence before. It seemed so extraordinary and unheard of, but then a lot of things were unheard of to her at eighteen. The theater had put an ad in the paper for one hundred extras to work for only two marks. The people who performed were from all walks of life, and they were willing to work for only two marks because of their love of the opera, the theater, and the excitement of performing. That was why, Maria soon learned, the theater had to have an all-night rehearsal. It was because these people had regular jobs during the day, and they could only practice at night.

She arrived at the theater with no idea what to do. Her first scene was as a reveler on Venus Mountain; the stage actually moved up and down. This was the ballet scene that took place right after the overture. Chiffon curtains hung across the entire stage, fans blowing on them to create an eerie, cloudy, and misty effect.

The whole production was amazing to her. She had performed many times here, but she never saw the full potential of the entire theater utilized, and what a production of this scope entailed. She thought to herself that people never know what goes on behind the scenes at a theater. *Tannhauser* was her first real experience with the huge mechanisms of scenery changes and the moving stage.

This opera had twice as many scene changes as other operas normally have. The scale, the size of what went on backstage, was worthy of the lofty scale of Wagner's imagination in this grand opera. Sometimes, a performance needed to create the illusion of hills or steps, and the whole stage or parts of it would be moved to create the illusion. This was a rare event because of the number of people involved.

The stage itself was divided into three parts that would rotate up and down through several stories as the staged scenes changed. The whole stage, the entire thing with the scene that just finished, would descend with the scenery, actors, singers, and dancers. It went down about two stories to stop at a platform where everyone exited it, and stagehands removed the scenery onto a loading dock on the right side, while another crew took the next scene off of a loading dock on the left side and set it up. For large performances like this one, work crews sometimes loaded and unloaded truckloads of scenery while the performance was going on.

She noted how strict they were about safety measures with the performers when they were raised or lowered while standing on the stage. No one was allowed to move at all. There was a guardrail around the stage, but if an arm, a hand, or even a piece of costume got caught, it would be an instant tragedy. If one fell off, that individual would fall onto the mechanism and be killed instantly. She had heard stories about stagehands that were occasionally killed because they fell. The whole operation with the stages and the machinery was about four or five stories high, all behind and below the theater.

Once the scene was set up, the whole stage would move to the rear of the building, where the performers would take their places for the next scene. They would literally freeze for the ride up to the stage level. This wasn't always a quick ride. Sometimes the wait could take twenty minutes to a half hour while the present scene was in play. The stage would then begin its slow ascent behind the stage currently in use, hidden by the backdrop for that scene. She thought to herself how quite amazing it was what the people in the audience do not see.

When the cue for their scene came, the front stage would drop out of sight, and their stage would move to the front of the staging area while a third stage rose up behind them prepared for the next scene. What struck Maria as even more amazing was that it was also possible to rotate parts of the stage while all or part of it was going up or down for a scene, like the mountain of Venus, which required that type of motion.

The opera opens on the Venusberg, the mountain of Venus. All Maria did on Venus Mountain was to wave her arms gracefully, holding scarves that fluttered in the fan breeze; the dancers represented the sensuous revels of Venus's world. This was fairly easy, so she figured that the rest of the evening would be a breeze.

Later, she was a page for Wolfram von Echenbach, one of the main characters that played opposite Tannhauser. However, she was not just an ordinary page, she was the head page. Because old Wolfram was the lead role, he was always first to do anything by virtue of his important position in the opera, and Maria, as the head page, had to be there to lead the other pages.

Since she arrived at the theater just a little while before the performance, the stage manager talked her through what she had to do. It certainly seemed easy enough. There was really no dancing involved, all she had to do was carry a silver tray with a goblet on it and present it to Wolfram for her first performance with him. Later on, when the characters began a singing competition, she was to give him a lute to accompany his song. It all seemed easy enough, and she was sure that she could improvise anything needed for those brief moments.

The size and scope of these Wagner operas was huge, almost beyond comprehension. There were stage people called captains that were in charge of sending the various groups on stage on cue. There was one for Maria and her group, the pages, one for the pilgrims, one for each group of hunters, and so on. Of course, none of these captains knew her since she wasn't at the dress rehearsal the night before. However, each group was choreographed, knew what to do, and was prompted by these captains. The performance was underway. She was confident that she could carry her tray without too much difficulty. She was standing there with her group; next to the pages was a group of hunters.

The captain of the hunters had them marching out on cue. All of a sudden, he came up to Maria, put a flag in her hands, and said, "What are you doing standing here. Here, take this flag and get out there with your group." She tried to protest, but the man was persistent, so she took the flag and followed this group of spear-wielding hunters up the mountain. She thought that the captain would have figured out that this was not quite right. Here was a group of rugged, hairy hunters dressed in hunting gear followed by a short page with a yellow pageboy wig, purple tights, and a black leather vest with a royal crest on it carrying their colors up a mountain to hunt.

When she got to the other side of the stage, the stage captain of a different group of hunters carrying bows and arrows, who also did not know her, yelled at her, "What are you doing here. Get back over there," as he handed her a different banner for this group of hunters. She followed them toward the back of the stage. Then she heard the music and realized that her cue to carry the tray out to Wolfram was coming up. The captain of the pages was frantically motioning her to get over to pick up her tray. She broke off from the group of hunters she was following, and marched alone down the mountain over to the curtain, and ran so fast behind the curtain to the other side of the stage that she could have won an Olympic Medal for the dash.

She got there barely in time to take up the tray and walk on stage to give Wolfram his first drink. She was breathing so heavily that the opera singer playing Wolfram paused momentarily to see if she was all right. Then she carried the tray off and had only to wait for one more cue. Her "grand" part in *Tannhauser* would soon be done for the night. She kept thinking to herself that this was the end of her young career. She was doing everything, it seemed, to make the worst possible impression on the director.

However, she was not lucky enough to make the worst impression. It became disastrous. She went off the stage behind the wrong curtain, and the same captain that started her mess began to yell at her in hushed whispers so the audience could not hear.

"What are you doing here, you idiot? You should be on the other side of the stage," He whisper- shouted at her. She tried desperately to protest and explain that she was a page and not a hunter, but her words fell on deaf ears.

"Don't argue with me, or you'll get fined. Now quickly take this flag and get out there."

So she went on the stage, the idiot page following the spear-wielding hunters up the mountain. She thought to herself that her life in the theater was surely over. What could be worse?

Suddenly, she heard a whisper- shout from the left side of the stage; it was the captain for the pilgrims. As she walked off the stage behind the hunters toward him, he asked, "Who are you? Where did you come from? What are you doing? You must be with the pilgrims."

"But I... " Maria started to open her mouth to explain when he took her flag from her, and handed her the banner for the pilgrims, and pushed her on stage. She was beyond desperation. Tannhauser, Wolfram von Echenbach, and Walter von der Vogelweide were about to begin the tournament of song in the Minstrels' Hall. She could see the captain of the pages waving at her furiously to get over to the side of the stage. But it was not so easy this time to march away from the hunters. She had to make an exit that was not obvious, or it would detract from the performance. She slowly worked her way to the left of the stage to the side curtain, threw the banner at the captain, and zoomed behind the curtain to the other side of the stage. She could hear the music begin her cue when she was about halfway to her mark. Gads, the thoughts that went through her head. She would be lucky to sweep the floors after this. Why did she let these people push her around like this? Worst of all, she knew that Wolfram was going to start to sing, and his lute was not going to be there for him. By the time she got to the group of pages, they had already begun to file out to serve the singing competitors. So now, instead of being the lead page, she was the last page, but it did work out. The second page served Wolfram, which bumped all of the other pages up one person, and put her at the end.

She was so out of breath, and must have looked so frightened or bewildered, that the opera singers all had a smile on their faces. That offered about as much support as one could get on a crowded stage in the middle of a performance. When this scene was done, so was her work in *Tannhauser*. Maria quickly slipped to the dressing room, changed into her clothes, and sulked all the way home.

When she arrived home, her mother asked her how it went. She wasn't at the performance because it was too late for her to get a ticket. Maria cried a little, but she was more discouraged than anything. Her mother listened very attentively at first, but as her story unfolded, Maria could see Anna trying not to smile. Finally, a grin crept across her face; then a smile; then a chuckle, and by the time Maria finished her story, they were both roaring with laughter, and she felt much better.

Chapter 4

Maria did not have much time to worry about what was going on with the rest of the world. She knew Germany was getting bigger. The Nazis had invaded Poland and divided it up with Russia all in the name of Lebensraum. Goebbels was encouraging artists in the name of the Reich to perform and create for the next millennium of the Reich. So, she just tried to concentrate on her work and let the world do what it must as disturbing as that might be.

She finished her studies at the conservatory, and she realized that she had to make some profound decisions about what she wanted to do with her life and her career.

"I know I have to start in the chorus line, but I don't want to stay there. I want to be a prima ballerina as soon as possible," Maria said to her mother.

"I know dear. So just start here in Frankfurt. You have a place to live, and you will be close to home and your family," Anna replied.

"I know Mama, but there are so many people competing to work here. And they are so content once they start in a position that it would take years to move up. I would be an old maid before I could even be a solo dancer. Those dancers have the security that there will always be a good job for them as long as they maintain their high standards of practice and performance. They also have the advantage of living in a large city."

There were too many people competing for a limited number of positions. The ballet corps had thirty-six dancers, and all of them had seniority. The turnover rate of dancers leaving a large theater like Frankfurt was very low.

Maria wanted to advance faster than that. She was an impatient young artist who was sure of her talent. Aside from a few disasters like *Tannhauser*, her ballet instructor at the conservatory considered her to be one of the best pupils she had ever had. Maria thought that it would be better to be a solo dancer at a younger age than stay in the chorus line for years before getting a break.

"The best strategy to advance," she surmised out loud, "is to apply at medium-sized theaters where the move upward might be a little faster. After all, everyone wants to work in Berlin or Frankfurt, and that leaves many excellent opportunities in smaller towns."

"I see what you mean. It is hard to watch your children grow up and move away, sweetheart, but I will help you however I can," Anna went on.

As the year wore on, Maria received numerous offers from many smaller towns. This was really good for her because she wasn't sure that she was doing the right thing. The fact that several theaters wanted to hire her was reassuring. She considered them all very carefully, but there was finally an offer that caught her eye; it was from Gelsenkirchen. Based on her application and recommendations from the conservatory in Frankfurt, they offered her a position as a chorus dancer. It paid half as much as Frankfurt, but it was a start, a stepping stone. It was a good place to build her reputation as a dancer, and she had the potential to move up more quickly there.

She and her mother took a trip there for Maria to go to the tryouts. Gelsenkirchen was much larger than Maria had visualized it. It was situated in a relatively flat area in the heart of the Saarland, and it seemed to have much more industrial areas than Frankfurt.

The theater itself was much older and smaller than the opera house in Frankfurt, but it was elegant in an aristocratic way. There was a park with beautiful gardens next to it. Swans swam regally in its reflecting pool. The theater itself had a terrace in the back that overlooked the park. Maria was immediately drawn to it.

"I can walk here to get away from the hectic practices during breaks," she said.

"This is a beautiful place for a theater in a city this large. They did a good job on it," Anna responded.

The inside of the theater was well kept. It seemed a bit too ornate Maria thought to herself. The auditions were held in the theater itself, on the stage. There were only two positions open, and about twenty candidates had been summoned. Maria changed her clothes in a dressing room, went to a practice room to stretch and warm up, and entered the theater to await her turn.

She realized that she was up against some very talented dancers as she scrutinized their every move. She felt nervous, but she understood her abilities. Her confidence grew as she mentally compared the dancers to each other and herself, so when her opportunity came, she felt that she was as prepared as she could be. It was similar to her experience at the conservatory entrance audition.

By the end of the day, the panel of judges had made their decisions and posted the results on the theater bulletin board so the losers could read them. Two names were conspicuously absent. They were Maria's and some other girl named Thea. Maria was elated and felt much taller than her petite five-foot two. The ballet meister, Anna, summoned each of them separately to tell them of the panel's decision. Maria and her mother then immediately left the city to return to Frankfurt.

Maria spent the summer getting ready to move to Gelsenkirchen. Her mother had already decided to come with her and rent an apartment so she could watch Maria's career grow. Her brothers could take care of themselves; they had moved out on their own, so Anna didn't have much to keep her in Frankfurt. Karl and Heinrich encouraged her to go with Maria. Since she would otherwise be living alone, Anna agreed. "Why not?"

"I will tell you what. I will keep our apartment in Frankfurt. That way we will always have a place to come home to when we get homesick," Maria told her.

"Ya. If we go stir crazy in a smaller town like Gelsenkirchen, we can always return to Frankfurt for a day or two to maintain our sanity," her mother replied.

Mini and her mother had to stay in Frankfurt so Mini could finish up her work at the conservatory, but Maria and Mini made a solemn vow to try to work in the same place once she graduated. Maria was elated because the operhaus in Gelsenkirchen had one of the best reputations in Germany.

When Maria arrived in Gelsenkirchen, her first assignment was to work on the chorus line, but within a month, the ballet meister, Anna, started her as an understudy for the solo dancers. Anna said that Maria was good - one of the best young dancers she had seen in a while. Her opinion meant a lot to Maria because Anna had been a solo dancer with Gertrude Steinweg just the year before. Steinweg was known as one of the best, if not the best, choreographer in the German Theater.

The theater association helped Maria and her mother relocate to Gelsenkirchen. Through the Catholic Church, they found a family with whom they could stay until they found an apartment. The family lived on the outskirts of town, which made for a long commute to the theater, but they only lived there for about a month. Then, with the help of the theater, they found an apartment closer to the center of town.

Within a month, Maria met a very nice girl from Stuttgart who had also just moved to Gelsenkirchen into the same apartment building. She had long, dark brown hair, and she was about the same size as Maria.

"Did you audition last spring?" Maria asked.

"Yes. Did you?" The girl answered.

"We were the two who got the jobs then. What is your name?" Maria asked.

"Thea. What's yours?"

"Maria." She answered.

"You know we look a lot alike. We could almost pass as sisters," Thea said.

"I thought the same thing. I bet we even like the same things," Maria replied.

They immediately became close friends. They walked to and from work together, they rehearsed together, they ate lunch together; and in the evenings, they went to the movies together. And as their friendship grew, they even started to act alike.

Thea once confessed that one of the main reasons she liked Maria was because she liked her mother. She missed her parents. It was very unusual for anyone to bring a parent along with them to work in a new city. Most of the younger performers were not yet married and had recently left their parents and families, so Anna was like a substitute mother for all of them. Many of the performers liked to come over and visit with her. Even the older ones who were married, loved having her around. She was like an *Oma,* or grandmother, to them. It gave them all a sense of family.

A Promotional Poster created during the first year at Gelsenkirchen. Thea top left, and Maria second from the right.

That year, Maria did get a few solo dances, but none of them were showstoppers. Then one day, Anna, the ballet meister, asked her to lunch. This had become a regular routine ever since Anna recognized Maria's talent and stage presence. They became good friends, and Anna gave Maria every opportunity to advance. She was an extremely creative and original choreographer, and Maria was somewhat in awe of her abilities. They both admired each other's skills and abilities without the usual jealously that could creep into relationships on the stage. Their relationship was very similar to Maria's friendship with Thea. People did not feel threatened by Maria. They liked her and admired her talent. Her sense of humor and self-deprecation usually kept them in stitches. She made the laborious and often torturous practice sessions tolerable because she took advantage of any opportunity to spice up a performance with some off-the-wall antic.

Anna did not appreciate what Maria did to some of her choreography, but some of it she loved. Sometimes after practice, they would play off of each other as they created new dances and combinations in the practice room. Sometimes Maria was secretly honored to see some of her "fun stuff" show up in a new creative and professional routine hatched in Anna's mind.

At lunch that day, Anna had a new idea for a production. Instead of doing a classical ballet like <u>Swan Lake</u>, <u>Copellia</u> or something similar, she said, "What about a circus?"

"A circus?" Maria asked half-asking and half-agreeing. "That sounds great, and it would be fun too."

Anna's idea was to have several dances representing the different elements of a circus. There would be a grand parade to open it. There would be an elephant and its trainer in a dance, a juggler dance, an acrobat dance, a tightrope dance, and a magician dance. These numbers would be recapped with a clown dance at the end.

Maria thought it was a great idea and said, "It seems a bit short for a whole evening of ballet."

"That is no problem," Anna replied. "I have choreographed a new light ballet set on sand dunes on a beach. It is also short, and should round out the evening of entertainment."

"I think that sounds like fun. It will be something entirely different from the usual run of the mill evening at the theater. Where do you come up with these ideas? Do it," Maria urged.

"I will. Thanks for the encouragement. I wasn't sure it was such a great idea at first."

The next week, Anna held meetings with the director, stagehands, costume people, lighting people, and scenery technicians to determine the logistics of the proposal. They all liked the idea and thought it was within the capabilities of the theater to put it on. So they started work on "An Evening at the Circus."

After everything was approved, Anna asked Maria, "Do you want to be a clown?"

"Me? Absolutely. It fits my nature perfectly. I can do on the stage what I do everyday, and get paid for it. Oh yes, that number is for me."

Anna said, "Me too. Let's do a clown number together. " Just as they often did in the practice room with routines, they built their enthusiasm and excitement by outlining ideas and trying routines out in front of each other.

The next day Anna, came in and said that her husband wanted to be in the circus as a clown too. He was an actor with the theater, and they had just gotten married. Although he couldn't dance, he could fill in with pantomime. The three of them had great fun creating this dance. However, Maria ended up doing most of the dancing while Anna helped her husband with his cues.

Of course, there were some minor problems along the way with the whole production. There was a dancing horse in one of the numbers. Thea and another girl named Dodi played the horse. Neither one wanted to be a horse because they would be hidden inside a costume, but Thea ended up being the horse's head, which meant that Dodi was the other end. She was a cute blonde girl with an ego as big as the theater. She put up a fuss that was unbelievable. She did not get her way though, and she grudgingly played the part of the dancing horse's ass.

She was able to handle being a horse's ass hidden inside a costume until the programs came out that listed the dancers and the parts they played. When Dodi saw it, the tantrums started all over again. She even began to cry, but it was too late. She was locked into the dance, and Anna was not going to change anything at that late date.

Dodi and Thea's dance was actually a showstopper because the horse number was so unique. The front of the horse would sometimes be doing a different dance than the back part. The audience loved it, so Dodi ended up being happy after all because when she removed the costume to take a bow, the audience shouted, "Bravo." The audience loved the whole production because it was such a departure from the standard theater fare.

The clown number was the last one in the production. There was a big backdrop that looked like the inside of a circus tent with the spectators in the background. This was unique because there were holes cut in it where some of the heads and arms of spectators would normally be, and real people stuck their faces and arms in these holes to applaud and make motions. Someone even had the idea to pop popcorn and create an authentic smell for the production.

Maria's clown routine was fun. The basic idea of the whole dance number was to briefly review and exaggerate all of the previous numbers in the show through dance and pantomime. Anna, her husband, and Maria started the number by making fun of the trainers and the jugglers, and then Anna and her husband moved off the stage. At that point, Maria had a long solo in which she walked on an imaginary tightrope on the floor holding an umbrella above her head. She danced and did magic tricks that didn't work. The audience was roaring with laughter. Maria could barely hear the orchestra over the laughter. She had formed a bond with them, and they kept laughing harder. Even she started to laugh.

When the number ended, the audience was immediately on their feet with a standing ovation. She bowed several times, and then the curtain came down. The entire cast came out on the stage, except her, and took a bow when the curtain reopened. The curtain closed and opened again, and again, they all bowed. Then she walked out, and the audience roared. The applause welled up into a crescendo of bravos and thunderous applause.

The curtain closed again, but the thunder kept up. The stagehands did not open the curtain again, so this time, Maria went out through the middle of the curtain. If you are called back a third time, they do not open the curtain, but two stagehands open the center for you. When she went out, she applauded back at the audience, laughed, and went back. They kept clapping. She came back out; they roared. She would do something silly like sit on the edge of the stage with her legs dangling down into the orchestra and count the number of people in the front row as she pointed at them. She then put her hand over her mouth and pretended to do an exaggerated laugh. One could hear the laughter of the audience amid the applause. She went back through the curtain. They called her out again.

By the fifth curtain call, the stagehands had lowered the iron curtain that was behind the fabric curtain for fire prevention purposes, so she had to go through a door in the iron curtain as well as the curtain in front of it to take a bow.

She must have been inspired because each time she went out to take a bow, she thought of something crazier to do. At about the fifteenth curtain call, the director gave her some roses that were on the stage from an earlier number. The audience assumed that they were given to her for the number of curtain calls. So when she went out, she held them up in appreciation, took a deep sniff, and fainted for the crowd as a gag. As she fell, she could see Dodi out of the corner of her eye, standing off stage with the bottom half of the horse costume wrapped around her, and glaring at her. Anna was standing there clapping, and she blew Maria a congratulatory kiss. Anna apparently saw the creative, improvisational wonder of what was happening on the stage.

No one was leaving the theater. Maria had become a one-woman show. She was overwhelmed. No one ever did curtain calls through the iron curtain more than once or twice. In all, she was called out twenty-two times. She knew that she had broken all records for curtain calls. She knew at the time that something magic and big had just happened.

After that performance, Maria was given many solos and recognized as somewhat of a prodigy. Anna even used some of her choreography in the ballets. She received accolades from performers and critics all over Germany.

Maria and her costume handler backstage.

Chapter 5

Near the end of her second year at Gelsenkirchen, Maria sent out letters to different theaters in Germany seeking employment in a higher position. She enjoyed working in Gelsenkirchen. Besides she had established her reputation as an excellent performer, but the theater there was not large enough for her to be promoted fast enough. No one in a higher position was leaving the Gelsenkirchen Theater, so she was stuck as a chorus dancer with the occasional highlight of being a solo dancer. In fact, she had more solos than her position called for because Anna felt that she was such a good dancer. In addition, Anna had decided to take a position in Hannover, and Maria felt that this was an opportune time to move on.

"Do you think I'm doing the right thing?" Maria asked Anna, the ballet meister. "Am I going too fast?"

"No Maria. I think your plans are sound. Anyone else I would tell to get some more experience, but you learn so fast, and your are talented. You remind me of me," Anna responded.

"Thank you so much. You don't know how much I appreciate your support," Maria replied.

Anna understood Maria's ambition completely and wrote references lavishing praise on her. She told Maria that she would miss her, but she understood that Maria wanted to move on and up.

As offers arrived in the mail, she scrutinized each one carefully. There was a hierarchy of positions in the theater with ever higher prestige and pay. The hierarchy was: chorus dancer, chorus/solo dancer, solo dancer, assistant ballet meister and ballet meister. Most chorus dancers did not usually move up the ladder quickly. Many were content and could make a good living. However, Maria was ambitious and wanted to fulfill her dreams.

An offer came from Halle to become a chorus/solo dancer. The pay was much higher, and she had the potential to do more solos. She had also been persuaded in letters from a casual friend, Anny, who had attended the conservatory with Maria, and moved to Halle to dance in the ballet corps. Anny told her how great the theater was. It was old and ornate, but had been renovated so that it was very modern. The ballet meister was innovative and forward thinking. She wrote that the city had beautiful parks that meandered along the river. The hills around the city were dotted with medieval castles.

With these images and a good job offer, Maria and her mother took a trip there to see what the theater and the city had to offer. They liked what they saw. The theater was better than Anny described it. The position and the pay were acceptable, so Maria auditioned and was hired.

It was the summer of 1941. In the past two years, she had seen newsreels of Hitler walking through Paris, and Hitler meeting with Mussolini and Hireohito to make an alliance. It was bewildering to know that all this was occurring. At first, the propaganda led her, along with the greater mass of Germans, to believe that it was good that all Germans were finally united in one country. However, it bothered Maria that it made no sense; Paris and France were not a German culture. There seemed to be a current of revenge in the reports. This made her and her mother uneasy.

They heard that the British had planned their first air raid on Berlin, and now Germany was bombing London. They were very alarmed because Maria had already contracted to do some summer work in Berlin, and she could not get out of the contract. The bombings had started after she had signed the contract. The last thing she wanted to do was go to a place where someone was dropping bombs. However, in spite of the unsettling circumstances, the two of them packed up and went to Berlin.

One of Maria's primary responsibilities in Berlin was to perform in what was called *Sommerblumen am Funk Turm,* Summer Flowers at the Funk Tower. She was to be one of the *Blumen* or flowers. As it turned out, this was a huge Nazi propaganda production celebrating the completion of the world's largest and most powerful radio transmitter. Although Hitler was not there, all of the other top Nazi officials, including Joseph Goebbels, the Minister of Propaganda were there. She had never been fond of the Nazis, and the thought of performing for them or their cause distressed her. She tried several times to get out of her contract again, but she could not.

There were parades and productions on a grand scale. The entire city was covered with red, white, and black banners bearing the swastika. There was a huge cast of 106 dancers. She danced with a group of five other girls. Half of them were dressed like men, and they did a couples' dance. This was not unusual in the theater because most of the able-bodied men were drafted into the army whether they wanted to go or not. Maria was the leader of her group. Goebbels sat in the front row of a raised stand as he watched the parade and dancers pass by. Her group was required to stop directly in front of him and perform as an orchestra to the side of his stand played music. He smiled at her and gave her a little wave. He then took a note pad out of his coat and wrote something on it while pointing at her, talking to the man next to him.

Maria saw this, and it made her nervous, but she shrugged it off thinking that he would want them to perform at some other event. She was repulsed by him, but forced a smile at the ugly little man.

This whole great event made her realize for the first time of what a power Germany had become, and that she was a reluctant part of history by dancing in this production. The parade was a gigantic pageant. It was almost medieval. It was a strange mixture of goose-stepping troops, naive artists, horsemen, occult floats, and children. It was a sea of humanity surrounded by banners several stories high.

Later that evening, fireworks blazed in the sky for an incredibly long time. An orchestra played as the sky burned. The finale was a huge firework display as large as a one-story building way up in the sky. Hitler's face jumped out of the darkness, and filled the backdrop of the night for a few moments, and burned out as it fell to the ground. Maria thought to herself that it was too bad that it wasn't the real Hitler's face melting into the darkness. A month after that event, Germany attacked the Soviet Union.

The rest of the summer, Maria danced at the Rose Theater in Berlin, which was fairly uneventful after the *Funk Turm*.

Picture from *Sonnenblumen am Funk Turm* Maria is the second from the left.

Picture from *Sonnenblumen am Funk Turm.*

Maria and her mother went to Halle several times that summer when Maria would get some time off from the Rose Theater, but it was impossible to find housing there. The summer went too quickly, and suddenly, the theater season was on them, and they still hadn't found an apartment. The theater was not as helpful as the one in Gelsenkirchen when it came to finding housing for their personnel. They ended up living in a hotel for half a year because they could not find anything. There just wasn't anything available.

But on the rare occasion they could find a potential place to live, the people were extremely rude. They went to look at one apartment where the owner interviewed them with the door slightly cracked open, and when Maria told him she was in the theater, he said, "We do not rent to circus people," and slammed the door in their faces.

"Circus people! How dare he," Maria said.

"He is obviously uncultured, sweetie. Forget it," Anna said.

"Circus people. Ach," Maria sputtered.

Mini and her mother were there also. Mini and Maria had kept close contact with each other by mail since they became such close friends at the conservatory. Mini had started out studying to be a pianist, but she chose ballet instead. She had wanted to do both, but there was only enough time in her life to do one or the other successfully as a career, so she spent an extra year at the conservatory studying ballet. They wrote to each other often and got together whenever she and her mother returned to Frankfurt. Mini tried very hard to land a job at Halle so they could be together. They were very happy when they found out that they would be together.

Back: Mini, Bumpus, Maria
Sitting: The Haas

Mini and her mother were having the same difficulties that Maria and her mother had finding a place to live. Mini and Bumpus ended up living in the same hotel where Maria and the Haas were staying. That was an excellent arrangement, though, because that gave their mothers someone to pass the time with in this hostile town. Both girls worked long hours, so their mothers entertained each other. The four of them lived in the hotel a while longer. Mini's mother was a short, pleasantly plump, and round lady who really deserved a better nickname. Anna's nickname was "Haschen" or "Haas" which means the little rabbit, but she was anything but little. She was short with a bit of a Wagnerian profile. Bumpus and Haschen looked like they could have been sisters.

Mini and Maria worked hard that year. They did matinees, evening performances, and weekends to develop their skills and their reputations. Of course, this required hours of constant practice that kept them at the theater. As a result, their mothers started to get bored because they had nothing to do while Mini and Maria spent so much time working. They eventually started to get into trouble of one sort or another as they tried to figure out things to do with their time.

Mini and Maria had very little spare time to do much of anything other than work, but they did try to go to the movies once or twice a month. It was at one of these movies that Maria saw a newsreel about the Japanese attack on America in December. Because the United States seemed so far away and protected, it was jarring. There was always a sense of uneasiness now. She could even see it in the faces of the theater patrons as they tried to escape for a few moments in the world of the theater. The whole world was at war now.

One of the most interesting things she saw during those newsreels was a view of the New York skyline taken by German U-boats in New York harbor. The commentator told them that it was not so surprising that Japan could hit America with a sneak attack if the U-boats could lay right there in one of the busiest harbors of the world completely undetected.

Maria did not like working in Halle. Although Mini and Bumpus made life a little easier, the city itself was cold. The ballet meister was weird. The ballet meister Anna had written about had left, and this man took her position at Halle at the same time that Maria started work there. His choreography lacked creative flare, and he was effeminate.

"Only if you have a man, can you have the deep feeling to connect with the audience at an emotional level," he would repeat often in the practices, flaring his arms in grand circles.

"Mini. Do you think he is a warm brother," Maria asked using the slang for homosexual.

"Oh yes. I have heard rumors that he is very warm. Just look at how he acts."

"Well. There is nothing wrong with my emotions when I dance. I do not need a man to find them. Especially his kind of man," Maria declared.

As a result of her discontent, Maria started sending out applications to other theaters about a month after she started work in Halle. One of those applications went to the theater in Wuppertal. Gertrude Steinweg was the ballet meister there, and surprisingly, she personally replied to Maria's request, writing that she was coming to Halle in the early spring to look over the talent there. She had a formidable reputation in the theater in Germany, and Europe in general. She had been the first solo dancer at the Moscow Theater for ten years before she came to Germany as a ballet meister and choreographer. She was currently the choreographer at Wuppertal and was looking to expand her ballet corps there. Anna, the ballet meister at Gelsenkirchen, had told her about Maria and her incredible talent, creativity, and improvisational skills. And, of course she knew of the legendary clown dance with its record-breaking number of curtain calls.

At the time, Maria was dancing in *The Doll Fairy*, a light ballet. All of the dancers were very nervous the evening of that performance knowing that Steinweg was in the audience. It was unnerving having someone of her caliber in the audience evaluating their every move. Maria wanted to get out of Halle, and desired the opportunity to work under Steinweg. Her nervousness forced her to concentrate on things that usually come naturally to a dancer.

She was sure she overreacted. She concentrated even on where her fingers were as she did each ballet combination. She felt rigid, like a robot in a tutu - a confident robot, nevertheless. She knew the dance steps inside and out during their practice sessions. The practices they all cursed always came in handy in situations like this, but it allowed too much time to think about trivial things.

Maria felt that the performance was technically good. She knew that she had danced flawlessly. Then there was a knock at her dressing room door. Maria opened it to find Gertrude Steinweg herself standing there. She stammered, "Come in. Please."

"Anna was correct when she said that you were a very competent dancer. I certainly did not waste my time coming here," she said.

Maria was surprised. Steinweg looked much smaller in person compared to the titan Maria had imagined her to be. She was personable, and quite friendly.

The other dancers huddled outside her dressing room door and tried to listen in on their conversation. Maria was star struck because of Steinweg's fame and reputation in the theater. She felt honored merely to meet her, yet here she was in her dressing room telling Maria what a good ballerina she thought she was. She set up an appointment for the next day so she could get more information. Maria thought to herself how amazing it was. Normally, a dancer had to go to the theater where she had applied to be interviewed. It was most extraordinary to have a ballet meister come out in the field to interview someone. Especially Steinweg.

In the interview the next day, Steinweg offered Maria a job in her ballet corps. She needed a chorus-solo dancer, and she offered the position to Maria. It was a promotion as well as a move to a larger theater. Maria might have had to stay in Halle another year if she had not received Steinweg's offer because the government was not letting people move from job to job so easily anymore. However, Steinweg had a lot of influence, and although she was not a Nazi, she had enough personal charisma to convince Goebbels himself to let Maria work with her. Besides, the war was starting to heat up, and Maria thought that Wuppertal would be a safer place for her mother and her to live. She had heard rumors that it was being spared bombings because of its strategic location. She had also heard that Halle was a dangerous location for possible air attacks because it was a strategic rail center in the eastern part of the country that supplied Hitler's war ambitions in to the east. Maria was so happy, but she did not know until then how well known she was throughout the theater community in Germany.

Much to Maria's relief the season came to an end, and none too soon for her. She and her mother were glad to get out of the city when the season ended in Halle. However, one day, the theater director came up to her and asked her to do some summer theater because he needed some dancers and wanted to use her.

She said, "No. Don't take it the wrong way, but I do not like Halle."

She didn't want to stay there a minute longer than she had to. He told her that the pay was very good, and he offered to let her and Mini play a small part for a couple of performances. She talked it over with her mother and Mini. Mini and her mother were just as eager to get out of Halle as Maria and Anna were, but they figured that they could use the extra money, so they agreed to do it.

Halle was a beautiful old city, and they were going to perform in *A Mid Summer Night's Dream* set in the castle courtyard by the Halle River. Outdoor theater in Germany was always special and splendid.

Maria played a bee and Mini was some other kind of a bug. Their parts required them to buzz around the actors. After one performance, Maria decided that she did not want to be a bee for the summer, but she agreed to go the length of the show. At the end of the last performance, she was beed-out. It was one of the most bizarre things she had ever danced. It did not even require any technical skill. After the performance, she came home and told her mother to pack. "Let's get out of Halle, now."

She and Mini knew that even though they were the best of friends, they would have to go their separate ways if they wanted to pursue their careers. Neither of them liked the idea of splitting up, but Mini went to the theater in Hannover, and Maria went to Wuppertal.

"Let's make a sacred vow that we will never forget each other. You are the best friend I've ever had," Mini cried at the train station.

"We can see each other in the off-season. You and Bumpus can come to the Black Forest and visit with the Haas and me. We will always be together," Maria sobbed back.

Bumpus and Haas both held handkerchiefs to their faces, wiping away tears and straightening their hats. When the signal came to board the train, they all embraced each other separately and in a group hug. Mini and Bumpus slowly but deliberately picked up their bags and got on the train. They entered their compartment and stowed their bags.

Then they opened the window and shouted out to Maria and Haas. "We miss you already."

Slowly, the train began its movement toward the opening in the huge building. Maria and Haas waved their handkerchiefs, while Mini and Bumpus waved back. Then the train slipped out of view around a curve.

Maria and her mother decided to spend most of the summer in the Black Forest after visiting Frankfurt for a while. It would get them away from the cities where all of the bombings were going on. Her mother, her aunt, and Maria had been going to different places in the Black Forest for vacations since she was a little girl in Frankfurt.

This summer, her aunt had found a place called Wildbad. It was a famous and expensive spa nestled at the end of a local train line in the western part of the Black Forest. She did not have to work hard to convince them to go there to escape.

When they got there, it turned out to be quite expensive, and there seemed to be a lot of Jews there. Maybe it was one of the few safe places left for them. It was too expensive for Maria and her mother, so they went back one stop on the train to Neuenbürg to try to find more affordable accommodations. They were always looking for nice, clean, quiet, and inexpensive places to vacation.

It was so beautiful there. The forest rose up the mountains all around them and touched the crystal clear blue sky dotted with wispy clouds. They had heard that there was a small village at the top of the one mountain called Waldrennach. So they all hiked up there to see what it was like. When they arrived there, they found one small inn in the village. A farm lady named Gertrude owned it. To no one's surprise, it was called Gertrude's Inn, and since it was affordable, that was where they planted themselves.

This place was so out of the way and surrounded by beautiful forests dotted with small, flower-filled meadows that they fell in love with it instantly.

Maria said to her mother, "You know, this would be a nice place to live. We could escape from it all, including the war here."

"You are so right," Anna said.

They spent the rest of that summer visiting Frankfurt, the spa at Wildbad, and looking for a place to rent in Waldrennach. Finally, they found a little place just big enough for the two of them above a small house. Maria immediately leased it for a year to be sure they could keep it.

Chapter 6

Steinweg worked them like slaves at Wuppertal. Maria's anticipation and excitement were tempered by the grueling workouts. She decided that Steinweg must have been a slave master in another life. She would often work them for two hours at a time without breaks. The steady beat of her cane haunted Maria in her sleep. She fell asleep counting the relentless beats of the routines Steinweg pounded into the floor. She was good, but she was a taskmaster. However, she was not without feelings.

Food was strictly rationed by now because of the war. People barely had enough to sustain them. So one day Steinweg interrupted the exercises.

"Do you all have enough to eat? I feel like I'm always hungry. If the war doesn't kill us, the lack of food will. We should get more rations for ballet dancers. We work harder than heavy laborers. I bet a construction worker couldn't keep up with us," she said. "I'm going to go the ration office, to see what I can do."

Maria had not thought much about being hungry, but she was tired of eating cabbage and potatoes. This seemed like a wonderful idea. After all, they were only receiving about a quarter of a pound of meat per person per month, and about an egg each per week. It was not easy, but they did not feel too hungry.

Steinweg made several arguments at the ration office for more food. First she told the officials that ballet dancers were not just the lovely final entertainment product they saw on stage. She explained the many hours of hard work that made up a performance. Secondly, she compared the dancers to laborers and soldiers, although this argument almost made her gag. She was too dignified to believe that, but she knew how to get results. Finally, she appealed to their patriotism. She pointed out that the theaters helped keep up the morale of the people as she echoed the words of Goebbels.

The ration officials told her that they would have to go through the "proper channels," and that they would call her as soon as they heard anything. She also made a few phone calls when she returned to her office, but no one knew to whom.

A couple of weeks later, a telephone call came for Gertrude in the practice room. It was extraordinary for practices to ever be interrupted. She took the receiver in her hand and spoke for a few moments in hushed tones, but the only words that could be heard in the silenced cavernous room were. *"Danke Schön. Schuss."*

The next morning, Gertrude went to the ration office. When she came back, she was extremely proud. She had won. They had given her ballet company extra rations for each member. All thirty-six of them were elated.

She had procured for each of them an additional quarter pound of bacon, a quarter pound of sugar, a half-pound of flour, and a bottle of wine. The entire ballet corps thought that the bottle of wine was a nice touch, but they could not figure out why it was included in the ration. But it didn't matter; they were rich. Gertrude took good care of them.

Wuppertal, like all other theaters in Germany, had a Wagner week. It usually started with *Der Ring der Nibelungen*. Because Wagner week occurred at different times in different cities, theaters were often able to share some dancers from different theaters for this occasion.

Wagner week in those days was like some German religious experience, and Wuppertal was no exception. Men dressed in tuxedos while women dressed in sequin dresses, diamonds, and furs - the best clothes in the world. The foyers of the theaters were decorated with palm trees and scenes from some of the operas. With all this opulence, it was difficult to believe that there was a war going on, especially since all Germans were on rations. However, it was a great escape from the harsh realities.

People literally fought for tickets for the performances during this week. It was even impossible to get tickets for standing room only. The people with SRO tickets were dressed as well as everyone else. Sometimes during Wagner week, depending on the city, there would be parades and fireworks in conjunction with the operas.

During this festival of Wagner, the theaters usually doubled the size of the chorus, the orchestra, and the ballet corps. Everything was done on a grand scale. This celebration in Wuppertal was one of the grandest in Germany, it seemed to Maria. The performers from the Stadts Oper came from Berlin to double the size. Hans Knappertsbusch was hired as the guest conductor for that week also. Maria knew that it would be a great honor to dance under his baton.

Steinweg asked her if she wanted to play Flosshilde in the first act of *Das Rheingold* along with Brunnhilda and Schwanhilda. Maria immediately accepted because she saw the opportunity to do anything different from ballet alone as a chance to learn more about the art of theatrical production. The roles of the three Hildas were operatic roles sung by opera singers, but in certain scenes, ballet dancers filled in for them because of some of the agility required.

Maria, "Brunnhilda," and "Schwanhilda" had to start practice several weeks before the rest of the cast because, beyond their dance routines, they had to learn flying stunts; they also had to learn to mouth the words to certain arias. Maria was always fascinated with the wonderful illusions that could emanate from the stage with some creative slight of hand. To her, this was the most interesting part about performing. What seemed mechanical and unattractive on the stage actually tricked the audience with a completely believable, flawless scene.

In the opening scene of *Das Rheingold*, the three Hildas were suspended by ropes to create the illusion that they were floating in the Rhine River protecting the gold that was hidden there. In this scene, the three of them were floating just off the bottom of the river. The stage was immersed in a greenish twilight, and there were fan-blown chiffon curtains rippling in front of them to simulate being under the water.

As they floated and mouthed the words, the opera singers were on the stage hidden behind the scenery singing their parts. Like most opera singers, they were either too big or too afraid to be suspended. Besides, it would be almost impossible for them to sing hanging in the harness because it wrapped so tightly around the torso. The audience thought they were seeing the actual opera singers through the dim lighting and the waving chiffon. This illusion was created since the costumes Maria and the two other dancers were wearing were identical to those worn by the opera singers. In addition, the long wigs they wore covered most of the top part of their bodies and hid them.

Maria quickly had her desire for new learning experiences put to rest. It was disconcerting to be lifted so far above the stage. None of the performers enjoyed being suspended, flying around the stage. Just a year earlier, a ballet dancer had broken a leg and almost got killed when a suspension rope snapped.

Maria almost dropped out of the production one day at rehearsal. The cast was about halfway through the first act. She was suspended about fifteen feet above the stage when she heard her rope stretch. She suddenly dropped several inches, and she let out a scream when she heard a second stretch a few seconds later. Knappertsbusch stopped the orchestra, and the stagehands lowered her immediately and slowly to the floor.

"This is not safe. I do not want to fall, break a leg, and never dance again," she screamed.

"Don't worry," the director responded. "It's perfectly safe. The ropes just stretched a little bit." He put his arms around her and tried to comfort her. Her legs were still dangling as she strained to reach the floor.

The ropes would not reach to the floor, so the stagehands had to help her out of the harness as she hung there like some helpless, animated puppet.

The ropes were thoroughly checked and replaced because they were worn and a pulley had broken. Maria was reassured that it was safe, but she had to practice the whole process several times, building a little more confidence each time until she was comfortable with the part again.

During their stay in Wuppertal, Maria and her mother visited her brothers, aunts, and uncles and tidied up their apartment in Frankfurt several times during the year.

The season was almost over, but the bombings were becoming more intense everywhere, every day. The Americans had declared war on Germany, and they started bombing the country in August of 1943. Maria knew that the sooner she and her mother got out of the city, the better off they would be. Every night, bombers would come roaring out of the mountains and head south to bomb cities in the Ruhr region. Wuppertal had not been bombed, but the daily routine of practicing air raid drills and the nightly ritual of the bombers droning through the darkness was disconcerting.

Maria and her mother had heard on the radio that Frankfurt had been hit hard the day before. The radio was reporting that it was the worst bombing there so far. They were anxious about their family, and they wondered if their apartment was still intact, if it was gone, and if any of their belongings survived in the cellar.

During that week, *Tosca* was scheduled to play in Wuppertal. It was a straightforward opera with no dancing in it. The ballet corps was in a lull, so Maria asked Steinweg if she could go to Frankfurt.

"Oh Gertrude, I'm so worried about my brothers. My mother won't be able to sleep until she knows if they are all right. We can't get through by telephone. Do you suppose I could have a few days off to see how my family is while *Tosca* is playing?" she pleaded with Steinweg.

Gertrude said, "I understand completely. Just go. You won't be missed. We don't have anything for a couple of days except practice. I hope everyone in your family is OK."

Maria thanked her even though she didn't think Steinweg had the authority to do this. Nevertheless, she and her mother took off for Frankfurt that afternoon.

Of course, irony reared its ugly head when one of the lead opera singers became ill that same afternoon and *Tosca* had to be canceled because there was no understudy. It was very rare that performances were canceled, but when this happened, there were backup programs that could be used to fill in on short notice.

In this instance, Gertrude had a ballet ready. It was one that she had commissioned. She had hired a composer to write the music for her, and she developed the story and the choreography.

It was rather unusual. It was set in a castle where three large paintings adorned the walls. The frames were huge because the dancers posed in them as real life figures. Five dancers played the Schreckensteiners, who were the people depicted in each painting. Each painting then came to life, and the dancers acted out a story about the painting in dance. It had a very unusual name too. It was called *Die Fünf Schreckensteiner*.

The butler told the story through dance. It was almost as much pantomime as dance. Steinweg tried desperately to catch Maria before she left for Frankfurt, but it was too late. She was gone. Gertrude had danced in this ballet before, and she had played the part of each of the Schreckencteiners, including the butler. In this performance, she played the butler, Maria's part. The Schreckensteiners were a comic bunch, so Steinweg was having a wonderful time. Gertrude told no one that Maria was gone. She just took her place in the ballet.

Die Fünf Schreckensteiner   Maria is the bald butler on the left.

When Maria returned a couple of days later, Gertrude said, "You didn't need to come back so soon. I thoroughly enjoyed dancing in front of people again for a change. You know. I never get to dance in my own ballets. I never really get to dance in anything as the choreographer."

Steinweg was able to pull it off because there were only ten dancers in the whole production, not the whole ballet corps. She was happy to be on stage again even for a little while.

Maria and her mother only stayed in Frankfurt for one day. The family was OK, her apartment was untouched, and their belongings in the cellar were intact. The city did not seem as bad to them as the radio had made it sound. With a little peace of mind, they returned to Wuppertal.

Gertrude was clearly disappointed that Maria came back so soon, but Maria took over the role of the butler, which she had studied, and Gertrude complemented her by telling her that she was almost as good at it as she was. She genuinely liked and trusted Maria and the two of them became as close as their different professional roles would allow.

One day, the whole ballet corps was afraid to go into the practice room. Steinweg was in a bad mood. Everyone knew when she was in a bad mood because her waist-length hair would be down instead of in the tight, dark brown, and neatly wrapped bun they were accustomed to. She worked the dancers hard enough when she was in a good mood, but when her hair was down, she made them wish they were dead.

When Maria arrived for practice that morning, the other ballet dancers were standing out in the hall talking. None of them would go into the practice room, so after she changed into her tights and ballet shoes, Maria went in alone.

When she walked into the room, Steinweg was leaning against the ballet bar with the mirrors behind her. Her dancing staff held tightly in her right hand, she had a scowl on her face that could freeze water.

Maria just walked over to her, looked straight at her, and said, "You have your hair down today."

Steinweg simply glared at her.

There was a long silence where Maria thought to herself that she had made a serious strategic blunder. Perhaps her relationship with Gertrude wasn't as good as she had thought. "You look like Pocahontas," she went on.

Slowly, Steinweg's face melted into a smile, and she said, "This was going to be a bad day, but you just changed all that. I like you, Maria. Your sense of humor is so refreshing. Pocahontas, huh? Go tell the others that it's safe to come in."

Chapter 7

In the early spring of 1944 in Wuppertal, Maria got a break that would build her reputation in the country. She was gaining all of the wonderful experience that one could get from studying under Gertrude Steinweg. The few months of her personal attention and tutelage was like having three or four years under a lesser choreographer.

One night at about midnight, there was a fateful knock at her apartment door. She opened it to see Gertrude standing there holding a piece of paper in her hand. Even the neat bun of tightly wrapped dark hair had long wisps floating around it. She came bustling in, in a dither, waving the piece of paper saying, "You have got to help me. You have got to help me!"

Maria said, "Settle down. Here, have a seat." She led Gertrude to the large, overstuffed sofa by the door. "What in heaven's name is wrong?" she went on.

"We are putting on *Maske in Blau*," Gertrude said, her voice slightly out of breath and shaky.

"So, what is so terrible about that?" Maria asked.

"Don't tell anyone, but I don't know one tap step, and there are several tap dances in this operetta." I know that you know how to tap dance because I have seen you playing at it in the practice room. Could you please do the choreography for this one for me?"

Maria couldn't believe her ears. Gertrude Steinweg, a woman of such a reputation, a woman who had studied ballet in Russia for ten years, a woman who could write her own contract anywhere in the world and was sought after as a ballet meister at every theater in Germany is asking me to choreograph a ballet for her because she dosen't know how to tap dance. How strange. How deliciously wonderful, Maria thought to herself. "I would love to, but I'm sure you know how to do some tap."

"I only know a few steps. I never had any reason to learn it because I'm a ballerina. I certainly don't know enough to choreograph even one dance. Besides, I have a phobia about tap dancing. In Russia, we were told that it was a decadent western plot to hypnotize the proletariat. I just never considered it because of the consequences from the Communists," Gertrude told her.

"Oh my," she said, "that is a problem. Of course, I would be happy to help you out. But this is not Russia. You don't have anything to worry about with tap dancing. *Maske in Blau* is only a light operetta," Maria answered.

"Good. Could you come in a couple of hours before rehearsals in the morning to get to know the music," she asked.

Maria told her, "I know the music. We did this operetta in Frankfurt, and I was in all of the tap numbers as well as most of the other dances."

"Wonderful, wonderful. It is up to you, then. I am turning the whole thing over to you. I won't be there. I will be out of town for a couple of weeks. I need to get away for a while anyway," she said. Her whole face seemed more relaxed and smoothed out behind her heavy makeup.

Maria worked very hard on *Maske in Blau.* She knew quite a few tap steps, and she could even remember entire dances from the Frankfurt production. Luckily, there happened to be a Fred Astair movie showing at that time. She had seen his movies before, so she went to try to pick up a few steps from him. She was so taken with some of the routines that she went back and sat through the movie five more times with a paper and pen to write down the routines.

Set in South America with lavish scenes, the operetta was a smashing success. Everyone loved the dancing and the choreography. Maria received critical acclaim, and became recognized as a choreographer. The headlines in the paper marveled at the work of this brilliant new choreographer. Gretrude was happy for Maria, for the accolades and good reviews the critics gave her. It was probably because it drew attention away from her and her perceived inadequacy at tapping. This was a situation that worked out very well for everyone involved.

Maria center stage right in *Maske in Blau.*

Sometime during the middle of the year, several things came together that caused Maria to apply for other positions. She was becoming a close friend with Steinweg, but Gertrude had hinted that she might be taking a position with the Vienna State Opera, one of the most prestigious theaters in Europe. Nothing definite, just a thought. Maria asked her out of loyalty if she would mind if she took a position elsewhere. Maria felt obligated to ask her, especially since Steinweg had come to her specifically to ask her to work in Wuppertal. Steinweg told her that it was a great idea, and she could only advance at the rate she wanted by being ambitious. Gertrude offered to write a letter of recommendation. Maria's scrapbook and portfolio of professional recognition was impressive by now.

There was a major problem that developed that year with Franz, the first violinist in the orchestra. Maria wanted desperately to leave to get out of that situation.

She was not exactly sure how or when it started, but Franz, whose violin they tried to save in the first bombing raid on Wuppertal, had fallen hopelessly in love with her. He was good, a true virtuoso. He was a great violinist in the true sense of the word. He was occasionally called to other cities as a guest violinist. Cologne, before it was bombed out of commission, liked him so much that they always asked him to come and play in *Paganini*.

About half way through the year, Franz greeted Maria at the stage door as she was leaving after a performance late one evening.

"May I walk you to the *Schwebebahn* and then home?"

Maria gladly accepted his offer since it was so late, and she knew it wasn't out of his way. He and his wife lived next door to her mother and her. She didn't think much of it.

The next night, he was waiting at the stage door again, and again Maria just thought he was being nice to her. She appreciated having the company late at night.

However, he started to show up there every night. His conversation became a little bolder, and he would ask her to stop for a drink on the way home. Maria became concerned, but it seemed like an innocent offer.

The first violinist of an orchestra was second in command after the conductor, so Franz had a private practice room where he would not be disturbed as he practiced. One day, a few weeks after he started walking Maria home, he saw her through the window in the door of his private practice room and stuck his head out to say hello as she was walking down the hall. She stopped to respond out of courtesy when he suddenly grabbed her, pulled her into this small room, and tried to kiss her. Maria pulled herself away from him, slapped him in the face hard enough to leave a welt, and stormed out of the room.

That night, she left through the front door of the theater to avoid him, but he somehow knew what exit she was using. He stopped her outside the door.

"Please let me escort you home. You don't understand. I did not mean anything bad. Believe me."

Maria said, "OK, but don't try anything, or you will be in trouble."

On the way home, they had a long talk. It was time to clear up the situation because it was out of control.

"You have a lovely, caring wife. Why do you want to ruin a good marriage over me? Look, I really like you. You are a nice person and all, but I'm not the least bit interested in you romantically. Your wife is a good friend of mine. She is my mother's best friend here. We are all good neighbors. Think about what you are doing to your relationship with her. Please leave me alone and go back to her," Maria told him.

The next day, Maria told Annalise, a ballet dancer who lived in their apartment building, what had happened and asked her if she would walk home with her after the performance that night. She was glad to help Maria, but it didn't matter. No matter what door they tried to leave through, no matter what door they tried to sneak out, he somehow knew where they would be. Then he would insist on escorting the two of them home. All the while, he chattered with Maria as if Annalise was not even walking with the two of them.

The theater had strict rules about this kind of conduct. The females were always closely protected from infatuated patrons who would try to see them for less than honorable reasons. Maria and Annalise didn't want to report Franz to the theater officials. Besides, they didn't think that anyone would believe them because of his brilliant reputation as a great artist. So they asked another ballet dancer, a girl from Oslo who lived near them, to join them.

Franz would greet them all at the exit "de jeur" and escort them all home. He would make small talk, but he would always sit right next to Maria on the train, and somehow manage to get next to her on the walk home from the station. The three of them tried ignoring him. They tried embarrassing him. They made jokes about him, but he persisted.

Then one day, Franz stopped Maria in the hall and said, "I have to talk to you. Please don't deny me, Maria. Please."

Maria told him, "I don't have time," and started to walk away.

"Please, Maria," He pleaded, tilting his head and looking deep into her eyes.

"I'll give you fifteen minutes. Not a second more," she said.

"I took a long walk by the Wupper River, and I know there is only one thing that is true. I love you. I love you with all my heart. I can't live without you," he explained.

"You are married. You have a beautiful wife." Maria felt as if she sounded like a broken record because she had this conversation or a variation of it, with him many times. However, this was the first time he said that he was hopelessly in love with her.

"It's just not going to happen. I do not love you; I think you are a nice person, but you have got to get a hold of yourself. I would appreciate it very much if you would just leave me alone. I don't want to hurt you, but you have got to get it into your head that I just do not love you," Maria told him.

"I have nothing left to do then, except to kill myself," he stammered, tears welling up in his eyes. He walked away. Maria had no idea how to stop him.

The next day, he met her in the morning on the sidewalk in front of her apartment, and walked her to the train station. He followed her on the train and walked her to the theater. He was like a shadow. His attention was intensifying. He was stalking her, but she couldn't tell the police because he wasn't doing anything against the law.

Meanwhile, his wife and Anna were becoming fast friends, and she was becoming suspicious. Her name was Gerti. She was a beautiful, slender woman with an aristocratic face. The three of them talked. She understood that Maria did not provoke or encourage what was going on with Franz. She knew that Maria was doing everything she could think of to discourage him because Anna had told her everything that was going on.

One night, Maria came home from work to find a pound of butter sitting on the table. This was very odd since one couldn't buy butter, even if one could find it on the black market.

"Where did you get the butter?" she asked her mother.

"Franz gave it to me," Anna replied.

A sudden feeling of terror came over Maria. "Give it back. Get it out of here," she shouted.

"Sweetheart, I thought of that with all of your problems, but you can't buy butter in this town. It's been months since we've had any." Butter cost 169 marks a pound on the black market. Maria was momentarily tempted to keep it because it was a real treasure, but she knew she could not.

Maria took the butter to work with her the next day. It was one of the rare days that she was able to do something alone. Franz had left her alone that morning, perhaps thinking that the butter was enough for one day. Maria was angry. Enough was enough. She felt that he was trying to sway her mother, and she made up her mind that he must leave her mother out of this. Determinedly, she marched down the hall, opened the door to his practice room, and threw the butter at him.

"Take that and leave me the hell alone," she shouted and slammed the door. It slammed so hard that the glass cracked. Her anger had the opposite effect. The more she mistreated him, the more aggressive he became.

But that evening, he was not at the door waiting for her. When she arrived home, Gerti was sitting there with Anna weeping wildly. Anna had told Gerti that Maria was going to return the butter back to him. Gerti knew how much he was in love with Maria, what he had gone through to get the butter. She was afraid that he might harm himself. He was sure that the butter would succeed where his other efforts had not. It was like a last desperate attempt to win Maria's heart. He had lost his sense of reality.

"Didn't Franz come home with you?" she asked sobbing, dabbing her eyes with a handkerchief.

Maria replied, "No."

"Oh, I just know something is going to happen to him. We've got to find him. He's getting suicidal," Gerti said. By this time, Gerti, Anna and Maria were all talking with each other openly about how to handle him.

Maria had hoped that the butter incident would calm him down, but it had made him more depressed.

"He's probably at the Wupper River," Gerti said. "But I don't think he can drown if he jumps in because it's not deep enough."

So the three of them wandered up and down the banks of the Wupper looking for him, about an hour each way. It was past midnight when they finally found him sitting under a bush sobbing.

The three of them had formulated a plan to deal with him when and if they found him. They all agreed that Anna wouldn't say anything. Maria went up to him first, and she talked to him very seriously. None of her sense of humor could work here. She spoke with him for quite a while, saying the same old stuff. She couldn't seem to find any new words to help him. She thought to herself that Gerti was the wisest, most understanding wife she had ever known.

Eventually, the three of them talked openly. Anna remained silent. He loved Maria completely, and Gerti loved him, but she just wanted to be anywhere but sitting on the grass under that bush on a warm summer evening.

As they walked, Maria told him, "I haven't been left alone walking to the train from the theater or home for months. Besides, take a long, close look at Gerti. You are the luckiest man on earth. Please treat her better."

After that night of crisis, Franz did leave Maria alone. Her life began to take on some normalcy again. She even began to feel safe going to and from work.

His work began to decline. He didn't practice any more. He spent most of his time wandering along the banks of the Wupper. Maria thought that she even heard some errors in his playing during performances.

A few weeks later, however, he appeared again outside the stage door. Her heart began to pound. She couldn't take anymore of this. He held an envelope in his hand.

"See here. These are divorce papers. Gerti is leaving me. Maybe we." His voice trailed off, and then there was a hopeful look in his eyes.

She said, "Absolutely not. You have got to leave me alone."

The season was almost over. She knew that she was leaving in a few weeks, so she told him, "If I leave this theater and go someplace else, I do not want you to visit me. Don't call me. Don't even send me a card. Just leave me alone. Totally. Do you understand me, Franz? It is not going to work, ever." Maria ran down the street to escape from him.

With all of that in mind, she wrote a letter to the theater at Gelsenkirchen indicating that she would like to return there to work, and that she was interested in the position of ballet meister. She knew that she could work there anytime because she had left with such a good reputation. In addition, Steinweg would give her an enviable recommendation.

When the letter arrived from Gelsenkirchen, Maria couldn't wait to open it. But when she did, she was disappointed. They had already hired a ballet meister, but they wanted her as first solo dancer or prima ballerina. As she read on, they added to that the position of assistant ballet meister. That meant that if anything ever happened to the regular ballet meister, she would take over. She couldn't believe she had moved up this far in such a few years.

Chapter 8

The Present

Maria closed the diary and stared out the window of the musty attic. She was amazed at the deliberate and steady progress of her career. She had forgotten that she had developed a degree of recognition and fame that she had planned and worked for. She realized that she had been a career woman ahead of her time in how she did this. But until she arrived in Wuppertal, the war was something she tried to push out of her mind. It seemed that the war caught up with her the moment she moved there. At Wuppertal, everything that could thwart her began to mount up. She had run from the Nazis and from stalking admirers only to find refuge in worse events.

The memory of Maria's first bombing and the sad concert on the side of the hill outside the armory that she had read earlier, was still fresh in her mind, so she leafed past the entry on the bombing of Wuppertal, and began to read again.

A few days after the concert, her mother left for the apartment Maria had rented in the Black Forest. Maria had a difficult time convincing Anna to go while she stayed in Wuppertal, but she finally convinced her that it was the best thing to do. Anna was pleasantly plump, and she could not move very fast. That lack of mobility was a liability now that the bombs had come to Wuppertal. She would be far better off, and much safer, deep in the Black Forest where there was no cause for the bombers to strike. Anna left a few days later.

Maria was scheduled to stay the few weeks that her contract was yet to run, and then she would join her mother. The next night, she was sitting alone in her room reading a magazine. She missed her mother even though she was happy that she was safe. Maria looked forward to the next day when she was supposed to pick up the new suit and hat she was having tailored. She had just returned from the final fitting a few hours before. She was very excited about getting a new suit. All of her clothes were tailor made, which made her look like a model. It was a small bright spot in her life at this point especially the hat because she was known for the smart hats and outfits she wore. Suddenly, the sirens began their incessant wail. The distant drone of bombers became an inescapable thunder of machines churning the evening silence into a froth of terror.

Maria had learned from the destruction of the earlier bombing to run for a bomb shelter the moment she heard a siren begin it's warning. To stay in an unprotected building was suicide. She grabbed her purse and the small suitcase she kept by the door for this purpose and bolted down the flight of rickety stairs of her apartment building. Other people were running out of the building just as fast. In their panic and haste, they ran into each other.

The closest bomb shelter was about three blocks away. It was built under a park in front of the old Eberfeld Opera House. Just as she and the group from the apartment breathlessly arrived at the door of the bunker, the bombing flares went off with a crack like lightening that had a lingering, ghastly hiss. The door to the bomb shelter was closed tightly. Maria and the others in her group tugged at it without any effect. They all beat on it desperately with their fists. Their screams were punctuated by the eerie whistle of falling bombs concluded with volleys of explosions.

Someone inside must have heard their desperate screams. The door opened a crack, and they all slid through the life-saving opening. As soon as they were inside, they stopped, mesmerized by the sea of people sitting on benches and the floor. Maria thought to herself that they looked like a surrealistic audience scrutinizing her as she entered the stage. Some were standing, and others some were huddled in small groups on benches and on the floor. Mothers tried to comfort their children; husbands tried to calm wives; old women wept and wiped their eyes; and old men sat and looked helplessly on in despair.

Behind the crowd and just inside the door were several halls with rooms off them. None of them had doors so that the wounded could be quickly and easily moved in and out. Doctors and nurses were stationed there to take care of wounded people. As Maria worked her way further into the depths of the shelter, walking around and over people to get away from the door, she saw a woman on a table in one of the rooms off the hall. The woman had gone into labor and was giving birth to a baby even as the bombs were falling. In another room, the doctors were wiping blood off the head of a man who had been injured.

Maria could hear the bombs exploding in muffled roars of anger as they tore through the city. There was a direct hit on the bunker. It shook the ground and knocked out two of the air vents. The air raid seemed to last for hours even though it was only thirty or forty minutes long. With the great number of people in the shelter, the air quickly became stale, making breathing a labor. Another bomb hit the entrance and caved in the only ingress and egress to the shelter.

Maria had found a spot against an inside wall. She thought how fortunate it was that her mother was in the Black Forest, but she felt helplessly alone. She did not know anyone around her. Everyone was a stranger, and she wondered how her life had come to this huddled in a bunker with no air and no way out. She wanted to cry; she wanted to be in bed as a little girl, pull the covers over her head, and make the thunder go away.

Suddenly, a Nazi SA soldier who was sitting on a bench stood up and shouted, "*Verdamte Krieg. Das ist doch schrecklich,*" meaning "Damned war. This is terrible." With that, he tore his Nazi medals off his uniform, threw them on the floor, and ground them into the concrete with the heel of his boot.

Another bomb hit the shelter just as he finished as if to punctuate his anguish. No one said anything. No one dared say anything. They just watched the drama as they tried to shield themselves from falling concrete and debris. The cement dust clogged their lungs as the air became thicker and thicker. Then another bomb knocked the shelter, and the percussion flung Maria and five other people to the opposite wall.

The people were panicking as the thought of suffocating in the shelter spread through the bunker. Some women began to holler that there was no other way out. Others held their families closer as the tempest of terror from the sky began to deny them life.

Abruptly, the debris fell away from the entrance as several soldiers with shovels pushed the rubble aside. Some soldiers filed in rapidly, while others continued to widen the opening.

"Everyone out of here now!" the commander barked. "Go out through this hole and run as fast as you can. There will be soldiers posted every ten meters to guide you to safety. As people climbed up the pile of rubble to the opening, two soldiers, one on either side, grabbed their arms and lifted them out of the deathtrap.

There was no panic now. The civil defense air raid training had taught people that survival came from clear thinking. When Maria climbed up to the opening, she was so light that the two soldiers threw her into the air. With her little case intact, she landed on her hands and knees right next to the body of a dead woman. She had just a moment to look into the woman's blank eyes, and to see the bodies of dozens of dead people who did not get into the shelter and perished when the bomb hit. Without time to reflect on their plight, she was instantly pulled to her feet by a soldier who told her to run in the direction he pointed as fast as she could. It was a wide street, and everyone was supposed to run down the middle of it. The bombing had subsided, but a building next to Maria disintegrated as a delayed bomb went off. She was knocked to the ground and pummeled by small debris.

Someone helped her to her feet, and she began to run again as she held onto her hat with one hand, and her small suitcase waving violently in the other. The soldiers shouted to the people and pointed them in the direction they were supposed to run. The whole street was on fire on both sides. Flames were trying to grab her from the center of the street. As she ran, the wall of a storefront collapsed and fell on a woman carrying an infant in one hand and desperately pulling a young girl along with the other, crushing them all. Maria stopped for a brief second, but she was knocked down by someone running behind her. She knew that there was nothing she could do for any of them, so she wept and ran and ran and wept. It was difficult to breathe because of the thick smoke and the lack of oxygen. The fire was consuming the buildings along with the very air she needed to survive. It roared as if to taunt the people trying to escape.

Maria's legs were aching, but the soldiers kept urging the people along. Finally, she found herself on the outskirts of town. There was a caravan of Red Cross trucks stationed there waiting to take the people to safety. She was headed for a truck when she bent over with her hands on her knees to catch her breath. She was in excellent condition because of her training, but she was completely out of breath and needed a moment to catch it. As she stood there, her legs spread swaying back and forth, a woman came up to her and grabbed her shoulders to steady her.

"Come with me, child. Our house is a kilometer from here. Well out of town. You will be safe there. They don't bomb that far out."

"Oh thank you. Thank you so much," Maria gasped, out of breath.

They began to run again. The woman asked a couple more random people to follow her to safety. The trucks were filled to capacity, and Maria would not have been able to get to a shelter anyway.

The woman and her husband owned a small house, but they tried to make the half dozen people they had salvaged as comfortable as possible. They all sat wherever there was a place to sit, on the sofa, chairs, the floor.

"Here. I think we all could use a little of this," the man said as he poured a small glass of cognac for each of them and passed the glasses around the room. The wife offered Maria some bread and cheese, but she could not eat because she was nauseous from the acrid smoke. Her main labor was to breathe better.

"You are all welcome to stay the night. I don't think it is safe to go back into town. Indeed, I don't think that there is much of a town to go back into. In the morning, it will be much easier to figure out what's going on."

Maria found a place to sleep on the sofa, and began a fitful slumber, listening to the distant sounds of a city trying to rescue itself.

The next morning, the couple offered their "guests" a cup of very weak coffee. Maria took it and ate a slice of bread. She thanked the people for helping her and promised to remember them after things returned to normal.

Maria's next goal was to return to her apartment and try to get back to normal. However, as she walked deeper into Eberfeld, the realization that her home was gone began to set in. When she came to the street where she lived, she saw that there was nothing left of it. All the buildings on her block were nothing more than huge piles of smoldering rubble.

She sat on a heap of debris across the street from what used to be her apartment, put her face in her hands, and sobbed. She thought to herself, "Those old steps wouldn't have saved me this time."

After a few minutes, she gathered herself and set out to find a train to take her to Frankfurt. She found no one from the theater. Steinweg's apartment building was gone. No one was where he or she was supposed to be. When Maria found the train station, it was leveled. Railroad men and soldiers were repairing the tracks. There were no regular trains left there, but the railroad workers had put together a train from the good cars that had survived the last bombing. It was a regular local train that was headed for Mannheim. Since that was as close as she could get to Frankfurt, Maria boarded it. She immediately fell into a deep sleep induced by the security of the familiar clacking of the train wheels on the track.

Mannheim was more intact than Wuppertal. The trains were more regular, so Maria took a local from there to Pforzheim. The ride there was filled with anticipation. The terror of the previous night was melting as Maria anticipated seeing her mother again. The countryside was less scarred. The first pine trees of the Black Forest seemed like the blanket she had wanted to hide under the night before. However, as the train rattled through the suburbs of Pforzheim, it was obvious that it had been bombed hard. Her heart sank. Until now, she had not worried about her mother. A sudden terror gripped her. No place was safe. Pforzheim was only a couple of stops away on the local from Neuenbürg. She should not have sent her mother here to die.

As the local train chugged deeper into the forest, however, her fears began to subside. The land again was untouched. Anna had no idea that Maria was coming, so when Maria showed up at the door they hugged each other and they both cried.

"I'm so glad I sent you here," Maria sobbed.

"I'm so glad you are here, sweetie," her mother sobbed back.

Maria told her about the horrific bombing the night before, and Anna just wept. "But I am here now, and I am staying here. There is nothing to go back to in Wuppertal."

Chapter 9

When Maria moved to Gelsenkirchen near the end of the summer, it was a lot like putting on a comfortable pair of shoes since she had lived there before. She knew her way around the city, and she knew that some of the same people she had befriended earlier were still there. Best of all, Maria thought to herself, Thea was still there. Thea, however, was amazed that Maria had returned as the assistant ballet meister. She was still in the chorus, but she was filled with joy and congratulations for her dear friend.

"Maria, I'm so happy for you. You really deserve this position. You are good," Thea told her as they met, embracing at the train station.

"Oh Thea, I'm so glad you are still here. It is so wonderful to have an old friend to talk to and share with," Maria replied, hugging her.

"Tell me every little thing that you have been doing for the last two years," Maria went on.

Thea did not have much earth-shattering news, but when Maria told her about her experiences in Wuppertal, Thea cried. She was moved at Maria's story about Franz, and she was scared to death about the bombings.

"Oh God. They are not bombing Gelsenkirchen yet. You have made me so scared. I don't think I could have lived through what you did." Thea trembled as she spoke.

Maria assured her, "You learn to survive. I think we are safe in Gelsenkirchen. It looks like it's not an important military target, or it would have been bombed already."

Maria quickly learned that luck and timing are very strange sometimes, and can provide opportunities - unexpected opportunities. One of those opportunities presented itself within days of her arrival in Gelsenkirchen. The regular ballet meister, Monika, had hurt her leg and had to have an operation in a city up on the North Sea. She would not be able to work for at least six weeks.

Maria saw this as another one of those breaks that could change her life. She was especially lucky because she was starting with the ballet corps from scratch. In other words, she knew that she did not have to live up to any expectations, nor did she have to undo the training of another choreographer. It was a lucky break.

The fact that Thea was there was very beneficial for the both of them. Maria never gave her any special attention that might upset the other dancers, but they spent their free time together. Their friendship picked up where it had left off. In another fortunate instance, there was a vacant apartment in Thea's apartment building the right size for Maria and her mother, so she took it. Thea shared her apartment with a roommate, another ballet dancer.

One afternoon, as Maria and Thea were leaving practice to go home, Maria asked her, "Are you going straight home?"

Thea said, "Yes. Why?"

"Do you want to walk together?" Maria asked.

"Of course, you silly. We always do anyway," she said.

Maria replied, “I just don’t feel safe for some strange reason.”

“My, you are full of angst. What are you worried about?”

“I don’t know. I wonder if there’s going to be a bombing or something.” Maria replied.

“I certainly hope not. I couldn’t handle it,” Thea said as she glanced up at the blue sky, wincing at the thought.

As they walked out of the theater, Maria was momentarily frozen in her tracks. Franz was standing on the steps with two little packages in his hand.

She whispered to Thea, “I had a feeling there was something wrong. He is the violinist that almost drove me out of my mind in Wuppertal. Please stay real close to me. He’s not dangerous, but we will never be able to get away from him.”

“I. . . I just want to give you a going away present,” he stammered holding the brightly wrapped packages toward Maria with both hands. “Go ahead. Please take these. I promise never to bother you again if you will take these.” He clearly hoped that if Maria took these gifts, she might love him and be with him forever. He had tears in his eyes and was obviously in emotional pain.

Maria felt sorry for him. Her heart was crying for him, but she knew that if she showed the slightest interest or emotion, she would never be rid of him. “I will only take it if you absolutely promise to leave me alone, and never show up in my life again.” She tried to be tender and firm at the same time.

“I promise,” he whispered. It almost sounded like a death gasp. He pushed the little packages toward her.

She took them from him, feeling compassion that she dared not express.

Wiping a tear from the corner of his eye, and trying to muster a small smile, he said, “Goodbye Maria. I will always love only you.” He turned and walked away with stooped shoulders.

Maria thought that there was something very final in his voice this time. She felt that he would finally leave her alone.

When she arrived home and walked through the door, Maria said to her mother, "Guess what happened to Thea and me today? I bet you will never guess."

"I have no idea. You received a promotion maybe? Do those two packages have anything to do with it?" Anna asked.

"Well, yes. And who would give me presents?"

"Oh, no. Not Franz?"

"Yes, Franz. Thea was with me. At first I thought that it was all going to start again, but I think he will leave me alone from now on," Maria told her.

"How can you be so sure? Remember how obsessed he was in Wuppertal?" Anna asked.

"No, he seemed resigned. I felt so bad for him, but he gave me the impression that he would leave me alone from now on," Maria told her mother, tears of compassion filling her eyes.

"We can only hope so, sweetie."

"He did not sound or look like he would bother Maria again. I think that he will leave her alone," Thea added.

Maria put the packages on the kitchen table and debated whether to open them or just throw them away.

"Open them now. I'm dying to see what's in them," Thea urged.

"Honey, you have nothing to lose. Besides, you should at least know what you are throwing away," her mother added.

Finally, after some urging from Thea and her mother, Maria decided to open them. One package contained a small bottle of Channel #5. Perfume was more difficult to buy than food and must have cost at least a week's salary on the black market. The other package held a clear, ten-carat topaz. These gifts were so extravagant for the times that Maria felt guilty about having them. However, she decided to keep them. It made her pity for Franz all the more poignant. She thought to herself how he had given up his wonderful wife. His work was suffering, and the one thing he loved the most had rejected him. Maria wanted desperately to help him, but she did not know what to do.

Several weeks later, she heard that Franz had been killed in an auto accident after he stepped in the path of a truck in Wuppertal. That was the official story, but she knew in her heart that it was no accident. He had given up. She wept for him and prayed for his soul.

The highlight of those first six weeks was a wonderful benefit the theater put on. It was a variety show in which the stars would perform one or two of their favorite numbers. Maria choreographed all of the dances. First, the opera singers would sing a special aria. Then the ballet corps would perform a solo, duet, or a dance chorus number from a popular ballet. A magician would also perform. It was great evening of lighthearted fun. One of the actors was running around on stage chasing the opera singers with a butterfly net while they were singing. It was amazing to see the stars, especially the opera singers, display such a sense of humor in public.

The orchestra conductor was quite impressive in his act. He sat at the piano and asked the audience to shout out songs they would like to hear him play. He then played short excerpts from about thirty songs that ranged from obscure classical music to beer drinking songs. The show was a hit, and reviews touted it as one of the most creative evenings the theater had brought to the community in years. Special mention was made of the "new young and brilliant choreographer who brought the whole production together into an integrated evening of hilarity and art."

Promotional picture for the Gelsenkirchen Theater.

Maria bonded well with the whole ballet corps, the orchestra, and the stagehands. They all worked together extremely well. They were like a family. Maria put everyone at easy with her self-deprecating humor. As a result, they worked twice as hard and enjoyed the work. When Maria came into the practice hall in her tights with a small drape around her hips and her hair in a tight bun, they would all joke for a while, but then they turned to the serious business of developing dance routines. The practices usually consisted of bar work, turns and jumps across the floor, and then hours of practicing new ballet combinations of steps, developing the nuances of the choreography. The practices gave each dancer an awareness of all the other dancers' motions and ability. They could become so synchronized that if one dancer forgot a step, he or she could pick it up from the other dancers with a slight glance.

The work schedule was rigid. This was something Maria had learned from Steinweg. Maria strove for the same perfection in her dancers that she demanded of herself. The dancers were expected to show by nine a.m. There were no exceptions for tardiness. There was an automatic five mark fine. They would warm up from nine to ten, take a fifteen-minute break, do exercises from ten fifteen to noon, and then take a thirty-minute break. No lunch other than a light snack was allowed because it slowed down the dancers. Then from twelve forty five to two forty five, they would continue to do exercises and learn new steps and combinations of steps that would be used in dances during the performances. This was the customary pattern of workout and teaching the choreographer's dances. Precision and grace were the outcome. Maria's schedule for the dancers was a little more rigid than usual because of the short noon break, but then she dismissed them a little early to compensate for the time. Besides, no one seemed to object because they all got along so well.

After six weeks Monika, the other ballet meister, returned. She was clearly jealous and intimidated because everything went so well in her absence. In fact, it was clear to everyone that Maria was a better, more creative choreographer. Besides, she had notebooks full of ballet combinations she had compiled while working under Steinweg. She had gone home each night in Wuppertal and carefully recorded "the Gertrude's" genius on the stage. Maria even wrote down the crazy routines they created when no one else was in the practice hall.

When Maria was choreographing for those six weeks, she, of course, gave herself the solo dances. She could do that as the choreographer, and not one of the dancers thought she was trying to steal the show. They could see the clarity of her motions, her poise, her balance, and her perfection. They thought she should do the solos.

However, when Monika returned, she was supposed to share solos with Maria. In some theaters, depending on their size, there might be a first, second, and sometimes a third solo dancer. Maria was basically the second solo dancer, and should be given some solos and duets, but Monika choreographed dances in which she put Maria in the back line.

One day at a rehearsal, Maria asked her on stage, "Why are you putting me in the back line? I am a solo dancer."

No one had ever dared to confront Monika because she was an insecure vindictive person who could do damage to the career of an aspiring ballerina.

"I don't know what you are talking about. You get your solos," Monika retorted.

"I will not dance in the back line," Maria answered stubbornly.

Monika did not know what to do when Maria confronted her, so she grudgingly moved her into the third line from the back, not the front line, like she was one of the chorus dancers. This was like a sarcastic slap in the face of a solo dancer.

Maria was incensed. She strutted out of the line and directly up to her. "That is not what I am here for." Maria really did not want Monika's job; she just wanted what she had worked so hard for. She stormed off the stage, and she went straight upstairs to the office of the director of the theater.

Maria was greeted by his secretary.

"May I help you, Fraulein?" she asked, somewhat startled to see someone in this high office in work clothes.

"Yes. I want to see Herr Director Licht."

"Would you like to go change your clothes first to be more presentable?"

"No, I need to see him now. There is a problem with the ballet corps that needs to be corrected," Maria said emphatically.

"One moment please." She turned and pressed a button on her desk and asked Herr Licht if he had the time to speak to, "What is your name and position?" she inquired of Maria.

"Freulein Happersberger. Assistant ballet meister and solo dancer," she said impatiently looking blankly around the room.

"Send her in," the voice came over the intercom.

"My, what can be so important to bring you to my office in your dance clothes?" Herr Licht asked.

Maria explained the situation trying, not to sound petty or childish. She knew what her position entailed, and what her position description was. Herr Licht listened attentively, and he was in complete agreement with her. Besides, this was not the first complaint he had heard regarding Monika.

He immediately summoned Monika to his office out of the rehearsal hall. With Maria in the room, he pointed out to Monika that personality conflicts would not be tolerated, and that she needed to follow the terms of the contract when it came to assigning parts in ballets. A second solo dancer, he told her, was supposed to do some solos.

"This is the last I want to hear about any of this, or there will be consequences." With that, he dismissed them.

They went back down to the stage where Monika immediately and grudgingly rearranged the ballet. The tension on the stage was obvious, but the other ballet dancers were happy at Maria's victory. They were not very fond of Monika. Maria did not have any problems with Monika for the rest of the year, but she did get some minor revenge later on when she tampered with some of Monika's productions.

Chapter 10

During the early part of the year, Maria would glance at the headlines in the newspapers. Russia was defeating the German army almost daily. The Americans and the British were defeating Rommel in Africa, and in May, the British began bombing the Ruhr. She could not keep up with the war. Things were happening so quickly. Italy was under siege, and air raids were creating firestorms in Hamburg and other cities. She had heard rumors about the treatment of the Jews in Poland, but she just did not want to believe them. After all, she was German, and she could not comprehend Germans being as brutal as the rumors characterized them. She was bewildered when she heard that Himmler had ordered the total annihilation of the Jewish ghettos in Poland. Her brother, Heinrich, had been drafted into the army, and he was fighting in Italy somewhere. He was not a Nazi, but when he got drafted, he had to serve or be shot. Furthermore, his whole family could also be in danger if he refused. Many non-Nazis were literally forced to fight for a Germany they did not believe in.

One day, while Maria was practicing in the ballet room with the other dancers, the phone rang. One of the girls went over to answer it. It was for Maria.

"It is a gentleman caller," she said, batting her eyes at Maria in an exaggerated manner and giggling at the same time as she handed her the receiver. It was a Heinz

Happersberger, and he wanted to talk to her. Maria told security that it was all right to send him up, but when she hung up the phone, she wondered why. She thought it was Heinrich playing a joke on her by calling himself Heinz. However, that made no sense since he was supposed to be in Italy. Besides, he knew that no one, including close family, was permitted to disturb her in the practice room unless it was an emergency.

She thought she had been tricked. Because she was a solo dancer, and easily recognizable, she had extra security to protect her from fans that became overzealous or infatuated with her. All of the female performers were closely protected. Admirers could often be very resourceful when they wanted to meet someone from the theater, so security was always very tight around them.

Suddenly, the din of the ballet room was broken by a knock at the door. When Maria opened it, there was a dashing soldier in an army uniform standing there. There were no Nazi markings on it, but she looked at him suspiciously and asked, "Who are you?"

He replied, "My name is Heinz Happersberger. I saw your name on the Litfasaule." These were the round posts on every street corner that had posters tacked to them.

"I am researching the family name of Happersberger. It is a very rare name in Germany, and when I saw your name on the poster, I had to ask you about your family. You see, I was separated from my father as a child, and I am trying to find him. He abandoned us years ago," he said.

He seemed to be honest enough, and he reminded Maria of her brother, so she told him about her family history as far back as she could remember.

"Well let me see," she said, looking at the ceiling. "My father's brother went to England and lived there for about a half a year; then he moved to Australia. My father died when I was five, and the only living relatives from him are myself, my mother, my mother's sister Herta, my two brothers, Heinrich and Karl, and their families."

"I have only found two other families with this name in Germany, and now I have found you. I have traced the Happersberger name back several hundred years to the Hapsburgs," he told her.

"My, that is interesting," she responded.

"If we are descended from them, then we have royal blood from the Holy Roman Empire. Our last name could be a corruption of the Hapsburg name to protect whatever nobleman took advantage of some medieval Frauline. We may be a stray branch of royalty."

"I'm afraid I cannot be of much help. I never looked into our bloodline. It is indeed very interesting. I can't wait to tell my mother. Please excuse me. I really do have to get back to work," she told him.

"I would love to talk more to you and your mother to see what she can remember, but my unit is moving out tonight. May I contact you when I come through here again?" he asked.

"Oh, please do. I am fascinated with the idea," she replied.

He turned to leave and promised to send her any information he might find.

Maria closed the door behind him, and the dancers immediately began to call her "Your Majesty." She made some regal strides across the floor and bowed to them.

There was no routine schedule in Gelsenkirchen any more. Almost daily, it seemed that the eerie howl of the air raid sirens would pierce the walls like the bombs that would follow them with the incessant drone of the bombers.

Every person in Germany had to take a civil defense course. It was usually taught at the police department. However, because the theater had such a diversity of schedules, they could not get there as a group. So the authorities decided to come to the theater to train them.

The training took place in the theater building where the civil defense authorities divided them into groups. The first group was the orchestra, the second the chorus dancers, the third the opera singers, and the fourth group the stagehands. These sessions were scheduled on Saturdays so that no one would have an excuse not to attend.

The trainers usually started with a test asking how the participants would respond in different situations. They would then discuss their responses with them. On the second day of training, the authorities explained the layout of the theater to them. As if we don't know it inside and out, Maria thought. They explained how to escape in case of an emergency. These were Nazi bureaucrats who took the whole affair very seriously. They actually bored the theater personnel to death.

On the third Saturday of training, there was supposed to be a mock bomb attack. All of the groups were required to participate in this exercise together. The instructors had marked areas with different-colored flags. The flags with yellow crosses on them indicated where Gelb Kreutz Gas, yellow gas, was located. This gas, if it touched your skin, burned through it and poisoned your nervous system. They were to avoid those areas at all costs. None of the theater personnel knew where these markers would be, but they soon discovered that they were placed in the stairwells.

Maria's group was scheduled to begin the drill. The instructors set off a horn; they all split up into pairs and went in different directions to escape from the theater. Thea and Maria were their own group. They did everything together. The others broke up along similar lines. They, however, never paid attention during the training sessions, so the two of them occasionally wandered into other groups. They had no idea where they were supposed to go. All they knew was that they had to avoid the yellow flags at all costs. The only thing they did right was to put their gas masks on correctly.

Two individuals from the opera singer group sneaked up to the roof using the stairs with yellow flags because it was easier than their prescribed route. Their assignment was to get to the roof and use the fire hoses to put out the fire. The conductor and his group had already sneaked up there through the yellow poison gas zone and had grabbed the hose.

The opera singers were leisurely walking and making small talk through their gas masks on their way up to the roof. As they stepped through the door, the conductor turned on the fire hose and soaked them completely. The tenor ran over to him, grabbed the hose, and wrestled him to the ground. Water was flying in every direction as the hose fired indiscriminately on the onlookers. Thea and Maria could hear the commotion - laughing, screaming, and running through the whole building. It was complete mayhem. The conductor won the match with the tenor and aimed the fire hose into the stairwell, hosing every one in there. He then ran down a flight and aimed it through a door, hitting the Nazi instructors. The stagehands then wrestled him to the ground and turned the hose on him. Everyone was screaming in fear of the dreaded water and laughing uncontrollably. Maria thought that it looked like something Stravinsky might have conceived - dozens of wet people running around with gas masks on screaming and laughing.

The Nazis barked orders at them, but they ignored them and intensified their chaos in response. The "artists" and the Nazis couldn't coexist. The Nazis couldn't control them. They thought they were nuts. The authorities threatened them, but they finally left in disgust at this "unpatriotic" behavior.

Throughout the years, Maria had many admirers and would-be suitors who sent her flowers and gifts. Occasionally, she would have a gentleman wait at the stage door in hopes of meeting her, but more often than not, security would be sure that it was safe for them all to go home without hassle by chasing would-be suitors away. As a matter of fact, it was almost impossible for strangers to get near them.

One day, a dancer in the chorus introduced her to a girlfriend of hers who worked in a department store. She was the daughter of the owner. Her name was Lise Lotte, and she was beside herself when she met Maria. She had never met anyone famous from the ballet before.

"Oh, I just love everything about the theater. I wish I could have been on the stage. I just love the opera. I want to dance in a ballet."

Maria could tell she was trying to impress her, and that she was star struck. "It's like any other job. It is mostly very hard work. The performances that you see look easy and good only because of the hard work that goes into them."

"I know. I understand. But I feel honored to be around someone famous," she replied.

"Well, I'm not exactly what you would call famous," Maria, said.

Lisa said, "You are too. I read about you in the newspaper all the time, and I see your pictures on the kiosks all over town. No. No. You are famous. At least a lot more famous than I am."

"Look, why don't I try to get you some tickets to some of my performances?" Maria asked her.

"I would love that so much," she said.

Lisa was a down-to-earth, honest person. She wasn't trying to befriend Maria to know a famous person. She genuinely liked Maria, and Maria liked her. They became good friends almost immediately. Maria was happy to meet someone who was not in the theater for a change. However, because of their schedules, they usually only saw each other whenever Maria went to the department store or when Lisa came to the theater to watch a performance.

A couple of months after they met, Maria had lunch with Lisa at the department store. Lisa was excited and animated because some gentleman who saw her working at the department store sent her flowers after he introduced himself.

"Oh Maria, he is so handsome that I practically swoon every time I see him. Besides, he is the nicest young man I have ever met. He is very, very rich, and my family approves of him," Lisa said. "I would like for you to meet him," she told Maria. "I told him about you, and he would love to meet you. His name is Dieter."

"Listen Lise, I don't want to meet him. He is your boyfriend. Why don't you get to know him better before you introduce him to everyone," Maria said.

After that lunch, Lisa went out on a few dates with him and kept Maria informed on the progress of their relationship. He was a complete gentleman. He never tried to impose himself on her. That wouldn't have worked anyway because she was a highly moral girl.

A few weeks later, Lisa urged Maria to meet him again. Maria thought that she was looking for approval from her. She told Lisa once more to give it more time.

A week later, at two o'clock in the afternoon, the phone rang in the ballet practice hall, interrupting the practice. This was the only way outsiders could contact them during work. Usually, security was so tight that someone had to hand-carry a message up to them.

Someone wanted to see her. She had no idea who. She shrugged her shoulders at the other dancers and asked who it was. The person on the phone announced his name. At first, it didn't register, but then she recognized the name. It was Lise's boyfriend, Dieter. Although Maria did not know him, she thought that he wanted to learn more about Lisa, so she had security send him up.

A few minutes later, there was a knock at the door. When she opened it, the ballet room became silent. Standing there was an aristocratic looking man. He had a slight mustache, and not one hair was out of place. He wore a full-length black cashmere coat, white gloves, and a long, white scarf. In his right hand, he held two long leashes connected to two perfectly groomed, well-behaved standard poodles, one white and the other black. In his other hand was a liter jar of caviar, and resting in the cradle of his arm were a dozen red roses. Maria thought how lucky Lise was. This gentleman was striking and noble-looking.

"Can I help you?" she asked.

"I brought you a little gift because I am never able to meet you," he said handing her the jar of caviar.

By this time, the whole ballet corps was looking over her shoulder to get a look at what he had in his hand. Maria could hear them oohing and aahing and whispering excitedly.

"Please accept this small gift. I would be most honored if you would accompany me to dinner this evening, Frauline Happersberger," he said, bowing slightly.

Maria replied, "Aren't you dating a friend of mine, Lise Lotte?"

"Well, I am, sort of. Please forgive my brashness. I knew she was a friend of yours, and I have been trying to meet you through her for weeks now, but it never seemed to happen. So here I am meeting you in person. My life will be shattered if you say no." He was so charming that she was momentarily speechless.

Then Maria said to him. "You have been dating a friend of mine just to meet me. I think that is terrible. How could you lead her on like that? I'm sorry, but I'm not interested in seeing people like you," she half shouted at him as she slammed the door and walked back into the ballet hall. The rest of the dancers had scurried back to their places and were acting like nothing happened. One girl ran over to the door and opened it a crack to watch him walk away. When she looked down, she saw that he had left the flowers and the caviar on the floor in front of the door.

In those days during the war, it was almost impossible to buy a loaf of bread, so this jar of caviar was somewhat of a spectacle worthy of a Wagnerian opera. Within a half hour, people were coming into the room from all over the theater to admire the liter jar of caviar. Everyone advised Maria to marry him. If he could afford caviar in these times, he could afford anything. But he could not afford her because she had to go back and tell Lise what had happened.

Maria took great care to give Lisa the bad news carefully. Lise cried. "Some rich people will stop at nothing to get what they want, and this was one of those sorry people." Maria told her.

"I know. I'm glad to know, but he was really my first true love," Lisa sobbed into Maria's shoulder.

"We are always warned about the dangers of people who are obsessed with us. We are told that some will stop at nothing to meet us. Why do you think security is so tight for us?" Maria asked her.

"I know. My mind understands, but my heart is breaking. I know it is not your fault." Lisa wept.

"This was the most devious trickery I have ever heard of," Maria went on.

Lisa finally realized that she was really lucky to have found out about this guy before she became any more involved with him. Most of all, she was glad to have a true friend in Maria.

When Maria returned to the theater the next day, she told everyone to collect anyone they could find in the building for a big surprise. By the time a crowd had gathered in the practice room, someone had found some stale bread. Maria announced that they were all going to celebrate by getting rid of the caviar. The crowd gathered around her in anticipation, and when she opened the jar, a big sigh arose from the crowd. Then a New Year's Eve atmosphere prevailed.

Ironically, everyone in the theater ate expensive caviar on stale bread while they couldn't find enough food to feed their families at home. The war was playing strange tricks with people's lives.

The air raids and the bombings were becoming a way of life. Not every air raid resulted in a bombing because planes would fly over on their way to another target, but everyone had to take shelter in the air raid bunkers, nevertheless. One never knew what was going to happen. The bombings and false alarms happened almost daily. Maria never became used to the horrific sirens and the hellish drone of the bombers.

One evening, the theater was presenting the operetta *Land des Lachelns* by Franz Lehar. The audience was in place, and the curtain went up at eight p.m., but when the overture had begun, the air raid siren went off. The whole theater - musicians, technicians, stagehands, dancers, and the entire audience - went quickly and very orderly into the basement that had been reinforced to be a bunker. The ushers barked orders and moved the whole crowd efficiently into the shelter of the huge basement of the theater. There was no panic, just a strange hushed sound of fabric brushing against fabric and muffled whispers filling the air.

Thirty minutes later the all-clear was sounded. The whole large group went back up into the theater. The audience went back to their seats; the performers to their places; and the technicians to their posts. It took thirty to forty minutes to get everything ready to go. The curtain went up as if it was still eight, and the overture began again.

Ten minutes into the first act, the air raid sirens wailed again. The whole theater - musicians, technicians, stagehands, dancers, and the entire audience - went quickly into the cellar again. The ushers barked orders and moved the whole crowd efficiently into the shelter of the huge basement of the theater.

Eventually, the all-clear was sounded. After the second air raid, it took less time for everyone to get settled. However, this time, the performance took up where it left off. Near the end of the second act, the sirens wailed again, and once again, the theater was evacuated to the cellar. This time, the all clear came at about one a.m., but the whole entourage returned to their places once more. It seemed like the performers and the audience was engaged in some surrealistic repetitious scene in a play from which they couldn't escape. The performers were all determined to continue, and the audience was determined to try to escape from the war for a little while, but for all their stubbornness, they all gave up for the night at about one two a.m. and went home. This situation was unique because there was usually only one air raid in an evening, but this night there were several. Maria dragged herself home from "nonperforming," and slept a deep sleep after she and her mother laughed at the bizarre story.

Maria left and Thea in the shelter under the theater for *Land des Lachelns.*

"I'm afraid you have to go to Waldrennach in the Black Forest. The bombings here are getting as bad as they were in Wuppertal," Maria told her mother.

"I knew you were going to say that today. I've already started to pack. Oh sweetie, I hate to leave you alone here. But I know you won't let me be until I leave for there," her mother said.

"Well, remember, you left just in time from Wuppertal. You know as well as I do that we would probably both be dead if you had stayed. You could never have run to safety fast enough," Maria told her.

I know. Just write every day so I know that you are all right."

"They are not bombing churches, hospitals, or theaters according to the radio. So I should be safe. Besides, I have to fulfill my contract, or I would go with you. Believe me," Maria said.

"You know, that assurance did not last very long in Wuppertal. You'll probably be with me sooner than you know." Anna said.

In the spring around Easter, Maria received a special ration of three eggs. This was like a treasure. She put them in a shallow bowl and set them on the dresser so she could admire them and feel wealthy. She fell asleep hungry and dreamed about a feast of delicious eggs.

Suddenly, there was a violent explosion. Maria had heard no air raid sirens. The windows blew in. The doors blew out. She was thrown out of the bed against the wall. A bomb had exploded across the street. She was dazed, but her only concern, having been torn from a deep sleep, was to rescue her precious eggs. She crawled around the room on her hands and knees, frantically searching for her eggs. Her hand then felt the wetness of the yolks and broken shells. She gave up. She felt hopeless, threw herself on the floor, and cried uncontrollably over the loss of her precious stash.

Then reality brought her to her senses as the close proximity of the falling bombs shook her to awareness. Maria had to escape from her apartment - and fast. She threw on some clothes, grabbed the bag she kept by the door for fast exits, and hurried down the stairs two steps at a time. The intermittent flashes of exploding bombs and flares that lit up the night sky provided the only light for her escape. When she dashed out the door, a pouring, driving rain slapped her in the face. Maria couldn't distinguish the difference between lightning, thunder, and exploding bombs.

She stopped momentarily to open the umbrella that she kept in her bag. Another bomb or clap of thunder hit. She didn't know which, but she took off running. The latch on her suitcase broke. Clothes were bouncing out of her bag, so she clutched it to her chest while holding her umbrella and running.

Without warning, there was a horrendously loud crash. Bomb or thunder, again she did not know which. It shocked her so much that she abruptly changed direction and ran directly into a brick wall at a full gallop. She bounced off it backwards and landed in a deep mud puddle. Her hat was knocked off, and her bag blew open, so she rapidly gathered together what clothes she could find and ran to the shelter about a block away.

She had never been to this particular air raid shelter before. It was unusual because it was above ground. She pounded desperately on the huge metal door. There was no answer, so she picked up a brick to beat on it. There was no answer. She screamed and used her umbrella, her fists.

Finally, someone opened the door and let her in through a crack. The people looked at her strangely. Usually, people ignored how other people looked under these circumstances because it was a matter of survival. However, she thought that some people even chuckled in the midst of this terror when they looked at her standing there soaking wet. She had wet clothes draped all over her. Her bag was inside out, and a frazzled, totally useless umbrella stood erect above her head for protection. The door slammed behind her. She maneuvered past people and sat on the floor in a corner. The last thing she perceived was the feeling of a warm blanket as it covered her shivering body. She fell asleep too exhausted and afraid to stay awake.

The all-clear was sounded at dawn. Maria was still groggy from the previous night, but she wanted to look for her lost belongings. She had a belt in the bag for which she had paid fifty-five marks. So when she found the large puddle, she got on her hands and knees and felt around on the pavement, looking for it in the murky water. She did find it. Her hat lay by the wall, upside down and filled with water. She grabbed it too. This small victory gave her the strength to cope with all this madness.

Maria asked some people about the unusual bombing patterns the Americans had used for the past several days. It was rumored that they were trying to hit a fuel storage tank, the biggest one in Germany. Later that day, she worked up the courage to walk across town to look at it. It had been hit, but it looked like an accordion that was still intact. The Germans had siphoned all the fuel out through underground pipes. She thought to herself that it was becoming difficult to survive. She felt an empathy with that damaged yet still intact storage tank. She thought to herself, "I feel like it looks."

Maria was thankful that Anna was already at the apartment in the Black Forest at Waldrennach. She was too old and too slow to run for shelter during the increasing air raids. Maria was not sure that her mother would have survived the last one. She was glad she was there because her mother had written that the planes only flew over the Black Forest; they did not drop any bombs.

One day after that bombing, Maria developed a powerful hunger for a good dinner. Every citizen was rationed food because the war was intensifying. But she figured that if she could convince a few people to put their ration stamps together, they would be able to make a good meal.

The next morning at practice, she asked, "Does anyone here miss having a good meal?"

"Boy, I do," one of the dancers answered

Another one added, "Food. What is food?"

"Here's my idea. We each get a quarter of pound of meat per month, but if we all pooled our meat, we could have one big meal," Maria suggested.

"Yeah. It sounds great, but what do we do for the rest of the month?" another chimed in.

"Come on. We all buy things on the black market anyway," Maria pleaded.

"She has a good point," another girl added.

"So, how many of you are interested?"

About six people chipped in some food stamps.

Maria was supposed to have the dinner at her place, and she was supposed to do the cooking, but there was one small problem - she couldn't cook because her mother used to take care of all that. Thea, of course, was no help. She could not cook either. So Maria asked a girl from the ballet corps, Ella, if she knew how to cook. She said that her husband was a cook in the army, and she thought that because of that, she could cook. Ella agreed to help her prepare a dinner.

They went grocery shopping with their ration stamps and decided to make pork chops. They kept raving to each other about how wonderful it would be to eat some good portion of meat for a change. They handed over their loot of ration stamps for the meat and a lot of potatoes and cabbage. On the way back to Maria's apartment, they bought some coffee from a man who ran a small black market operation out of his house. They felt like spies. They kept looking over their shoulders, expecting to get arrested at any time.

When they returned to the apartment, they carefully unwrapped their treasure of meat and laid the beautiful pork chops out on the table. They beheld their pinkness. They commented on their thickness. They smelled their rawness. They poked at the opulent slabs with their fingers.

"I remember pork chops," Maria said.

"I know," Ella replied. "Remember how we used to take pork chops for granted? We used to be able to buy this many or more anytime we wanted. Oh Maria, please tell me that this terrible war will be over soon?"

As they looked at each other, they felt a little silly to be doting over some cuts of meat this way, but the war and deprivation made people do crazy things.

Maria asked Ella, "How do you make pork chops anyway?"

"I'm not sure," she said "but I think you just put them in a pan and fry them."

Maria insisted, "I think you beat them. I know that you beat something before you fry it. My mother did it all of the time."

Her apartment was on the second floor. There was a restaurant on the first floor. Maria prevailed, and they decided to beat the pork chops, so she went downstairs and borrowed a mallet from the restaurant chef. She acted like she knew what she was doing so the restaurant owner wouldn't think that she was stupid. However, if she had told him what she wanted it for, he might have saved her a lot of grief.

When Maria returned back upstairs, Ella was no help. Maria decided that the chops needed to be pounded on a solid surface. However, the table did not seem to be stable enough, so she put them on the windowsill.

It was a warm day, the sun was shining brightly, and it was a Sunday; people were on their way to church. The two of them were getting hungry because they could smell the food smells drifting up from the restaurant below. Maria seasoned the beautiful pink pork chops with salt and pepper. Then she lifted the mallet above her head with both hands and hit the first pork chop with a shattering blow. The whole windowsill jumped up, hurtling the pork chops through the air to the street below.

Maria and Ella just watched helplessly as those beautiful pink slabs seemed to drift on the breeze in slow motion. Maria yelled to Ella to run down and pick them up.

She said, "No. You get them."

Maria replied, "No, you get them. I'm not going to go pick pork chops up off of the street." Besides, she figured that they would not lie around long enough for either of them to get down to the street to save them. She knew that anyone seeing pork chops falling from the sky on a beautiful Sunday would certainly thank God grab them and run. In a moment of sudden realization, they bolted for the door, flew down the stairs, and arrived on the street just in time to see a man run around the corner cradling the meat in his arms like an infant. The meal was gone.

Maria sheepishly took the mallet back and sincerely wished that she had paid closer attention to cooking class in her Catholic girl's school instead of always spending time in the hall.

When her guests arrived later in the day, they truly believed her fantastic story. Maria knew they felt sorry for her, but she felt the worst of all knowing that she had lost each of their meat rations for the month. They did, however, make the best of it and had a grand candlelight meal of cabbage and potatoes followed by fresh, strong coffee.

Chapter 11

Two days after the pork chop feast, Maria was sitting in her apartment studying dance routines for the ballet *Copellia.* It was nine thirty in the evening, and she was trying out steps as she held the notebook in her hand, saying the routine out loud as she did each step. Abruptly the wail of the sirens pierced the night air. She folded the notebook, stuffed it in her purse, took her coat and the small suitcase out of the closet, and left her apartment for the bomb shelter about a block from her house.

By the time she arrived there, she could hear the drone of the airplane engines as they neared the city. She quickly entered the cavernous cement building, and found a seat in the middle.

There seemed to be more children than usual in there. A few minutes later the doors closed and the first bombs began to find their targets. One bomb hit particularly close to the shelter. Some women shrieked, and children began to cry. One little girl next to Maria could not be comforted by her mother.

Maria dressed impeccably and wearing her trademark hat, moved closer to the girl and her mother and said in a soothing voice, “Don’t worry. Everything will be OK.”

The little girl, about eight would not stop crying.

"I'm afraid she is terrified," the girl's mother said.

"Did you ever see a ballerina?" Maria asked, stroking the girl's long dark hair.

The little girl paused for a moment to look closer at Maria, and calmed a little. The percussion of another bomb made her cry again.

"I'm a ballerina," Maria said.

"You are?" the girl asked.

"Would you like to hear a funny story?" Maria asked.

"Ok," she said still sobbing.

"Well, let me see. This happened right here in Gelsenkirchen a couple of years ago. I have this very good girl friend, Thea."

Maria proceeded to tell the story of how Thea and she were almost fired two months after they started. The theater was to put on a tragic opera, *Euridice*. A general rehearsal or Haupt Rehearsal in German theaters is equivalent to a dress rehearsal. It is to proceed as if it were an actual performance without interruption including all costume and scenery changes. Every element of the performance was to be carried out as if it was opening night and there was a full house in the audience.

"In this particular instance, we were rehearsing the complete opera *Euridice* by Christoph Gluck. The entire symphony orchestra was there. All the opera singers and the ballet dancers were in full costume. The curtain was set to go up on Euridice's casket, which was set in an open place, on a platform in front of an ancient temple at the top of three steps that ran the full length of the stage. It was a very large casket for dramatic effect.

A chorus of shepherds and shepherdesses were to sing a lament around Orpheus and the casket as he stood there. Thea and I were two slaves kneeling at the head of this mammoth coffin that was four feet by eight feet. We posed at the top corners, kneeling with our right arms wrapped in front of our faces over the top of our heads. The tenor, Orpheus, stood to the left of the casket with two slaves on either side swaying large plumed fans above his head. He looked like a pharaoh. But his costume was so stiff that one could hear the material scraping on itself as he walked across the stage.

Thea and I were dressed in sheer silk costumes that flowed easily with our dance. We wore a narrow gold band around our heads with an asp rising out of it in the middle of our foreheads. We also wore long, black shoulder-length wigs. Our hair almost looked like yours," Maria said, as she stroked the girl's hair again.

By this time some other people in the shelter were listening to escape their fears. Some more children moved closer to hear.

"Our makeup was heavier than usual for dramatic effect. As a matter of fact, it was so heavy that it was about the only thing I could smell on the stage. Our eyelids were painted black, outlined with gold and silver lines that came to a point somewhere on our temples.

When Thea and I came onto the stage to take our places, I looked at the tenor and then at the casket and said to him, "That thing is so big. All four of us could fit in there," I meant the tenor, Thea, myself, and the soprano backstage who was playing Euridice.

He said something to me like, "You are right, but do not start anything, Frauline Happersberger. I know about your silly antics, and I do not need any of that here."

"Suddenly, the conductor began tapping his baton on the music stand. The orchestra became silent as he said, "OK people. Let's go." With that he raised his baton."

"The orchestra played the entire overture and then began to play the opening scene. The gravest and most solemn scene of the entire opera was under way. Thea and I were kneeling at the head of the casket. On the correct musical cue, we slowly unwrapped our arms off the top of our heads and extended our hands out flat at about eye level with our palms up. We were like moving hieroglyphics. We then folded our arms back up over our heads to unfold them again three more times."

Maria placed herself on the floor and demonstrated to the little girl and her growing audience how she and Thea moved.

"The first time I unfolded my arm, I noticed that someone had painted new large black tea roses on the casket. I thought to myself that they were the most hideous things that I had ever seen. They were not there the day before. I wondered where they came from. I figured that when the audience saw those weird things, they would probably leave. Black tea roses. How strange. When I started to unfold my arm the second time I saw those ugly roses again and got a big grin on my face. As I finished the movement, I looked across my open palm directly into Thea's eyes. Thea normally had big eyes, but in the middle of all that makeup, they looked like serving platters. She looked back at me and got a grin on her face. We folded back up, but as I put my head back in the cradle of my arm, I started to laugh just a little bit." Maria looked across the palm of her hand, made a face at the little girl, and laughed.

The people around Maria were entranced. Some were actually smiling as she did the motions for the girl.

"By the time I unfolded my arm the third time, I was out of control. First I saw the roses. Then I slowly raised my eyes. I knew that I couldn't look at Thea, but when I looked into those eyes that looked like platters, the laugh I was repressing exploded. Thea gave me a quick dirty look as if to tell me to shut up, and then she started to giggle."

Maria started to laugh as she remembered the scene.

"Our next dance move was to slowly rise, extend our right arms in front of our faces, and slowly, gracefully, and solemnly move to the front of the casket then back around to the head of it again. I was already giggling so hard that my arm was bobbing up and down as I moved toward the front of the stage."

She stood up and showed the crowd.

"When I saw my arm doing this, I started to laugh even harder. What made it worse was that I could hear Thea out of control on the other side of the casket. I knew that this had to be a totally solemn and sad scene, but the more I tried to suppress my laughter, the louder it got. It reached a point where when I took in a breath, I snorted."

Maria was laughing uncontrollably now as if she were back there. The air raid was still raging, but a large portion of the people in the shelter were focused on Maria.

"Abruptly, the loud rapping of the conductor's baton cracked through the mournful music, and his considerable voice boomed. "Frauline Happersberger, what is your problem?"

"I'm so sorry Herr Conductor, but it's her eyes. The makeup makes them look so big. She looks so silly. And the tea roses. . . I replied trying to gain my composure."

"Thea, however, wasn't going to let it pass, so she blurted out in uncontrolled bursts of laughter, "No. It's her eyes. They are even bigger!" "

"If you two can get control of yourselves, we would all like to continue with this opera. Back to the beginning of scene one," he said, turning to the orchestra. "Everyone to your places," he boomed as he raised his baton on the podium."

"I sat there curled up at the head of the ugly casket trying to get serious, but then I could hear Thea giggling over the music. I thought to myself, think sad thoughts. There is so much tragedy in the world. You had such a hard life. After all, your father died when you were only five years old. You never really got to know him. How sad."

"I unfolded my arm somewhat sobered - I even was able to cope with the black and white tea roses - but then I unfolded my arm and looked into Thea's eyes. Not only did those huge eyes stare back at me, but Thea's makeup had also begun to run from the tears she produced by her laughter."

By now Maria was laughing as hard as she had in the original production, and some people in the bomb shelter were laughing just as hard with her.

"Oh my God. I thought folding my arm back up laughing uncontrollably. You never got to know a brother and a sister who died at childbirth. How completely sad. Sad. Sad. Sad!"

"As I unfolded my arm the second time, I shoved the sleeve of my costume into my mouth to try to suppress my hysteria. It only made me snort and laugh harder. At this point, the woodwind section of the orchestra was noticeably missing from the fugue. They were in the unfortunate position in the orchestra pit where they had a direct view of the two of us. The conductor continued with the score determined to get through the opening scene."

"The heavyset woman who sat in the prompt box at the front of the stage covered her face with the libretto. Her laughter pierced the solemn music with high-pitched staccato bursts that reminded me of a wounded hippopotamus. She was about that big."

A bomb exploded close to the shelter and momentarily interrupted Maria's story, but she continued. Her laughter was contagious. She was telling the story with staccato bursts of laughter. The little girl was curled in her mother's arms laughing at the silly story.

"As Thea and I started our procession to the front of the casket with our arms bouncing up and down, giggles and snorts bursting out of our noses, the brass section lost their composure and started to laugh."

"When he lost the brass section, the conductor again rapped his baton on the podium. Thea and I could hear the anger in the repeated raps. He chewed out the brass section, then he chewed out the woodwinds. When he finally began to reprimand us, his bellowing only made our laughter worse. He stepped off the podium, walked over to the steps at the side of the stage, up onto the stage and confronted us."

"OK you two. Walk through this scene. Just once I want to see you get to your marks right here" he shouted, positioning himself at the marks on the stage where we were supposed to pose at the end of their dance as the tenor went into his sorrowful aria."

"We went back to our starting marks at the head of the casket and began to walk through the scene. I tried thinking sad thoughts. I tried gagging myself with my sleeve. I tried not to look at Thea. The two of us made it through the first two arm unfoldings OK, but on the third one, I glanced at Thea for a split second. It just so happened that Thea took the exact same split second to glance at me. That was it. She laughed. Again, I tried stuffing my sleeve in my mouth. I was out of control. The sleeve just made me snort. The prompt lady was laughing uncontrollably too."

"Thea and I stood up in our dance and began our walk to the markers on the stage. I didn't look up at all. I just kept my eyes glued to the stage. I could hear Thea suffocating and laughing. "

"Then it happened. I saw the conductor's shoes, and as I slowly raised my head, I saw the knees of his pants, his belt, and then his chest. Each consecutive part of his body became funnier in my mind. By the time I looked in his face and made eye contact, I burst out into a roaring howl of laughter. His anger melted into laughter when he looked into my face and saw that the makeup on my beautifully painted eyes had run down to my chin. I could hear the "hippopotamus" piercing laugh. I heard chuckles coming from the orchestra. I saw that most of them were in tears. Then I heard the tenor start to laugh. His laughter built until he laughed so hard and loud that he threw himself over the top of the casket. The soprano backstage waiting her entrance cue was doubled over, holding her stomach. By then, the conductor was slapping his knees, also doubled over in laughter. The whole production was completely out of control."

"As the conductor began to slowly regain his composure, he said, "I don't think we will use the ballet corps in this opera at all. And you two. I don't want you anywhere near the theater during the performance of this opera, or you will never dance in this theater again," he said it, still chuckling. "I don't think the audience would appreciate *Euridice* as a comedy."

"Thea and I were thankful that this and the fifty-mark fine was the extent of his punishment because he could have done serious damage to our careers. So we stayed far away from the theater for the full run of this opera, but I was sure that the performers had difficulty getting through the opening scene after Thea and I were gone."

"All clear. You can go now," the guard at the door shouted. The people in the shelter were laughing so hard that they even gave Maria a little applause. The little girl walked out hanging onto her mother's skirt with a big smile on her face.

Chapter 12

Gelsenkirchen was located in the industrial Ruhr region. It had become a prime target for the allied bombs. This region was regarded as such a dangerous location that the theater couldn't even "lure" people there to perform. Consequently, the theater established a rule that no one could leave. No one knew where this "rule" came from, and the headmaster of the theater coerced performers to sign there new contracts a half of a year before the old ones expired. Contracts were usually renewed about two months before the end of the traditional theater season.

One day, Maria was summoned to the headmaster's office. His hair was coal black; he wore a monocle, and strutted around the room like a peacock. He arrogantly shoved the contract in front of her and told her to sign it.

Maria said, "I don't want to sign it. I plan to go to Berlin next year."

He sneered at her, "You have to sign it. You have no choice. It is orders!"

"With all due respect Herr Director, I want to check into this first before I sign anything," she stubbornly replied.

"We'll see about that," he snapped as he turned his back to her and stared blankly at some non-existent painting on the wall. "Dismissed!"

Maria was shaken and upset when she left his office. She wanted to get out of Gelsenkirchen because the intensity of the bombings was increasing. She knew that she could not handle many more air raids like the one in the rainstorm.

Later that day, she talked to Klaus, a tenor, who shared her desire to leave.

"Maria. Have you listened to the radio lately?"

"No."

"Well, Dr. Goebbels said in a speech last week that the German people have to support their young artists. That they are the bright hope of the future of Germany."

"Besides, he added, "The Nazis need them to keep up the morale of the people and the troops with their entertainment. That should give us some power to deal with the theater authorities."

A light bulb went on in Maria's head. That same night, she penned a letter to Berlin asking for a transfer for the summer months. She faked her patriotism and applied for a position to train dancers to entertain the troops. She hoped that this would get her away from Gelsenkirchen. A week later, she received a telegram from the Berliner Künstlergastspeilsdirection. They offered her a job. They wanted her immediately. The telegram stated that money was no object. They knew of her, respected her talent, and wanted her to work for them. Steinweg's recommendations helped. She was hired to coordinate and choreograph groups of people who would entertain the troops.

However, while she was corresponding with Berlin, the Theater Master called her to his office and waved the contract under her nose demanding her to sign it.

She said, "Oh No. Absolutely not! I do not understand all of these matters." She was careful not to give him any indication of what she was doing with her correspondence. In fact, she didn't tell anyone about it.

He glared at her with his cold, dark eyes and said, "You don't have much time, or else I will take steps. Besides, you do not get along well with people. You always seem to have problems with the ballet meister."

"I really must go," she said, and she got up and walked out of his office. He didn't like her, but now she knew he liked her less because of her stubbornness.

Several days later, he summoned her to his office again and shoved the contract in her face.

"I'm warning you. You can't take a contract anywhere else. We can't find replacements. If you don't sign this contract, you will probably end up in a factory. It really is out of my hands. You have two days to sign. You are dismissed," he snarled at her in a repugnant voice that spit the words at her.

Later that week, she received a letter from the President of the Reichstheater Chamber. He was fourth in rank from Goebbels. She was ordered to Berlin the following week to talk to him personally. There were no performances to choreograph for several days that week, and by chance, this lull coincided with her trip to Berlin.

She lied to go to Berlin. At that time, one had to register with the authorities to indicate which town they were departing, why they were leaving, and what their destination was. Maria told the bureaucrats that she needed to get to Frankfurt to visit her relatives, but she did confide in one other person, Ilse, a young dancer from Schleswig – Holstein. Ilse was an adventurous soul who accompanied Maria to see Berlin. She lied to the authorities too.

Maria miraculously was able to contact her mother by phone and told her the plan.

"I have applied for a summer position in Berlin to get out of Gelsenkirchen. It's getting bombed, but I don't think it is getting bombed as badly as Gelsenkirchen, so it might be a bit safer there." she told her mother.

"Oh sweetie, I'm so glad to hear that, but you will be so much further away there."

"I know, but I really have no choice. It may not help my career, but it will keep me alive," Maria replied.

Anna agreed. "You'll be much better off away from the ballet meister and the head of the theater, sweetie."

That night, Ilse and Maria went to the railroad station to leave for Berlin. It was after midnight. They had to finish the performance for that evening. While they were waiting for the train, they suddenly spotted the theater master, Herr Spitz, at the other end of the platform. They both became paranoid. They were not sure if he was following them. When the train pulled in, they boarded at one end, and he boarded at the other.

The trip was horrible. They stayed awake all night to avoid Herr Spitz if he happened to wander into their car. After the first hour on the train, they had worked themselves up into fantasies of Nazi murder and intrigue. Every passing shadow outside their compartment door caused them to shudder and fall into hushed tones. They figured that Herr Spitz would have to stab them because a gun would attract too much attention. And so it went on. They planned for one of them to survive so the survivor could tell someone, anyone about the dreadful death of the other.

"Why did I come along?" Ilse asked. "Berlin is not that important to see. I'm getting off at the next stop and heading back."

Maria responded. "Sh. Don't talk so loud. We should be OK. Besides, we are more than halfway there. Ilse, you will love Berlin. It is so grand."

"Oh, all right. You talked me into it."

Just then, a man walked by their compartment door, and they both shrank back into their seats.

"I can't stand it," Ilse whispered. "I'm leaving."

Maria grabbed her arm and pulled her down on the bench. " We are both getting carried away with this. Now stay here. We will be safe."

Finally, they arrived in Berlin, and Herr Spitz disembarked at the same stop. He seemed to be looking for something as he strained his neck to scan the huge train station. Maria and Ilse melted into the crowd, and did, in fact, lose him. Of course, they were never sure whether he was following them.

They found a small, out-of-the-way hotel where they registered for a room, unpacked, and freshened up. After lunch, Ilse went sightseeing while Maria went to the address on the telegram. That was the first time she became nervous. The building was huge. It was imposing. It was regal.

It's over. She thought to herself. I am finished as a ballerina. I will end up dead. Why am I so stubborn? Well, I have done myself in this time.

However, as she started up the long flight of steps to the entrance with its imposing square columns, she felt her resolve and courage return.

No! I will not sign the contract for Gelsenkirchen. I have come this far. The damage is done. I must follow through, she thought to herself. Maria was certain that the theater master had been to the office earlier in the day to give his side of the story and ruin her life. By the time she made it to the fifth floor, she had worked up her courage. She would convince them that she was one of Dr. Goebbel's young artists. She would not give in to them.

The president's secretary led Maria through two great doors and into the office. A large window with heavy drapes dominated one wall. The wall opposite it contained a huge fireplace. Between the fireplace and the window was a desk larger than the stage at the Gelsenkirchen theater.

Gelsenkirchen! Why did I think of that? Suddenly Maria's courage was gone. Idiot! She kept thinking to herself as she gazed around the cavernous room. Why do you make such problems for yourself?

Ten minutes later, the two huge doors swung open, and a well-dressed man entered. It was the president of the Reichstheater Chamber. She hoped that she could detect a slight smile. He took off his hat to expose a balding head, introduced himself with a subtle bow, clicked his heels together, and began to talk.

"So, you are the young lady who is causing our little Gelsenkirchen problem," he said rather softly.

Maria hoped that the conversation was leaning in her favor.

"I have heard a lot about you. Why won't you sign the contract at Gelsenkirchen?"

At that point, she told him about her offer to go to Berlin. She quoted from Dr. Goebbel's speech and told the president that the "illustrious" doctor urged citizens to support artists; that bureaucracy should not stand in the way of their advancement; that Reich artists would nurture the spirit of future generations for a millenium; and that she wanted to keep going up the ladder of success. She inspired herself with false passion.

I should have been an actor, she thought. I'm almost making myself sick with schmooze. I better stop while I'm ahead since I have no idea what Goebbels actually said in his speech. She stopped talking and wondered if she had said too much.

After a long pause, the president said, "I see that you have done your homework. You are a very ambitious and very clever young lady. And I do emphasize, clever. Do not worry about anything. Everything will be taken care of." He walked her to the door with his hand gently rested on her back and wished her good luck as he gently pushed her through the door.

Maria found Ilse waiting in the agreed-upon restaurant, and told her what had transpired. They didn't even stop to sightsee in Berlin after they left the restaurant. Ilse had done a lot of sightseeing that morning and Maria had been there before, so they took the next train. Mercifully, Herr Spitz was not on the same train this time.

When they arrived in Gelsenkirchen, they were more rested than on the trip to Berlin. They bought a bottle of wine and spent the whole train ride toasting Maria's triumph, laughing as they reminisced about the dreadful ride to Berlin.

In Gelsenkirchen, Herr Spitz ignored her for the rest of the season.

Anna took a train to Gelsenkirchen to visit Maria. She was lonely, and she worried about Maria. Maria was glad to see her. They cried happy tears and hugged a lot. The next day, they heard on the radio that Frankfurt had been bombed intensely the day before. The reports stated that it was the worst bombing in Frankfurt so far. Anxiety for the safety of their family mounted, so they decided to go have a firsthand look.

They caught the train from Gelsenkirchen to Frankfurt with a brief stopover in Cologne. While the train was in the railroad station at Cologne, the air raid sirens went off. Fortunately, they had remained on the train because it started to pull out of the station very slowly. Maria and her mother could hear explosions amid the sirens and the drone of the planes. As the train gathered momentum, they could see flashes of light from the bombs. At the same time, a train full of troops from the front was slowly pulling into the Cologne railroad yard outside the station. It was a medical unit, the kind with a large red cross painted on a white background on the roof of the railroad cars so that it would be recognized by the bomber pilots. It would not be blasted because it was carrying wounded soldiers. Suddenly, Maria's train lurched.

"Everybody!" The voice of a soldier in their car exploded like a bomb itself. "Get down now! On the floor! Now!" and he threw himself to the floor.

Maria grabbed her mother around the back of her neck and pulled her to the floor just as the windows shattered and the doors blew in, raining glass and debris on them. The train stopped. The soldier leaped up and ran out the hole where the door used to be. It seemed like a long time, but it was only a few minutes when the train started to move again very slowly. The soldier came back in to tell them that the last few cars of the train had been blown up by bombs, but rail workers and soldiers were able to detach them from the rest of the train so that it could proceed. Everyone on the train up to their car was killed. The saddest part of it all, Maria kept thinking, was that the entire Red Cross train had been demolished along with the back of their train. That useless loss of helpless wounded men made this one of the worst bombings Maria lived through. To look back at Cologne out of the train window was to look back on a burning city full of anguished death. The wounded and dead were scattered like some demonic child's toys all over the railroad tracks among the smoldering debris. Maria and her mother just huddled together, comforting each other and fearing what they would find in Frankfurt.

When Maria and her mother arrived in Frankfurt, they went directly to their apartment, which was in an old house near the center of the city. They were surprised to see as much of the city standing as there was after listening to all of the terrible radio reports of the "big" bombing. The city was horribly scarred, but their little place in the center of town had somehow survived the air raid. They went in and immediately started to take some of their possessions into the old wine cellar under the house. Those old cellars were deep and cool. They told their family that they were going to stay the night and head back the next day. Maria kept several apartments. One was in Gelsenkirchen where she worked. She kept this one in Frankfurt so she could visit "home" and her family, and she kept a third one in the Black Forest for vacationing. Now she realized that the Black Forest was probably the safest place to be.

The city seemed somewhat quiet since there hadn't been a raid for a couple of days. They were about ready to go to bed when the air raid sirens began to wail. The drone of bombers soon filled the night air. It was another attack. They ran into the cellar. This air raid was different from the one in Gelsenkirchen in its intensity. They could hear the whistling of the bombs over the sirens. Explosions ripped up the city and shook the earth beneath their feet. They could hear the distinctly different sound of an air torpedo followed by an explosion that rocked the ground. They learned later that it had taken out a huge department store two blocks from them and left only a large, empty crater. It seemed like thousands of bombers were raining terror from the black hole of the roaring, nighttime sky. They could hear wave after relentless wave of planes and crushing bombs punctuated by the antiaircraft fire.

Eventually, the attack slowed down a bit, and they decided that they had to get out of the center of the city if they wanted to survive. They cautiously climbed the stairs and made their way through a hall to the exit door from the cellar. Maria cautiously opened the door a crack. A rush of air pushed it wide open, pinning them behind it while a swirl of flame burst through and rushed down the full length of the hall. They both screamed, and Maria slammed the door instantly. They stood there terrified, unsure of what to do.

"What are we going to do?" Maria's mother shouted over the roar of the wind, the thunder of exploding bombs, and the howl of the relentless air raid sirens.

"Let's get back to the cellar - now!" Maria yelled as she pushed her mother toward the steps leading down to safety.

A few minutes later, they heard the upper door open and close. Maria's brother, Karl, burst into the cellar wearing an asbestos suit that was issued to all civil defense workers. He had been working for them for about a year. Flames swirled around him as he rushed through the door.

He shouted breathlessly as he tore off his gas mask, "You have got to get out of here now! This is greater than anything I have ever seen! The whole city is burning out of control! It's a firestorm! It's a hurricane made of fire!"

"What are we going to do?" Maria's mother shouted.

"Have you got your survival stuff ready?"

"Yes, it's over here by the table!" Maria answered.

They ran over to the table where they kept their survival gear. This was made up of one large vat filled with water and a pan filled with vinegar. They soaked two silk scarves for each of them in the vinegar and draped them over their heads. This way, they could see through the silk material while they ran. The vinegar filtered the air somewhat. Then they soaked heavy blankets in the vat of water and wrapped them around themselves - over their heads and completely covering everything. This was an important survival technique taught during the civil defense training in Gelesekirchen. Maria was glad that she had paid enough attention there to survive now. They grabbed their purses.

"Are you ready?" Karl shouted.

"As much as we will ever be," Maria answered.

"I hope my knees hold up," Maria's mother said as she made the sign of the cross.

"OK! Lets go."

Karl led them up the steps to the door. They huddled behind the door as Karl opened it, and a large swirl off flame licked the walls of the hall along its full length.

The air was a roar. It had a life of its own, filled with destruction. Karl shouted above the roar, "Run this way toward the river!" he pointed and pushed them toward the Main River. As they were running, the front of a building on the other side of the street took a direct hit and blew out, knocking down a man, a woman, and a young girl.

"You two keep running! I've got to help those people."

"But Karl! Karl, what about you?" His mother screamed.

"I'll be all right. I'm trained for this. You two just get to the river as fast as you can. You will be safer near the water." He pushed them toward the Main River and rushed to assist the small family. The Main River flowed through Frankfurt to the Rhine River.

The air seemed to be completely filled with flame. The wind was so powerful that it almost knocked them down as they began their desperate escape to the Main River four blocks away. It was roaring. The fire was roaring. The bombers were roaring. It seemed like God was roaring. The sirens wailed in anguish. The streets were melting, and their feet became bogged down in the soft asphalt.

Long arms of fire reached from the conflagration and tried to snatch them. Sometimes the wind pushed them forward; sometimes it almost stopped them. Bombs exploded behind them, on the side of them, and everywhere.

Maria's mother could not run to begin with. Now she was hobbling because her knees hurt her so badly, but she kept turning to look back at their house. It had been hit with a phosphor bomb. That sight was hellish. It was like a bright gold thick pudding that ran very slowly down the valleys of the roof, oozed into the eaves, and dropped to the ground in thick burning globs of fire. The slow motion of it was out of place, and yet strangely correct somehow for this raging inferno. Maria kept pulling her mother toward the Main River. But they could barely move. The heat was intense. Their feet were sinking deeper and deeper into the pavement, and the wind almost knocked them down and then picked them up again.

Suddenly, a small piece of phosphor splashed from a building through Anna's scarf and burned through to her neck.

"Help me! Help me, Maria! I'm on fire!" she screamed desperately.

Maria could barely hear her scream above the deafening roar of the firestorm and the bombers. Phosphor cannot be put out. It just lay there burning deeper into her neck.

"Oh my God!" Maria wailed.

She was not sure what to do. There had been no training for this kind of hell. She finally took the end of her wet blanket and grabbed the burning goo from her mother's neck. It burned her hand through the blanket, but she had removed all of it. It left a hole about the size of a half-dollar on Anna's neck.

They started to run for the river again when the wall of a building fell right next to them and almost crushed them. Maria was hit in the head by a piece of flying brick and knocked to the pavement. She did not move.

Her mother sobbed and screamed, "Maria, are you all right? Talk to me! Say something!" She knelt beside her and cradled Maria's head in her lap. "Dear God, please save my baby!"

Maria opened her eyes, looked up dazed, saw her mother through the haze of the scarves, and asked, "Where are we?"

"Oh, you're OK! Thank you, God. Get up! We need to get the Main River."

With that, Maria stumbled to her feet, and they resumed their flight toward the Main.

Finally, they got to the Romerberg square. The beautiful old buildings on the three sides of the square were consumed in the firestorm. Amazingly, the Romerberg itself, the ancient town hall of Frankfurt, was not burning. This was due to the fact that the city workers had dug a large hole in the square in front of it and filled it with water to pump on it to save it. Sandbags were stacked around the building as high as the second floor. Fire hoses, undoubtedly the only ones still working, were pumping water on the Romerberg. Not all of the hoses were working however, because they were melting from the heat of the fire and sinking into the asphalt.

Maria and her mother tried to rush but took only small, incredibly painful steps on the hot pavement. By some lucky circumstance, their blankets were soaked by the spray of the hoses. This saved them because their skin had begun to burn under their protection. The river was only about two blocks away.

People were running toward it from everywhere. They could hear screaming and wailing above the roaring wind and bombers. The banks were lined with hundreds of people trying to escape the flames. But to Maria's incredible horror, the river was no sanctuary in this hell on earth. The powerful winds of the firestorm had whipped up the river into large waves. The people closest to the river were being pushed into the raging water, and the others were unable to save them because the waves would pull those in the water away from the bank of the river.

Maria thought to herself, these waves are drowning people in the middle of an inferno. Hell can be no more gruesome than this. Oh God! Oh God, how can you let this happen?

The clothes and blankets on the people who were huddled on the city side of the crowd were catching on fire. So Maria and her mother started moving along the mob a few blocks to where the flames were not as powerful. It was easier to move there because the bank was lined with grass and concrete that wasn't melting under their feet.

People were throwing up everywhere and falling to their knees and flat on the ground. She did not know if they were dead. She did not want to know. She and her mother were retching too. There was barely any air to breathe, and what they breathed was acrid, putrid, and sickening.

They found a place behind a statue that shielded them from the heat somewhat and helped keep their blankets from bursting into flame. The air raid finally let up, and a bit later, the winds subsided. They were numb. Too numb to care. They milled around by the river for several hours asking people if they needed help, unable to really give them any assistance beyond a little human comfort.

"What are we going to do? Our house is gone. We can't go back into Frankfurt to find anybody. Oh God. What are we going to do, Maria?" her mother spoke as she sat on a curb and wept into her hands.

"I don't know. I do know, however, that we can't just stay here and do nothing," Maria replied.

Finally, she decided that they should make their way toward the autobahn and try to get out of the city. It was useless to try to go back to their house or try to find Karl or anyone else in the family. They wandered for hours to get there, but it gave them a purpose on which to focus and took their minds off the disaster. They found the autobahn, and then they wandered along the thoroughfare for a little ways. There was no traffic. Maria just assumed that there was no more transportation left. She was sure that the world as they knew it had ended.

Finally, they saw a train coming along a railroad track next to the autobahn. Maria ran over to the track and waved it down. Her mother caught up to her, puffing and straining. The train stopped. It seemed to be picking up stray people because it picked up a few more people after they boarded.

They did not know where it was going, but it finally stopped in a station in Mainz outside of Frankfurt. There, the two of them picked up a train for Cologne to return to Gelsenkirchen. All they had was their blankets and their scarves. When they were underway, the conductor appeared, asking for tickets. He demanded to know where theirs were and why they would even get on a train without them. Maria told him that if he had been in Frankfurt the night before, he would know why they had not bought tickets. After she searched in her purse for some money and paid him on the spot, he left them alone. Maria still had her purse and identification papers. These basic necessities never left their sight under any circumstances.

After they got back to Gelsenkirchen and collected their wits, Maria bought a ticket to send her mother back to their apartment in the Black Forest because they both thought that it was a safer place, and she wanted to get her mother to safety as quickly as possible. The apartment there was out of the way, having no large cities or industries near it. At that point, she prided herself with the foresight she had to get several apartments. Luckily, she was in a financial position to do that. She also resolved beyond a doubt to get out of the Ruhr region to Berlin at all costs. She figured that Berlin was so deep in Germany that it would not be bombed for a long time.

The season in Gelsenkirchen ended, and she went to Berlin. Her mother was in the Black Forest. Anna wanted very much to come to Berlin with Maria since she had been with her all along. However, Maria convinced her that it was better to stay since she couldn't move too fast. That lesson was quite clear in Frankfurt. After all, the bombs did not wait for someone to leisurely stroll to a shelter, especially a chubby lady who was better at waddling than running because of the arthritis in her knees. The scar on her neck was proof of that.

Maria also didn't take a vacation that year because she did not want to stay in Gelsenkirchen or near the Ruhr industrial coal region. She wanted to be "safe" in Berlin and have her mother safe in the Black Forest.

Chapter 13

Maria's work in Berlin was fairly routine and somewhat exhausting. The dancers were good, and some of the groups were starting to go out to entertain the troops. However, Maria did not know that the President of the Reichstheater Chamber was watching her and her work very closely.

One day, he summoned her to his office. The immense office had not changed any from her earlier visit. It was just as imposing and threatening now that she was working there as it had been when she went there in conflict.

"Frauline Happersberger, we have been reviewing your resume very carefully, and evaluating your talent. Have you ever heard of the Elite Corps of Entertainers?" He asked her. He was not wearing a Nazi uniform, but he had small Nazi pins on his suit.

"No, I have not, Herr President Director," Maria replied.

He walked around behind his desk, sat down in an overstuffed leather chair, took a cigarette out of an ornately engraved cigarette box, and offered one to Maria. She declined the offer as he lit his and drew deeply on it.

"This is a small group of artists made up of the most outstanding performers in each of their respective fields: a tenor, a soprano, a prima ballerina/choreographer, and a pianist. There will only be five of you. In your particular case, we need someone who has a wide range of dancing and choreographing experience - someone who can tap dance to Gershwin, and also interpret Bach or Beethoven into dance. This group will only perform for the officers, and even perhaps for Hitler or Goebbels."

Maria knew that it wasn't a request. The decision had already been made for her by people high up in the government, and she knew it. A knot formed in her stomach, and she suddenly felt faint. She was drafted into the Nazi cause.

"I don't know what to say," Maria managed to choke out after she caught her breath. She was very careful not to show any emotion.

She didn't say "yes" or "no." It was too terrifying of a thought to take full hold of her consciousness. She had been able to avoid the Nazis up to this point. She immediately tried to rationalize and look for some hope in that it would get her out of Berlin, away from the relentless bombings. She knew she had no choice.

"I'm not sure. . ."

"Come now, young lady," the Herr President interrupted. "You asked to come here. You did not hesitate to promote the Funkturm here in Berlin a few years ago. You will do quite well. I have been told that Doktor Goebbels and the Fuhrer himself have scrutinized these resumes. Of course, you will have to join the 'party.' "As a matter of fact, I'm a bit surprised that you are not already a member."

Up to this point, during the brief time Maria had been in Berlin, she had been training performers to go out and entertain the troops. Now she did some research on the Elite Corps of Entertainers.

Maria was introduced to the two performers who had returned from the frontiers. They were a husband and wife team, he a tenor and she a soprano, who had just returned from Lithuania. They talked of mortar attacks, life on the front, and the relative safety of the officers' locations where they had performed. They told her that they were treated like royalty. They stayed in the best accommodations because they were the special entertainment for the officers.

Maria did not know what to do. Besides, she felt coerced to take the position. She knew she had no choice. That meant she would have to join the Nazis. The Reichstheater Chamber offered her a salary that was astronomical. They had sent her a telegram indicating that money was no object. Her mind spun. She tried to rationalize that she would be helping many soldiers because she had heard that much of the army was not Nazis. They were just conscripts like her brother Heinrich who needed something to lift their spirits, so she reluctantly followed her orders. She felt somewhat broken, but she would survive. She was scheduled to sign the papers in a couple of weeks.

Maria did not sleep well. She met the piano player who was part of the Elite team. They formed an instant friendship. They rehearsed daily on a Beethoven piece. Maria was choreographing a solo piece for herself that would also highlight the virtuosity of the pianist. They only had another week to rehearse before they would go out to the front.

Maria was becoming restless. She could not contact anyone in her family. The telephones were completely unreliable; telegraphs could only be used by the military, not artists.

I will not sign the papers. I cannot sign the papers. I will not be a Nazi, she thought to herself.

You idiot. They will shot you on the spot, cut your head off, and kick it around in a game of soccer, she answered herself.

To live and compromise my integrity, or to die. What a choice. I know what I have to do. There was no one she knew well enough to confide in, so one lonely evening, she came up with a solution.

It was as if the bombs were following her. As soon as she started the rehearsals, the allies started bombing Berlin heavily, even during the daytime. The intensity of the air raids increased every day. She was very unhappy - repulsed to be forced to work for the Nazis. Terror of the Nazis forced her to get up and go to work in the morning and stay there all day. Fear for her soul if she joined them strengthened her prayers.

The bombings increased, more frequent and more intense every day. Maria couldn't stand it anymore. She was spiraling into deeper fear with each air raid alert. However, the bombing of Berlin was not like the firestorm in Frankfurt. It seemed like the allies were just bombing rubble for the sake of transforming rubble to dust. There was not much left to burn. She just wanted to be safe from the terror raining from the sky, away from the sirens, the drone of the killer planes. It had never occurred to her when she was in Gelsenkirchen that the bombers could penetrate this deeply into Germany. The propaganda had painted Germany as invincible.

Several days later, Maria was summoned to the Herr Director's office. She did not have to wait long. The secretary buzzed him on the intercom, and he told her to send Maria in.

"Come in. Come in Fraulein Happersberger. How is your work coming along?" he asked, smiling.

"Just fine, Herr Director. It is hard work, though."

"Yes, but we know that you are doing just fine. Now, I have a proposal for you. It seems that Doktor Goebbels has taken an interest in your work, and would like to meet with you personally," he said.

Maria stopped breathing, and looked up at him.

She was not able to conceal her astonishment at this comment. "No need to look so shocked. You asked to come here," he said.

Maria fell back in her chair and gulped a breath of air.

"He would like to meet with you over dinner on Wednesday," he continued. "Can you be there?"

"I, I don't know what to say," Maria stammered. She instinctively knew what the request meant. He was known for his interest in female entertainers. Maria's mind raced. She could think of no way to turn down the "invitation." "May I think about it?"

"Oh, I assure you. It is strictly business," he sneered at her. "Then, it is settled, Wednesday it is. I will give you the details tomorrow." He showed her to the huge doors.

Maria was sick to her stomach. She did not know what to do. She wandered aimlessly around Berlin trying to figure out a way to get out of her predicament. She realized that there was no easy solution to her dilemma. She was desperate.

The house where Maria lived was on the outskirts of the city, about an hour's commute to work. She lived with a friendly family that the theater had found for her. It was a husband, his wife, two small children, and two nieces who treated her like a member of their own family.

The next day, on the way back to the house after rehearsing all day, after spending several hours in a bomb shelter, she made up her mind to follow through on her secret plan and leave Berlin. It just wasn't safe anymore because of the bombing. She resolved that she could not work for the Nazis regardless of how much money she was getting paid. She would absolutely, never go to meet with Goebbels to become one of his trophies. She was also worried about her mother in the Black Forest because mail was not coming through anymore. She resolved to go there to "protect" her mother.

When she arrived home after work, she packed a small suitcase. There was an air raid going on at the time, and she could hear the bombs exploding all around. She wondered why they were bombing way out here. There were no strategic targets here, just neighborhoods. The family was huddled out in the crude little shelter the father had built for them in the courtyard.

With a resolve that bordered on hysteria and reckless disregard for her safety in the reality of the air raid, she ran out the door toward the train station. She hesitated for a moment and thought about joining the family in their crude shelter, but she wanted to get out of the city at all costs. She did not want to work in the Elite Corps of Entertainers. She didn't want any part of the Nazis. She decided that she would rather be dead than see Goebbels. She was focused on the relative tranquillity of the Black Forest. At that moment her personal safety was not a concern. She was already in the Black Forest in her mind.

Maria finally made her way to the railroad station. The air raid had ended about a half-hour before. She decided to take the next train that came through. She resolved to board anything and go in any direction, except east toward Russia, to get out of the city. She knew that she could manage a way to get to the Black Forest from anywhere other than Berlin. But she was not going to take a chance on approaching the Russians. While she was waiting in a panicked state, a train pulled in, bringing in soldiers from the Russian front. Just as their train pulled into the station, the air raid sirens went off again. The hideous drone of the bombers began.

Maria did not know where the bomb shelters were in this part of the city, so she ran along some tracks down into a subway tunnel to find safety. People scattered in every direction. Suddenly, she realized that there was not enough room for her, her suitcase, and a subway train. Then she remembered that the subway was a target of the bombs too. Just a week before, several hundred people had been killed when a bomb tore through the subway tunnels. People were rushing past her to get deeper into the tunnel when they suddenly started to scream and run in the opposite direction. Maria turned and ran to get out of their way. Then she heard the rumble of a subway train coming up behind her. As she looked back over her shoulder, she saw the headlight of a train pop around a bend in the tunnel. She ran with all of her strength. Some people next to her fell. She was going to try to help a man up, but the train was upon them. She jumped back and threw herself flat against the wall of the tunnel, her arms thrown above her head with her small case dangling from her thumb. The train rushed by. Some others were able to get out of its way, but some were thrown like toys before it as it sped by. Maria staggered out of the tunnel, dazed. She made her way to the platform, and she threw herself in a heap on the landing, not knowing if the wailing she heard was her own weeping or the agony of death broadcast by the air-raid sirens.

There was no use trying to buy a ticket by this time. The whole terminal, as huge as it was, was in chaos. It had not been bombed, but there was no civil order. Maria scurried onto the first train that was heading west, and it just so happened that it was heading for Frankfurt. It was crammed so full of people that she could not get on it. She started desperately to chase it, screaming for help. Some soldiers inside heard her and reached out the window. She jumped onto the entrance stage and hung onto the railing. They took her suitcase and then pulled her to the side and in through the window. She felt so lucky. She just wanted to get out of Berlin at all costs, and she would have gone anywhere to accomplish that goal. But getting on this train headed west would make it much easier to get to the relative safety of the Black Forest and her mother.

She did not know that this train was carrying soldiers from the eastern front to hospitals in Frankfurt. None of them were Nazis. It was like being in the middle of a terrifying nightmare. It was so crowded that people had to sleep standing up.

Wounded men were lying on the floors, occasionally punctuating the steady progress of the train with a moan.

About two thirds of the way to Frankfurt, while Maria was in the middle of an uneasy nap sitting on the floor under the window with her small case wrapped under her legs, the train suddenly lurched to a stop. She was jostled awake and stunned by the percussion of a bomb that hit the back of the train. Only the last few cars were lost, and the surviving soldiers were able to loosen the train from the debris and start it moving forward. The front part of the train never left the tracks. It took several hours to rescue the few survivors. The anguish she had felt at Cologne flooded her soul once more when she looked back and a saw the same scene of death and pain as if it had been transported through time to this bleak, burning, and ravaged place. Maria was numb from exhaustion, desperation, and now a deep sense of tragedy. She wondered if this was what her life would be like until it was ended by a random bomb falling from above.

How ironic, she thought to herself. The tears of God should fall from heaven to heal Germany, but heaven is no longer up above. Satan is splashing tears of laughter wrought of phosphor and TNT across the world. Everything is backwards, inside out and upside down. What is right is wrong. What is life is death. Nothing makes sense. Maria cried herself back into an uneasy sleep.

A few hours later, the train began to slow down to a stop. The screeching of the brakes and the sliding wheels again woke her. The tracks in front of the train had been bombed. She could hear bombers approaching again, but this time, it was dark and all the lights on the train were shut off until they passed. All of the men on the train and any of soldiers who were able went out to help repair the tracks. Maria looked out the window and saw a huge crater in front of the train.

Oh God, she thought. I will never get out of this alive.

It took all night and the rest of the next day to repair the tracks safely. Men were carrying stones for the rail bed in their coats folded like sacks; soldiers used their helmets, and even the women carried them in anything they could find. Others were pulling up pieces of railroad track from behind the train and carrying them around to the front. Everybody on the train worked together and did whatever they could to help the desperate situation. People shared food that they had brought with each other. Others took food out to the men. Maria felt so helpless because she didn't have anything to share. She only had her suitcase, so she piled her belongings on the floor and gave it to a soldier to carry stones.

Finally, they were ready to move ahead again. Maria had her case returned and stuffed her few belongings into its dirt-covered compartments. Everyone disembarked from the train to make it as light as possible since the patchwork was shaky to say the least. The train began to move slowly forward. One could feel the tension in this unlikely group of makeshift construction workers as the engine began to move. They would glance into each other's eyes and look back to the train, hanging on to each other as they watched.

As it moved forward, the gravel shifted, and the locomotive listed to the left as a hushed whisper of horror came from somewhere in all their throats. But then the ground stopped shifting, and the train made it over the patch in an eternally slow creep. Once it was safely past the repair, everyone got back on the train, and it continued toward Frankfurt.

The train finally pulled into Mannheim, where Maria disembarked. She figured out that it was closer to Waldrennach and the Black Forest than Frankfurt. She immediately boarded the next train to Pforzheim. From Pforzheim, she was able to walk to Waldrennach, where her mother was living. Each step in the tranquility of the forest gave her a little more hope. However, she now had the nagging fear of being pursued by the Nazis.

Maria went up to the door and knocked in anticipation of seeing her mother again. She wanted to surprise her, so she decided to knock. Anna opened the door, burst into tears, and hugged Maria for a long while. Maria hugged her back just as hard. At last she had something meaningful and tangible back in her life. That gave her hope.

After they recovered from their reunion, Maria's mother told her that the farmers did not like city people. They distrusted anyone that came there during this time of peril. Maria assured her that this was a small problem compared to what was happening in Germany now. They both chuckled.

Maria sank into the big, soft chair in the living room with a cup of weak hot coffee and told her mother what had happened. She was completely horrified at Maria's stories about Berlin. But they were so happy to see each other that all the bombings seemed to melt into a memory. Anna assured her that there had not been anything like that there. Maria felt safe at last. She went to bed and slept deeply for the first time in weeks, but she could not shake a sense of uneasiness that nagged at her as she drifted off to sleep.

Chapter 14

The next day, while Maria and Anna were listening to the radio, one brief announcement sent cold shivers through Maria. The announcer stated in his stream of notes that no one in Germany was to leave their present location under any circumstances in case they were needed for emergencies where they were. He never said it, but the true message was that the war was going very badly for Germany. She was very concerned about that ruling, and she remembered the brutality of the Nazis. She was sure that the Nazis would catch up with her and kill her and her mother.

Maria looked at her mother and started to cry. "They are going to kill me, and then they are going to kill you, mama. Worse, they will kill you first and make me watch. We have got to do something."

"Maria, I haven't seen many Nazis around here. They are not too popular here. Besides, this is so far from any big city that it will take a while for them to figure out where you are," her mother tried to comfort her. "Who knows, maybe the war will be over soon."

"I have an idea," Maria said. "They already think I was going to be a Nazi, so I will let them think they're right. I never signed the papers, but maybe I can make them think that I'm sympathetic."

Maria had been told by her landlord that there was a small factory in Waldrennach that manufactured watches. It had been converted to a factory that made airplane parts for the Luftwaffe. She knew that it was a matter of time until someone checked her papers and sent her back to Berlin, so she decided to go to the factory and volunteer for work. If she could convince the management that she was of much more value to Germany building parts for the war machine than working in the theater, she would be able to stay with her mother and remain far from the heavy bombing. It was a gamble, but she figured that Germany now needed people to help build parts more than it needed artists. She planned to use all of her acting ability to accomplish this.

Waldrennach was situated half way up the mountain east of Neuenbürg. Maria lived in the first house on the left as one entered the village. The Burgermeister's house was four doors down from Maria's house, and the gamekeeper's house was on the other side of the street mid way between them. There were eight to ten houses on both sides of the main street that dead-ended into another street. That street was only three blocks long in either direction. The small factory sat at the north end of it, a small pension called Gertrude's Inn sat just to the south of the intersection, and several houses were scattered between them on either side of the street. Small trails meandered off into the woods from behind the peasant houses.

The next day, she set out to find the factory. It was a rather small building on the outskirts of town. She did not go there until after noon because it took her all morning to build up her courage. Another reason she waited was that every morning at exactly eight am, eight airplanes would fly between the mountains and fire machine-guns at the town. They shot anything that moved on the streets. They even shot through the windows of houses. They fired on anything and everything. They were very regular and predictable, but Maria did not want to take a chance that they might catch her out on the streets at some other time should they decide to change their schedules. In some strange way they, seemed less threatening than the bombs, but they were equally dangerous if not more so, just a little quieter, and there were no wailing sirens to warn her.

Maria took the morning time to draft a letter to the president of the Reichstheater Chamber in Berlin to explain that she was in a small village, and that, for the time being at least, since she was there, she was going to volunteer to work in a munitions factory. She tried to explain her panic from the bombings in the hope that it would be a sound reason for leaving Berlin. She made it clear that her contribution to the Reich would be far more valuable that way.

She also stressed that her work was completely voluntary, and that there would be no cost to anyone, especially the government, since she did not expect to get paid while working for the greater glory of Germany. However, she gave Furtzheim as her address so she could not be so easily found. She gave the address of a destroyed house so she could pick up her mail at the post office.

Furtzheim was also a long distance from Berlin, and she hoped that with the war going as badly as it was, that they might not have the time to be concerned with a small fish like her. But she never realized that she was no longer a small fish, having been drafted into the Elite Corps of Entertainers.

Maria found the factory, but she was surprised at the small size of it. She had always thought of a factory as a huge complex with large billowing smokestacks and a lot of noise and activity, but this was the size of a large house, and just as unassuming.

When she entered the door, she had to wait until a hard-looking man wearing a monocle swaggered up to her. His face appeared contorted. He did not look like she imagined a foreman to look. He was balding, and his eyes radiated hate. To her right was a small office. Next to her was a small desk. Behind the man, she could see approximately twenty people sitting at various machines doing different activities.

The place had an oily metallic smell mixed with perspiration and perfume. It was nothing like she expected a factory to be on the inside either.

"What is your business Fraulein?" he asked sharply.

"I have just arrived from Berlin and would like to volunteer to work in your factory." she replied.

"Do you have any experience in this type of work?" he asked. She could feel his eyes scrutinize her through his monocle.

"No," she explained. "I was a dancer in Berlin. I just arrived in town and plan to stay here. Berlin is being leveled by bombs. I wish to volunteer to work in your factory." She never mentioned the fact that she was a prima ballerina engaged in high-level artistic work there.

"We do not need cheap dancers here," he barked.

"Oh no, I was in the theater. A ballerina," she replied. She saw Nazi medals on his suit, so she measured every word as if she were playing a verbal chess game for her life.

"Oh, I see. You think working here will be easier than living in Berlin. I do need the help, but I must check with the authorities. Until then, you can start first thing in the morning. Seven o'clock sharp," he snapped.

"I can save you the trouble. Just this morning, I wrote this letter to Berlin," Maria answered. "If you would sign it to verify that I will be working here, I will gladly send it for you. Of course, you know we will have to wait for a reply before I start work." Maria knew that she would not have to work until Berlin Okayed it.

"For someone who is so patriotic, I would think you would not want to wait for a reply. The Fatherland needs you now Fraulein," he spit the words at her as if he were shooting a gun.

"That may be true, sir," she answered. "But I have to get my affairs in order, and see if the Reichstheater Chamber approves this."

He signed the letter, snapped it in her face, turned with a jerk, and strutted away. She knew she had bought some time before she would have to start work, but she was deeply concerned that she might end up back in Berlin, or if this Nazi had his way, end up worse.

Maria and her mother quickly fell into a routine. Every morning, they would go into the cellar until the eight airplanes finished their strafing. They would then emerge, go the Burgermeister's house, and get his wagon to help clear underbrush from around the neighboring forest. This was civil work so that troops could have visibility under the trees. After a couple of hours, they would dispose of the brush, return the wagon, go home, and eat dinner. For six weeks, dinner consisted only of potatoes. There was no black market here to procure a variety of goods. Then they would listen to the latest radio programs and propaganda for the rest of the evening.

The war was not going well for Germany now. The German army attacked Avranches and failed in August. Then they were driven out of Paris. The Russians were closing in from the east and took Romania. The allies liberated Vardun, Antwerp, and Brussels, and the American troops reached the Siegfried Line. The radio broadcasts were becoming increasingly more alarming.

One day, as Maria and her mother were on their way to clear some brush, a couple of airplanes approached. The two women were concerned, but not overly so because it was the middle of the day way past the time that the eight planes shot at the village. The two of them did watch the planes closely, however. The pilots had seen them and headed straight for them. They let loose of the cart and jumped into a deep ditch alongside the road. They were amazed that the planes started firing their guns at them and swooped right across the top of the ditch. There was no time to be afraid because they came so fast. Maria was astonished at how she could press herself so deeply into common earth to eke out every last inch of the depth of the ditch.

"Don't move!" Maria shouted to her mother. She was careful not to move anything but her mouth even though she was face down. "Act like you are dead."

"Don't you move anything, either!" Anna shouted back.

Neither of them moved a muscle as the planes made a second pass and fired again. The pilots must have been satisfied the second time that the two of them were dead, and they flew off and fired into other parts of the forest. The two of them just lay there for about ten minutes; they did not move a muscle, did not say a thing.

Finally, Anna asked, "Are you all right?"

"Yes, what about you, Mama?" Maria asked in return.

"I'm fine," Anna answered.

With that, they cautiously crawled out of the ditch. Ironically, they were more upset that they had to walk most of the way down the steep incline of the mountain to retrieve the cart and pick up the sticks and branches it had spilled than they were about being shot at. They grumbled all the way back up the hill about the discourtesy of these pilots who did not come on the regular killing schedule.

Maria tried to make light of the incident. "The allies are so inconsiderate. They make a schedule, but you just can't rely on them. You would think that they would let us know that they were coming so we could have dinner ready for them."

As time went on, Maria was getting used to this routine; she just kept putting the nagging worry about the response from Berlin out of her mind. No Nazis had showed up. Then one day, after about two weeks, she received the letter from Berlin at the post office in Furtzheim. Her hands were trembling because she did not want to go back to Berlin, nor did she want to be sent away to some Nazi "correction" area.

"Here, you read this," she said as she handed the letter to her mother. "I can't stand reading it."

"As if I am any better at this than you are. Thanks a lot." Anna responded.

Maria closed her eyes, clenched her fists, and hoped and prayed. The request was approved.

Apparently, Herr Mehrmund of the factory also received a letter because that same day, he sent a woman from the factory with a message. Maria was summoned to be at work at seven o'clock the very next day.

Then Maria's mind started to race. She had been ignoring reality for a while. She wondered how she could survive working in a factory. Was this what all her hard work in the theater had brought her to? Then she consoled herself with the thought that it would be a very brief employment because it seemed like the end of the war was very close.

The next morning, she bounded from her bed extra early so she would be sure to get to the small factory on time. She remembered quite clearly the earlier warning of the overseer. She dressed, ate breakfast, walked down the stairs to the street and began her walk to the grimy little factory.

Maria had never paid much attention before, but there was a large bunch of geese wandering around the farmhouse next to theirs. They were usually docile and under control because one of the family was usually around. However, at this time of the day, no one was around except her. She looked at the geese, and they looked back at her. They then started to move toward her. The whole group moved in unison, slowly at first. She stepped backwards a couple of steps. The geese sped up and started to honk. Maria moved backwards a little faster, almost falling down. One goose came close to her and tried to nip her. That put terror in her heart. She didn't like being chased by animals that should be docile. She knew that she could not even hide in a ditch from geese as easily as she could from airplane fire, so she started to run.

She just took off and ran into the woods. About ten geese were right on her heels, hissing and chasing her into the woods. She wondered to herself how these clumsy birds could keep up with a trained ballerina. Yet they kept up. They honked and fussed, and they escorted her all the way to the factory.

Although Maria did not want to go there, she was never so happy to see a place of sanctuary. She opened the door, ran in, and jumped up on the small desk by the door. One particularly aggressive goose chased her into the room and kept honking and hissing at her as she stood out of breath on the desk. The overseer and several workers came over and chased the goose out the door.

He then turned to her and snapped, "So! I see we are late already, and it is only the first day. You, Frauline Happersberger, are going to be watched very closely by me. I strongly warn you that if you foul up whatsoever, you will be very unhappy at the consequences. Now get over there and get to work." He pointed to an empty chair at the end of a line of people seated at machines.

The factory was dimly lit. There were three rows of machines with fifteen or twenty people sitting at them drilling something. It was called a watch factory, although it was producing parts for airplanes.

One of the other workers took Maria to her station, and taught her what to do. It was a repetitious mindless task. She took a small cylinder of metal and clamped it on a small drilling platform parallel to her body. She then pulled down on a lever on a piece of machinery directly in front of her that drilled one tiny hole the size of a pencil point in the metal. She removed that piece, threw it in a box, and then repeated the operation.

All of the grinding noise unnerved her almost the moment she walked in the door, and the procedure was not challenging enough to distract her. However, she kept reminding herself that it was safer to be here than in Berlin. Each time the drill bit met the metal, the grinding noise sent shivers up her spine. After a while, Maria stopped to rest because her arms were becoming tired and heavy from the repetitive movements.

A fat woman, a supervisor, came over to her and told her not to stop. "He will not allow it."

Maria gave her a dirty look and continued with the task. Within a couple of hours, she was completely nervous. Her legs became antsy. They wanted to dance, not support a pair of hands drilling holes in metal. She finally stood up, stretched a bit, and went to the restroom. She assumed that this was all right since several other workers had done it already without incident. The walk to the primitive smelly room was too short. As she walked past the other women, they would glance up at her, but then immediately avert their eyes. They were mostly farmers who simply concentrated on their work. She was able to use the restroom without incident so she went again in about another hour. On the way back to her station, Maria noticed a woman inspecting the holes that the workers had drilled.

There was something different about her. She was not like the others. She was dressed plainly, but her clothes were very high quality and quite expensive. Her hands were soft looking, and her face was flawless even without makeup. She carried herself differently from the other women hunched over their drill presses.

"You're not from here, are you? Where are you from?" Maria asked.

The woman replied, "You don't look like you're from around here either. Where are you from?" Turning the attention away from her.

"I came here from Berlin. The bombing was so bad there," Maria told the woman.

Maria thought the conversation was going well and wanted to prolong it when the woman suddenly interrupted her and said, "We're not allowed to talk. Mehrmund will get mad and take it out on everyone."

Mehrmund! It had not occurred to her until just then that she did not even know the overseer's name. This knowledge gave her something to focus on and helped her make it through that first, endless day.

The geese chased Maria every morning. She had to get up earlier every day so she could get to work on time because the geese tormented her. She tried going out the back door, but they found her there. She even tried climbing out of the window, but the geese seemed to know what she was thinking. Every morning, she would come bursting through the factory door in a terrorized dither.

Mehrmund scoffed at her, "Just grab one goose around the neck, and beat the others with it. That would solve your problem."

"I could not do anything like that. I don't want to hurt them," Maria replied.

"You cowardly ass. You better learn to do something, or you will be sorry." He made obscure threats.

Mehrmund didn't like anybody, and he couldn't get along with anybody. His only pleasure seemed to be in shouting at people and threatening them. He ruled his dim, little factory through intimidation.

One day, he confronted Maria outside the bathroom door. He put his hand on the door so she could not open it and literally spit the words at her. "You are pissing too much. You are slowing down production. Your pisses are cut off. No more. Now get back to your seat before I knock you out."

Maria shouted back, "I will go when I have to."

He raged back at her, "Here. In my factory, you work! You do not piss! Now get back to your station!" His hand was raised as if he were going to slap her with the back of it.

She winced at the volume of his voice and went back to her seat. She was not accustomed to being treated this way, but she held back her anger. Her relationship with him deteriorated steadily. He had made up his mind that she was a troublemaker. She would not cooperate with his demands. He moved her to another larger drill. He would watch her wince each time the grinding noise for each hole pierced Maria's ears.

After work in the miserable factory, Maria began to walk home with the woman who inspected the holes. She lived at the inn. It was in the same direction as Maria's house but a couple of blocks further on the same street as the factory. The woman didn't talk much at first, but as time went on, Maria was able to coax a little more than the state of the weather from her. The woman would avoid eye contact, usually looking ahead at the ground. Maria asked her to come visit her and her mother, but she never came to visit. She did tell Maria that her name was Edith.

Edith was a mystery that kept Maria and Anna guessing. Maria's mother had seen her walk by the apartment and thought that she looked so familiar. But she just thought that she looked familiar in the way that a person might seem familiar the first time you meet them. Edith was strikingly beautiful. She could not hide her beauty under a peasant scarf.

One day Edith was out of town, so Maria and her mother went to the inn to have coffee and talk to Gertrude. She was a jolly lady with two young daughters who owned the place. Both of her daughters overheard them talking and agreed. Edith did look so familiar.

According to Gertrude, the woman had lived at her pension for several months with her young niece who was about twelve years old. She thought that Edith looked familiar too. She added, that she must be well traveled because she had a trunk with stickers from all over the world pasted on it, some from as far away as Hawaii. She seldom ventured out of the inn to go into the village. But Gertrude could not get any information out of her either. She was not prying. They were just curious, and this gave them something to occasionally distract their minds with.

The next day, Edith and Maria walked home after work. Maria said again, "You look so familiar for some reason. It's driving me crazy. I don't mean to pry into your personal life. I guess I'm just too curious. I'm sorry I asked."

"That's OK. Someday you will know more about me," Edith replied. She said no more than that.

On their walks home after work, Maria began to tell Edith about her crackpot antics in the theater. Edith did not talk much, but Maria certainly did because it was her nature. And she really missed her life in the theater. She told Edith how she could hardly endure life here in the small village and how Mehrmund and her work in the factory was literally going to be the death of her.

One morning, Maria noticed a bruise on Edith's cheek, and of course, she asked her about it. Edith told her that, she and her niece did not have time to get to the cellar before the eight o'clock planes came that weekend. So she had thrown herself over the girl on the bed to protect her. The pilots had fired a bullet through the window, and it had grazed her cheek. Maria was stunned at the randomness of staying alive. She wondered if anyone was going to survive this war.

"You are so lucky to be alive," Maria told Edith.

"I know. That was so close. I could feel the bullet pull the skin off my cheek," Edith replied.

"I sometimes wonder how God decides who lives or dies," Maria went on.

"It's OK. We are still alive, Maria," Edith told her.

A few days later, Gertrude invited Maria and Anna for coffee to discuss Edith since she was out again. Edith never told Gertrude where she went on these monthly outings, but she would go out regularly once a month with her niece.

Gertrude said, "I would certainly like to look in that trunk of hers, but she keeps it locked."

"How do you know?" Maria asked.

"There is a big lock on it. You can see it for yourself. I really wouldn't look in it anyway," Gertrude replied.

"Of course not," Anna said, winking at Maria. " That would be wrong."

"You know," Gertrude mused, " I wonder if she could be a movie star or something."

That was too unbelievable. It just didn't fit in with this small town, or the factory work. So it passed, and the conversation went back to the war and how badly it seemed to be going. It never occurred to any of them that if Maria could be here sacrificing her fame and career as a prima ballerina, that someone else could be doing the same thing.

It was wonderful to have Edith to speculate about in that dreary, little factory. Maria spent hours at that drill occupying her mind with scenarios and fantasies about Edith's life. Then it crossed her mind, that Edith might be Jewish. It was a stupefying thought. It brought another reality of the war to her like a punch in her stomach. She could hardly breathe for a brief moment. It was just something that never crossed her mind. Something she never expected. A reality she had heard about, but never had to face.

After work on their way home, Maria asked Edith, "Why do you have your niece with you? What happened to her parents?"

Edith's eyes filled with tears, and she said, "I will tell you someday."

Maria quickly switched to telling a funny story about the theater and dropped the issue.

Several days later, on the way back to the inn, Edith said, "I think I trust you now. I was born in Hungary in Budapest. My whole family was in the movie business. My father and one brother were directors. My other brother was a playwright. My mother was a Hungarian actress. That is how I got into the business."

Maria suddenly realized that the woman was Edith Meller, a movie star.

"Why are you here? Why are you working in that Godforsaken factory?" Maria asked her.

Edith explained how she had received a call from her brother in Budapest that things were becoming dangerous for the Jews. There were terrifying stories about the disappearances of their friends, and he wanted to get his daughter out of the country as soon as possible. He wired Edith some money, which she didn't need, and told her to pick up the girl at the train station. When Edith met her at the station, she had a little nametag around her neck. There was absolutely nothing else to indicate that she was Jewish. She had one small bag, and that was all. When she saw her aunt, Edith looked at her, put her finger up to her lips to shush her, and shook her head no. She dropped her hand lower in front of her so it couldn't be seen by anyone else and motioned for the girl to follow her through the crowd. Once around the corner, Edith grabbed her by the shoulders and asked her if she was all right. She hugged her; then they cried together and quickly left the train station.

Edith knew that she was under surveillance too because she was Jewish and entirely too famous for her own good. Her ex-husband, who was not a Jew, was a movie director who still cared for her and truly feared for her safety. He devised a plan for her to spirit the girl out of Berlin, so Edith packed her bags before she went to the train station and took them along with her. She changed taxies several times on her way there. Then she and her niece changed taxies several more times on the way to meet her ex-husband in a car on the outskirts of town. He then drove them to a small village outside of Berlin, where he put them on a train for Waldrennach. He had discovered the small remote village on a trip to Wild Bad one time. He thought that this obscure village was out of the way, and a safe place for them to hide.

Edith's ex-husband and his new wife, who was also a famous movie star, came once a month and brought her money to live on and to pay for the inn. All of Edith's money had been confiscated in Berlin. She had also changed the spelling of her name to appear more German. She would meet her ex-husband in a secret place in the woods. This explained her mysterious monthly disappearances. Maria never asked her any more questions about it. She did, however, make up her mind to help protect Edith and her niece in any way she could.

After that, Edith told Maria many fascinating stories about the movie business, and the private lives of the stars, and Maria reciprocated by telling her about life in the theater. It helped both of them keep their spirits up.

Chapter 15

Put the metal cylinder in place, pull the drill bit down, hear the harsh grinding sound, raise the drill bit up, pull the metal cylinder out and throw it in a box, and then repeat the whole process over again. Maria did this endlessly. The minutes dragged into hours. The hours seemed like weeks and the days seemed like eons. Maria daydreamed about the theater to escape the unbearable boredom. She smiled to herself as she daydreamed about a caper at Gelsenkirchen.

Maria made some changes in a production that would make Monika, the ballet meister, miserable. There was a new, bizarre operetta that was written by a living composer. The director even wanted Maria to sing in it. She could dance, but she could not sing. He knew that, but he wanted her to sing because the story of the operetta called for two people with untrained voices to be singers in a seedy Chinese cabaret. It was a strange song about flowers and orchards and their beautiful colors. Of course, she had to audition for the part like everyone else. That is when the director discovered what Maria knew all along. Although she was the second solo dancer, and the assistant ballet meister of this theater, her voice was too "untrained" even for this short song. Thea won the part instead even though she could not sing much better than Maria.

The revenge plan began to unfold when Monika became sick again for a couple of weeks. As a result, Maria had to choreograph the operetta.

Most of the music and scenes were relatively easy to choreograph, and Maria was able to work up dances for each of them without too much difficulty. However, she was completely obsessed and intrigued with the cabaret scene. This was the scene where she almost had to sing, and it had such an unusual stage setting that she wanted to do something unique, something daring to liven it up.

The walls of the cabaret were decorated with dragons, Chinese pagodas, and other Chinese motifs. Tables and chairs were set around a small, raised circular platform that served as the stage for the cabaret floorshows. It looked like a round pagoda open on all sides with a sheer curtain draped around its full circumference.

In the first cabaret scene, Thea and another ballet dancer mingled with the crowd singing about lotuses. They were dressed like Chinese women, and their faces were painted white.

When their number finished, the nightclub act was to commence on the small stage. There were seven dancers in this number doing an Arabian dance on the small, round stage. It was too small for seven dancers, about ten feet across, and it was shaped like a pagoda, gazebo "thing." One dancer sat in the middle, while the other six danced around her in a circle. The small stage was so crowded that they could hardly move, but the script called for this strange milieu. The dancers were dressed in flowing, sheer, bright-colored, red, green, yellow, and blue Arabian costumes, while the two Chinese "out of tune" singers wandered around in the cabaret bellowing off key.

Maria was fascinated by the whole idea of an Arabian dance being done in a Chinese cabaret. This part of the operetta was somewhat lighthearted so she decided to change the scene just a little without consulting with the director.

She went into the ballet room, closed the door behind her to make sure that no one in the hall could over hear her, and said, "I have an idea. Who is willing to do something different with this weird operetta?"

All the dancers in the practice room started to chatter because they knew she had an idea that would challenge this production.

"What do you mean?" a voice emerged.

"I mean that this "modern" stuff is weird. It is nothing like the classical operettas. Maybe we can help its weirdness." She warned them, "We will have to keep this a secret until the night of the performance. Does anyone know if this theater has a big stuffed snake?" It should. Every theater has to have a stuffed snake."

"A stuffed snake?" One of the girls asked. "Why would anybody have a stuffed snake?"

"Well, the theater in Frankfurt had a huge, felt snake. In fact, every theater must have one. I'm sure of it," Maria said very authoritatively. "Any theater that has put on a production of the *Verkaufte Braut* has to have one," she said, thinking back to her earlier days at Frankfurt.

"What are you going to do?" one of the girls asked.

The others joined in excitedly, asking similar questions, their voices blending into an excited din.

Maria told them, "I've got an idea to change the Arabian dance in the cabaret a little."

"You will get in trouble for that," one girl said.

"Yeah, we will all get in trouble for that," said another.

"Don't worry about it. It is not that drastic. Besides, I will pay for any fines any of you get because of it," she told them. "Besides, Monika would love it," she added in a tone that they all understood.

"Now who wants to help me find a snake?" she asked.

Of course, Thea volunteered immediately, as did Helen and one other girl. It had become a quest for them. Maria was forming a friendship with Helen, and she knew that she would love to have some harmless fun.

"Where will we ever find a snake?" Thea asked.

"We have to go to the prop building. We will need to inspect the situation, and develop a plan. Theaters never leave their props unguarded," Maria responded.

So, the four of them set out to find a stuffed snake. As soon as they arrived at the entrance to the prop building, they knew that this would not be an easy task. A security guard patrolled the grounds and the building. His job was to protect the valuable props from theft, or from people like them who wanted to "modify" a production.

Thea and one of the other girls did a great job of distracting the security guard in front of the props building. It was like they had a degree in flirting. If he would start to turn his gaze from them, they would turn up the volume of their voices with questions and draw his gaze back to them. All the while, they stepped back ever so slightly away from the entrance.

He was clearly flattered to get all that attention. He had an incredibly boring job, and all that attention from two pretty ballet dancers distracted his focus from his job. As they talked, they continued to take tiny steps backward away from the door. He moved unconsciously toward them small step by small step away from the entrance. Meanwhile, Helen and Maria sneaked through the door into the prop building.

Maria thought to herself that this particular building was easy to enter. There wasn't even a lock on the door. Each city's theater had a different security arrangement. In Frankfurt, they would not even be able to get near the prop building without being interrogated or arrested; Maria thought to herself. This was so easy that it almost scared her.

When they got in, Maria was amazed. She had never actually been in a prop building before. She thought it was like a huge museum but more interesting. One area had nothing but backdrops; another, artificial trees and bushes. There was an area with nothing but row upon row of costumes, and there were shelves filled with boots, armor, swords, and wigs. One area had nothing but rows and rows of shelves with only hats on them. Another area of the first floor had all types of furniture stacked next to different types of mountains and their parts. There was even a special area with only chandeliers. Maria felt like they were "casing the joint" like two gangsters.

They found nothing in the dim light on the first floor. In the far corner was a staircase. They climbed it with tentative steps and came to the equally dimly lit second floor. This floor was a little less organized than the first floor. It contained props that were rarely used. There were even dummies of people and creatures. Even the monster dragon from Wagner's *Siegfried* was there, along with various other animal costumes.

Helen said, "How do you expect to find anything in here, let alone a snake? This is a cluttered mess."

"I don't know, " Maria whispered, "but I think we're getting close. Look. Here is an elephant. We are among the animals, and every theater has to have a stuffed snake."

Then Helen pulled on Maria's sleeve, pointing nervously at something near the elephant, and asked, "Is that one?"

There, sticking out from under a sheet that was protecting it from dust was a gigantic green felt snake coiled up in a pile about one meter across and a meter high.

"There it is!" Maria said a little too loudly and excitedly. "I knew it. Every theater has to have one."

Helen said, "Well let's get it."

"No!" she replied, "Now that we know where it is, we can come back and get it right before the performance. If we take it now, someone might notice that it is missing."

"Who would ever notice a missing snake? Who would even want to notice a snake? I don't think anyone knows it's here."

Maria said, "No, we know where it is now. We can get it when we need it. She was already working on "creative" choreography as they spoke.

They noted the snake's location, went back to the door, and peeked around it. Thea and the other girl saw them, immediately raised their voices and, maneuvered the guard so that his back was to the door.

Maria and Helen quickly slipped through the crack in the door, silently closed it behind them, and nonchalantly walked to Thea and the guard. Maria and the others acted like this was a chance encounter. Thea introduced them to the guard.

They chatted briefly, until Maria looked at her watch said, "We have got to go. It's time for practice."

"I didn't see you walk up. Where did you come from?" he asked. They all talked a while, changed to another topic of conversation so as not to be suspicious, and then left.

When they got out of range of the guard, they all giggled. Thea, Helen, and the other girl were trying to pump Maria for information about what she had in mind, but she wouldn't divulge anything except that they would have to wait until rehearsal in the exercise room the next day.

Put the metal cylinder in place, pull the drill bit down, hear the harsh grinding sound, raise the drill bit up, pull the metal cylinder out and throw it in a box, and then repeat the whole process over again. Maria snapped back to the irksome, dull job she was doing. She longed to be anywhere but in that sweaty place.

There was more excited tension than usual because this was a premier performance. The overture started. Thea, Helen, the other dancer, and Maria waited until the performance was under way to borrow the snake so no one would get suspicious. Helen was wearing three terry cloth robes over her costume. She was going to hide the snake with them. The robes over her costume made her look very fat, and very suspicious.

Thea and the other girl had the assignment to distract the guard while the overture was playing. He was taken in by their attention, and was more easily drawn from his duties this time because they were familiar.

Helen and Maria had to work quickly to get the snake. It was easy to get in through the door because of Thea's professional flirting. They ran up to the second floor of the prop building to where the snake was hiding out. They covered it with the three robes Helen was wearing. It was so big that it took all three robes to cover it. Then the two of them carried it out the door while Thea turned the guard to point at something near the stage. The snake was not an easy thing to carry. It was even more difficult for two ballet dancers to be inconspicuous walking around backstage carrying a pile of terry cloth robes with a green tail sticking out of it. A stagehand walked passed them and looked at the suspicious robes.

"These are for wardrobe. One of their people is ill tonight, so we are moving this stuff for them as a favor," Maria said.

He nodded at them and proceeded on his way.

They finally carried it to the left side of the stage between the curtains next to the round cabaret stage. They removed the robes and uncoiled the snake. It was about twenty-five feet long.

Thea whispered, "This thing is too big."

"Hush. Where is Helen?"

"I'm here," Helen said as she ran up to them behind the curtain. "Oh my God. That thing is huge. We better not do this." She hesitated.

"No. Now we all agreed to do this. You can't back out of it now. Besides, it will be so funny," Maria urged.

Everyone was in place. The music for the Arabian dance in the seedy Chinese cabaret was about to start. The cue came. The curtain on the stage in the cabaret opened, and there were the six Arabian dancing girls in a semicircle at the front of the platform. Thea's dreadful song came to an end. Maria and the others began to move in a flowing pattern around the stage to the right. As they danced, Helen came into view. She was sitting cross-legged on the floor in the center of the stage with the snake wrapped around her many times. Her arms were above her head with her hands clasped in what looked like a Budda pose. She wore a bright purple costume, but only the sheer veil showed past the snake. The rest of her was an ugly green, the color of the snake that was wrapped around her.

She was supposed to unfold her arms out to the side then down to her hips; then stand up and turn while the others kept dancing around her in a circle on that tiny stage. Well, none of them had ever rehearsed with the snake because it was impossible to hide it before the performance. The snake made Helen so fat that she could not move her arms lower than her shoulders. They had propped the thing so that its face stared directly into Helen's as if it was about to bite her. All the girls had grins on their faces, but Helen was brilliant; she never cracked a smile.

Meanwhile, the buffo and soubrette, the male and female lead singers in the operetta, were supposed to sing a romantic song to each other. The difference between a buffo and a soubrette and regular opera singers is that they usually dance and do stunts. The regular opera singers only sing, and use stand-ins for non singing scenes.

The buffo was supposed to begin singing, but he could not continue when he saw what was happening on the cabaret stage. The soubrette followed his line of vision and could not pick up on her cue because she had begun to laugh.

Helen could not move anything but her arms, so she kept repeating the same movement in her sitting position. Gazing cross-eyed into the snake's eyes, she could not get up to dance. She kept rolling to one side to stand up, but the snake did not allow her to get her hand close enough to the floor to push herself up. The singers tried not to look at the stage, only at each other, but it did not work. They just made up words and gestured a lot. They had lost their complete train of thought.

Maria was behind the first curtain where she could see everything that was going on. She could see the director behind the second curtain on the other side of the stage leafing frantically through his pad, but he could not see her.

Thank God he can't see me, she thought.

She could see Helen struggling, and hear the singers forgetting lines, making up mock laughter to hide the real thing. She could not see the conductor or the orchestra, but she heard laughter from them too. The audience was out of control.

She kept watching the director. He looked from the singers to the dancers and back again, shaking his head. His movements looked almost robotic. They were not smooth movements, but rather jerky and spastic.

Maria said to herself, this is the end of my career. She felt a kind of remorse - terror. She questioned her judgment, why do I do things like this? It must be the challenge. Oh, I'm doomed, she thought.

As the scene progressed, the director grinned and started to laugh. The singers were trying to kill time. The characters sitting at tables playing patrons in the cabaret scene were all laughing. Helen was stuck in a circle of giggling Arabian dancing girls wrapped in a green snake that was staring at her. The audience never knew that anything was out of the ordinary because it was the premier of a new opera. Usually, only the performers know when "mistakes" happen.

The next day, there was a knock at her office door. It was Jens the security guard. He knew her, but all he did was ask her name. "Frauline Maria Happersberger?"

"Yes."

"This is for you. And well deserved, I should say." He handed her a piece of paper and abruptly turned and began to walk away. It was a ticket that carried a fine for one hundred marks. This was the largest fine she had ever received since she was in the theater, but that was all that happened.

She looked up from the piece of paper and said, "I'm so sorry. I didn't mean to get you in trouble.

"Well, you and the others did. I'm on notice," he responded.

"I promise you, I will take all of the blame. It was my idea. I will see to it that you do not get written up," she vowed as he continued to walk away.

The director, however, did put out through the grapevine that if that kind of thing ever happened again, some people might find themselves back on the chorus line, or worse. Helen received a ten-mark fine that Maria paid for her. The ballet chorus dancers did not get any fines because they were "forced" to do it. Maria was able to keep everyone else out of trouble and made sure that she paid their fines and cleared their records.

Maria was wrenched from her reverie by a searing pain in her left index finger. She had not pulled her hand back from the drill fast enough and she drilled through her finger. A woman next to her reversed the drill and backed it out of Maria's finger. When Maria saw the blood pump out of it she became faint. The woman helped her to the cramped office where she applied some first aid.

Mehrmund charged from the other side of the factory and followed them to his office. He was bright red and furious. He thought that Maria had done it deliberately, but he had no choice but to dismiss her to go to the doctor in Neuenbürg located in the valley from Waldrennach.

The doctor was a very warmhearted, middle-aged woman with a kind smile. She assured Maria that it was a small wound, that the drill had only penetrated through the flesh, and that the bone was intact. Maria told the doctor briefly about how she was going stir crazy. The kind doctor understood what Maria was saying, so she insisted on seeing Maria the next week. The doctor made it quite clear that it was to be during the day during working hours. She understood Maria's frustration, and she was determined to get her out of that factory for a few hours if she could.

The following week, Maria left work to go down the mountain to the doctor's office. That morning, the village had been strafed twice, and Maria heard from the talk in the factory that a seventy-eight year-old milkmaid in Waldrennach had been killed. However, when she arrived at the doctor's office, there was a crowd of people standing around talking and weeping. The charming woman doctor in Neuenbürg had been killed in the usual strafing raid that morning.

Maria had no choice but to go back up the mountain and go back to work. Mehrmund actually laughed when she told him the news about the doctor. "Good. Maybe I will get some production out of you after all. Now get to work," he snarled through gritted teeth.

Chapter 16

A week to the day after that, Maria drilled through the same finger again. She was already a nervous wreck, but the pain was unbearable, and she needed to see a doctor. Mehrmund flew into a rage and accused her of treason at that point, but he allowed her to return to the doctor's office.

Some troops had come into town, and one was a doctor who had taken over the woman doctor's practice. Maria was terrified that he would side with the overseer. However, when she walked into his office, she stopped dead in her tracks and just stared at him. He stared back at her. They looked into each other's eyes for a few seconds. They were both speechless. He was rather short, but with a muscular build, and very handsome she thought, with light brown hair combed straight back.

"I am Doktor Dietrich. Peter Dietrich. You may call me Peter," he said, as he looked deep into her eyes. "Where are you from?"

"I am from Frankfurt," Maria answered. She forgot about the pain in her finger. "Where are you from?"

"Me. I'm from Berlin. "He answered.

"I just came here from there," she told him hesitating for a moment in fear that she had said too much.

Every time their eyes met, Maria felt as though they were looking deeply into each other's soul; then suddenly they would look away in embarrassment. Maria was attracted to him, and she could discern that he was attracted to her.

He abruptly finished up dressing the finger and said, "I'll see you back here in two days to be sure there is no infection." He jokingly added, " And to be sure that you do not drill through any more of those lovely fingers."

Two days later, to the total fury of Mehrmund, Maria left work to return to the doctor on the doctor's orders. Mehrmund seemed madder than usual from the color of his face. It gave Maria a sense of some small control over her life to be able to walk out on that self-important jerk. Not only that, but she was a little excited because the new, young doctor was so handsome and friendly. She remembered how they had looked at each other, and she thought that he was as attracted to her as she was to him.

When she arrived at his office, they talked for a long time. He indicated that he just needed a little background on her. He asked her about Frankfurt. He seemed to be probing at what she was doing here in this small village. Maria saw that he was flirting with her, but she was cautious about what she told him.

She, in turn, asked him about Berlin and how he came to be in this small village. He told her that his battalion had been supporting the troops fighting on the Russian front. When defeat finally came, his medical unit sent out some men with a white flag of surrender. When the Russians discovered that they were a medical unit, they put him and the other doctors to work caring for their own wounded. He told Maria that they had no choice, so he cooperated rather than be shot. In addition, the Russians could not hold the great number of prisoners they were taking, and they began to send the least threatening ones, such as doctors, back to Germany. After his battalion returned, they were split up. He and his aide were assigned to this town because it had lost its civilian doctor earlier.

Maria told him about her life in the theater, which seemed to intrigue him. Finally, she opened up to him and told him that she was going crazy in the factory. Sitting still was making her legs crawly, and being anywhere near Mehrmund made her furious. Peter listened to her complaints and said that he would think about her problems.

A few days later, she was sitting at her station when she suddenly developed severe chest pains. Her breathing became shallow, and she panicked. She had to get to the doctor's office because she was sure her heart was going to stop. One of the office workers assisted her down the hill and ran up the other to fetch the doctor, who then met her halfway down the mountain. He told the other worker to return to work because his official concern was for Maria's safety. He escorted her the rest of the way to his office, holding her steady.

After she entered his office, she told him that not only could she not breathe, but she also had muscle aches everywhere in her body. He examined her lungs, her heart, and everything else.

Finally, he said, "I can't find anything wrong with you, but just to be sure, I will send you to the hospital for x-rays."

Maria was genuinely worried and replied, "I live way up there on that mountain." She pointed to Waldrennach, "You work down here in Neuenbürg, and the hospital is way up there on that mountain on the other side of Neuenbürg." She pointed at the other mountain. "My lungs will not be able to take it."

He told her not to worry and gave her a note so she could leave work the next day to go to the hospital. Peter wanted to escort her home, but he had an important appointment that he could not break. She left his office, and as she approached the end of the walkway, the air raid sirens went off. The planes appeared so suddenly that she could not run back into the house. They sprayed their bullets at her, but she was able to jump into some dense shrubs in front of the house. However, one of the pilots had seen her. They all banked their planes sharply, but this time, one began dropping some small explosives while the others fired at her.

Maria thought to herself, none of the strafing attackers have ever done that before. They are throwing little bombs.

Peter rushed out, grabbed her, and pulled her into the house. He then pulled her into a small fruit cellar under the kitchen. They huddled against each other. Smoke began to filter into the small space, choking them. It smelled like the bombers had added tear gas to the bombs to force the people out into the streets to make them easier targets.

Maria was trembling while Peter just spoke soothingly and petted her hair between deep coughs. Shortly thereafter, the attack subsided, and the two of them ventured back up into Peter's office. The smoke had dissipated, so they knew the house was not on fire. Apparently, only a small shed outside had been hit, and that was where the smoke came from. Peter soothed their burning eyes with some clear liquid he took out of a cabinet. Then he poured two small glasses of brandy.

"Here. Drink this. It should help calm your nerves," he said as he handed her a glass.

He downed one shot in one gulp, refilled his glass, and sipped more slowly. They sat for a few minutes to be sure the planes would not return. Maria thought that he was handsome and strong. After they finished the brandy, he offered to walk her home. She was more than happy to have him as a companion. When they arrived at her door, he took her arms by the shoulders, turned her toward him, gently lifted her chin with his forefinger, and kissed her.

Maria pulled back, looked in his eyes, and kissed him in return. She then turned quickly, a bit embarrassed, and hurried into the house.

That night, she did not sleep well. She had forgotten what it was like to feel normal and not worry constantly. She felt like she had a protector at last.

The next morning, Maria got up early. She had been scheduled to be at the hospital at eight a.m. She dressed, ate a quick breakfast, and began walking to the hospital for the tests. However, when she came out of the door of her house, she was momentarily startled when Peter greeted her. She was completely surprised to see him at this hour. She was also pleasantly reassured that she would not have to walk alone. He kissed her lightly on the lips as he wished her a good morning.

They walked down the mountain hand in hand. On their way, they could see the hospital nestled on the side of the other mountain. They continued through Neuenbürg. On a beautiful day like that, with the sun shining brightly burning the mist off the mountains, walking along the quaint streets lined with unbombed houses, life almost felt normal. However, as they passed Peter's office, the bullet holes in the walls were a grim reminder of the ordeal that occurred the day before. They continued another four kilometers up the other mountain to the hospital.

Maria felt so good. To her, it was a beautiful day. It was a beautiful hospital. It was clean and efficient, and the staff was very friendly. Maria didn't think that a hospital this far from a large city would be so advanced. She spent the morning preparing for and taking the tests and x-rays.

Peter had kept himself busy with other details while he was waiting for her to finish up. The nurse gave her a large brown envelope containing the x-rays. Peter was waiting in the lobby for her, where he took the envelope from her hands.

"These are your x-rays. We can review them in my office." He smiled at her and winked.

"Am I OK?" she asked.

"We won't know until I have a closer look," he answered.

When they arrived at his office, he asked his aide to make them a cup of coffee. He put the x-rays up on a screen and remarked, "It is just as I thought."

"What is it?" Maria was afraid that she had something terrible.

"It is just as I thought," he repeated. "Maria, there is absolutely nothing wrong with you. Now tell me, what is your real problem." He already had a good idea what ailed her from what she had told him earlier.

"I hate this job. I am not right for this kind of work. I am a ballerina. I cannot sit still long enough to concentrate. The geese chase me every morning, and everyone gets up early to watch them do it so they can have a good laugh. Mehrmund has threatened to send me to some God-awful place. He is a Nazi. If I could just get my work hours cut to a half a day, I might be able to survive. Anything would help."

"I can see where your problem lies. You are in a tough spot. There is absolutely nothing wrong with you. You will have to go back to work," Peter told her.

His words fell on her ears like a death sentence. "I could drill through another finger - several fingers if it would help, "she said, holding up four fingers. Her hero was not rescuing her, the damsel in distress.

He replied, "Just go back to work for now. Let me think about this. I'll figure something out. Can you come to my office tomorrow?"

"I can't get off of work without an excuse," Maria told him.

"When do you get off then?" he asked.

"At five."

"Why don't we meet halfway and go to the cafe to discuss this more then," Peter asked.

"All right," she replied, hoping against hope that he would be able to help her with something.

The next morning was one of the most miserable that Maria had experienced during the whole war. She was Mehrmund's prisoner, and she knew it. He sneered and said, "Clean bill of health, Happersberger." He spit her name at her. He did not even use her first name. "Good! Now produce twice as much to make up for your treasonous foolishness, or I will see to it that you are taken care of."

She knew that she was either going to die in that factory or wherever Mehrmund sent her. The only thought that kept her sane was that she would meet Peter after work. She had fantastic daydreams all day - dreams that her handsome doctor would somehow take her out of the nightmare she was living, dreams that the war was over, and dreams that she was dancing again in front of appreciative crowds. Even the retched sound of Mehrmund's voice didn't seem to bother her much when she had those thoughts.

Finally, the workday ended. Maria darted out the door and headed for Peter's office. He was waiting for her at the end of the road where the houses of the village ended rather than halfway up the mountain as they had agreed.

He seemed somewhat excited. He said, "I have thought about this all night and day, and I have an idea that just might work. Come, let's go to my office," he said excitedly. He kissed her lightly on the forehead and took her arm to walk her the rest of the way down the mountain to his office. "No one will be able hear us there."

He had risked being seen with her by coming into the village. She knew the danger involved for him if Mehrmund saw them together.

She said, "I don't want to get you involved."

"Don't talk now. Wait until we get to my office," he said, putting his finger to her lips.

He unlocked the door to his office and held it open for her. When they went in, he had her sit on the table. He paced around the room, walking around the table and stroking his chin.

"You definitely have a problem with your leg. It originates in your knee and radiates all the way into your foot. It is a very logical problem that you have developed as a result of your dancing. I should have caught it right away from your complaints, but this type of disorder does not show up in x-rays." He had a grin on his face and winked at her as he spoke.

Maria picked up on what he was saying and doing. She played along with him since his aide was still working in the front office.

She said, "If I walk too long, I get such a pain in my leg that I start to perspire from it."

He looked into the outer office while they were talking and noted that his aide had just left for the day. "Good. He's gone."

She laughed and asked, "By the way, which leg?"

"Here is how it works." He said the technical medical name of the problem, but Maria could not remember it. She could not even say it. It was an ailment up under the kneecap that is quite difficult to pinpoint. It is kind like a back problem that will not go away, and cannot be easily proven.

"I will teach you the symptoms and how to react to any examination. First, you will have to lie down on the table. I will turn your foot to the right and then to the left," Peter told her.

"When I turn it to the left like this, don't say or do anything," he said as he turned her foot to the left.

"Now when I turn your foot to the right like this, you have to moan and groan. Now let's practice."

He turned it to the left, and she moaned and winced.

"No, no. To the left, nothing. Now let's try again."

He turned it to the left, and she made no sound. Then he turned it to the right, and she winced and groaned on cue.

"Good," he said, "but your groan is going to have to be more convincing. You are simply reciting all of the vowels in the alphabet. Do it something like this." He went on to make a ridiculous noise that sounded like a dying elephant.

They both laughed for quite a while at the noise when suddenly he leaned over and kissed her. This time, she kissed him back, and they embraced for a long time. They backed away from each other, and looked into each other's eyes, and then kissed again.

Peter said, "Let's practice more."

Maria asked, "The kissing or the moaning?"

"Both of course. We have to be sure that you. . . we. . . get it right," he answered.

They practiced the procedure a while longer making, more absurd noises. They were like two children carried away at playing. They would try to out groan each other, kiss, and laugh. They practiced long into the evening and fell in love with each other.

Mehrmund literally flew into a complete rage when Maria gave him a note from the doctor indicating that she only had to work half days.

"Now I've got you, Happersberger. And I will get your lying doctor friend too. I want this verified by a state Vertrauenartz, a state medical fraud inspector. You're a lying, treasonous bitch. You will destroy the war effort single-handedly with this kind of shit. I know that there's nothing wrong with you. This is a sudden new condition. All I need is proof." All of the workers in the small factory fell silent. They had never seen Mehrmund in such a rage.

Maria was surprised that he didn't pull out a gun and shoot her then and there. He went up to his office and tried to use the phone. She could hear him swearing, "*Verdammte telefon.*" It took several hours before the call went through. He stormed back up to his office and talked on the phone for almost an hour. Maria could see him gesturing and throwing his arms around wildly, but no conversation drifted through the din of the factory. She thought he would be on her back like a monkey, but he did not ride her the rest of the day, especially after he told her that she had an appointment with the Vertrauenartz in Furtzheim in two days.

Peter was able to borrow two bicycles for them to ride to Pforzheim. It was downhill most of the way, and it was the most reliable way to travel because the trains were not running on any predictable schedule anymore.

Pforzheim was in shambles from the bombings, but the two of them finally found the building. Only the ground floor of it was intact. Maria realized what a waste of time and energy the government was into. With the war going as badly as it was, they were more interested in prosecuting a small case like hers than winning the war.

Peter was nervous. He was distant – his mind somewhere else. He made her nervous. She made him nervous. They were both rattled. He kept rehearsing her verbally, but Maria was afraid that she would forget some important symptom. They hid the bicycles, and he walked her to within one block of the building and then slipped out of sight so that his medical uniform would not betray them.

Maria limped in through the front door. The room was bare except for the examining table, a desk, and a file cabinet. There was no nurse or aide present. Sweat began to bead on her forehead as she contemplated the seriousness of this encounter.

Suddenly, a tall, dark-haired man came into the room through a back door. Maria thought that his uniform seemed a little wrinkled for an officer, even though it had Nazi markings on it.

"So, you must be Frauline Happersberger."

She was alone in this place with a total stranger who held her life in his hands. She was afraid to be alone in there with him.

"Yes I am. I am here for a checkup." Her voice sounded shaky even to her own ears.

"Why are you at a Vertrauenartz office?" he asked.

"It is because of my supervisor. He does not believe the pain I am in."

"Well. You do know that it is a serious crime to practice fraud when the Reich needs all able-bodied workers for the war effort," he pointed out.

"Yes, I do. And I want to help." She lied. "But the pain distracts me so much that I can't do the work without going crazy."

He asked, "Where are you from?" as he looked her over top to bottom and left to right with his eyes.

She told him, "I am originally from Frankfurt. I was a ballet dancer." She was careful not to give too much information. She omitted any reference to Berlin. "I don't understand how this could happen to a ballet dancer like myself." She was gaining a little self-confidence as she talked. "It hurts so bad, I break out in perspiration," she ended.

He grinned at her and said, "*Bei uns in Stuttgart sagt'mer Schwitz.*" in a very heavy Stuttgart dialect that called it sweat.

She thought, oh my God, he's got a sense of humor. Maybe there is hope.

She said, "We say that in Frankfurt too."

"Lay down on this table here, and we shall proceed," he motioned to the table.

He did everything exactly the way she and Peter had rehearsed. She responded exactly like Peter had taught her.

Finally, the doctor said, "Yes, you've got (whatever it was she had)."

She knew that she had convinced him, so she replied, "You know, I have to sit so long at that job. I'm accustomed to much more exercise. If I could get my work time down to four hours a day, and get a little therapy, I might not lose the use of my legs."

He replied, "I see your point. A therapy program would be better for you. We will make it a half day of work and a half day of therapy. And you will probably need two or three days to stay off that leg to let it mend a bit."

She almost jumped up and threw her arms around him, but she could not let her face reflect any feeling, or she might betray her deception. He offered to walk her to the train station as he escorted her, limping, to the office door. She declined and left. She hobbled very dramatically down the street for the several blocks to where Peter was hiding. If the Vertrauenartz was watching or following her, he would have been convinced of her disability.

Peter came from around the back of the ruined building and whispered, "How did it go?"

"He believed me. Oh God, he believed me. I have three days off, and after that I only have to work half days."

"It was taking so long. I was starting to get very worried," Peter said, walking out from behind the building where he was waiting.

"No. No. I'm free. Well, half free. Oh thank you, thank you." Maria cried tears of joy as she threw her arms around him and kissed him. He smiled and kissed her back.

Peter then retrieved the bicycles from behind the building, and they rode back to his office. For the next week, they had secret rendezvous for dinner in locations where they wouldn't raise a suspicion if they were seen by any of the villagers. It was a wonderful week. Maria almost felt like the war was over for her. After dinner, they would take a long walk through the forest arm in arm; they would return to Peter's office, share some cognac, and make love.

Peter was from an extremely wealthy family. He even had his own butler as a boy. He told Maria that his family owned several houses in several locations around Germany and one on the Mediterranean Sea in France.

Sadly, the following week, the war returned to Maria's life. To her shock and dismay, Peter told her that he had received orders to leave for Frankfurt. It was war-related, and his services were needed more there than here.

"Maria, come with me to Frankfurt."

"Oh Peter. I want to so much, but I can't."

"Then promise me that we will pick up where we left off after this infernal war is over. I can't live without you. I love you." Peter kissed her.

Maria leaned her head back and looked in Peter's eyes. "Please don't go. I have never fallen in love before. Stay here with me. The war will end soon. The Nazis haven't found me here yet." She began to sob while Peter gently held her in his strong arms. She knew he was too honorable as a soldier to consider her plea, but she just wanted to be with him.

It was a sad departure. They had fallen hopelessly in love. Peter drove off in his car. Maria had never cried so deeply in her life. It was like he had died and she was mourning.

Maria's mother had talked to some of the townspeople about her ailment and the diagnosis, and word had drifted back to the factory before Maria showed up for her first half day of work.

When she did go back to work, Mehrmund was waiting at the door for her. His dark eyes glared at her with hatred and absolute contempt. Maria felt triumphant, but she tried not to show it lest he go berserk. After all, she had beaten him with the testimony of a government official. Nazi party or no Nazi party, she had an advantage over Mehrmund when it came to working with male officials.

"Come into my office now, Happersberger. We need to talk." He snarled the words, his lips visibly drawn back, exposing his yellowed, and tobacco-stained teeth.

"So you think this is some kind of game, do you? You think that you are above the laws of the Reich. You should be put to death. The Nazi authorities should come here and watch you and your treasonous antics." He paced around the small room, striking his fist on the table at the end of each sentence to emphasize his points.

"OK. I can give you a half a day, and I will give you a half a day, but at my other factory in Wildbad. You will begin your half day there tomorrow at six a.m. sharp. It was two hours earlier than her present schedule. If you are one second late, I will turn in your name to the authorities. If you are two seconds late, I will have grounds to shoot you on the spot. Now, get out of my sight before you live to regret it." With that, he kicked a chair halfway across the dingy, poorly lit office.

He had made it as difficult on Maria as he possibly could. Wildbad was at the end of the local train line, which was not very reliable anymore. When the train was running, it took about two hours each way. That basically gave her a full day including the travel time. Mehrmund knew that she allegedly could not walk well or ride a bicycle, and that there were no cars available to take her there. He had set her up, but she was still thankful because she only had to labor for four hours a day now. So she comforted herself with the idea of working four hours and riding the train for four hours.

The next morning, she made an extra effort to wake up early, and she arrived at Wildbad about an hour early. She was not going to take any chances with Mehrmund. She knew he meant business.

The factory there was much bigger than the one in Waldrennach. It was about twice the size. When she arrived, she was handed a time card the moment she walked in the door. She had never heard of such a thing. Maria had no idea how to use it. She couldn't imagine people taking a card and sticking it in a clock that automatically recorded the time on it. She was told that it recorded your starting and stopping time down to the second. Mehrmund truly meant it when he had said, "one second."

"Furthermore," the heavyset, loud-mouthed woman giving her instructions advised her, "every moment away from your station has to be recorded on this card. That includes bathroom breaks." She warned Maria that these were some of Mehrmund's very specific instructions for her. He was going to create a record of her every move. He planned to document every second of her activity.

"I will be watching you very closely," the fat woman warned Maria.

She was placed at a machine just like the one she had left behind. It did exactly the same thing, but it was much larger, and the drill bit was big enough to take off the finger of anyone careless enough to get one in the way. The factory was larger; the machines were larger; the noise was much greater; the lighting was dimmer; and it smelled. It smelled like a noxious mixture of sweat, oil, and smoke worse than the other one. It was so thick that she could barely breathe.

Suddenly, she heard a loud voice shouting over the din of the machines. She didn't even need to look up. She recognized the sharp nasty shrill sound of Mehrmund's voice as it cut through the noise like a bullet. A cold shiver ran up and down her spine. She couldn't bring herself to look up, to see the inevitable monster. His presence here explained where he was when he was not in his other factory.

There were fifty workers in the factory, all women. Maria asked the woman next to her what was going on. The woman was German, but she told Maria that most of the women were French since this plant was so close to the French boarder, and that he treated them all like prisoners. The woman he was shouting at could not even understand him. The more she could not understand him, the louder he shouted.

Terrified, she turned and looked back at the two of them. Then Mehrmund lifted his hand and slapped her across the face with the back of his hand.

Maria felt fury spring up in her chest. She could barely contain herself. It was the first time in her life that she wanted to kill anyone. Arrogantly, Mehrmund continued to strut up and down the aisles, swaggering, shouting, and abusing each woman he came to her station.

Maria had formulated a plan in her mind. If he even looked like he would raise his hand to her, she would pick up the heavy box of screws on the bench next to her and throw them in his face so hard that they would knock his eyes out. She was so angry that she was blind to the consequences of her actions. She did not care. She simply would not be treated like that, and neither should any other human being.

He started to strut down her aisle. The farm woman next to her said, "Don't say anything. He's mean. He will hurt you. Look at this." She turned her face so Maria could see the other side. It was bruised and cut from where he had repeatedly struck her.

Maria's heart raced. It beat harder with each step Mehrmund took toward her. She thought to herself that at least she would have a defense for attacking him. After all, she was German and the others were not.

Finally, he walked up next to her and stood there silently for a few seconds. Maria looked up into his evil eyes. He had a smirk on his face and said in a sarcastically sweet tone, "Good morning, Fraulein Happersberger. How are 'we' feeling this fine morning?" He used the imperial "we" to punctuate his sarcasm.

She turned her gaze away from him and back to her machine when his voice gathered a power and he blasted out, "Faster, you bitch. In this factory, we don't tolerate traitors. We will never win the war with subversive people like you around."

She turned back toward him, stood up the box of screws in her hand, and shouted, "We are not winning the war."

He lifted his hand in the air, and at the same time, she lifted the box of screws. He was bright red, and clearly furious. The hate in his eyes and face were almost overpowering. He saw the box and stopped his swing in midair.

He raged, "You get out of here. You get out of here now. I will see you dead, you son of a bitch."

At that, she threw down the box of screws and stormed out of the factory as fast as she could. She had only been there two hours. She had forgotten to limp as she ran out of the plant. She also knew that she and her mother were as good as dead.

When she arrived home, her mother said, "You're home early."

Maria started crying. "We are done for." She summarized the morning's events for Anna.

"I thought we would be safe from the bombings of the allies here, but it is Germany that is going to kill us in the end." Maria sobbed as she wiped the tears from her eyes with a handkerchief.

Anna comforted her, "Well sweetie, at least we are together. And we will stay together."

They planned. The next day was a Saturday, and Sunday would only give them one more day before they were taken away. They both knew that the Nazis would act quickly. They planned to run away, but they had nowhere to go. The French had broken through the Beffort Gap and were close to Strasbourgh.

Late Saturday, as they were packing, a neighbor told them that the planes had strafed the train to Wildbad in the morning, and that Mehrmund had been hit. His jaw and the whole bottom of his face had been blown off in the attack. He had been killed. He could not cause them harm now.

Within days, artillery fire began. It went on day after day - morning, noon, and night. It came closer, and Maria and her mother knew that the war would soon be over. The French had taken Neuenbürg and the hospital, and were now firing across the valley on their tiny village.

Chapter 17

Maria and her mother knew that the end of the war was very close. They had been listening to Radio Strasbourgh all night. It was an old decrepit radio that played more static than anything else. They had to listen to it huddled under a blanket with the volume turned to the lowest setting so no one would know that they were listening to it. People were actually being arrested for listening to an outlawed radio station by this time, and Radio Strasbourgh was considered a resistance station. It broadcast in German even though the French controlled it. Huddled under their blanket, they felt a little safe from the constant artillery fire that punctuated the announcements on the radio. The announcer had been blaring constantly about how the Russians were closing in on the Eastern Front; the English and the Americans were closing in from the Northwest; and the French were advancing from the Southwest. They were telling the people to hide in the forests - to seek any place they thought would be safe for them. Maria and her mother did not know what to do, but then neither did anyone else. Eventually, they turned off the radio and went to bed, unable to sleep as the artillery kept pounding the countryside.

The next day, they roamed all over the village, desperately looking for a car, a cart, or anything that they could use to put some of their belongings in and run.

At last, they were able to rent the small wagon-cart from the Bugermeister. It was the one they had used to clear brush earlier in the year. It was difficult to decide exactly what they should take, so they loaded onto it what they could. They took off into the woods to hide, pulling the loaded wagon behind them. No one had any idea what would happen when the foreign troops would move in, and Maria and Anna had no more of a notion about what would happen than anyone else. All they knew was that they wanted to hide anywhere. They were following directions from the radio. Some other people were doing the same thing. Villagers scattered into the woods.

They were pulling the cart across an open field when a man in what looked like a soldier's uniform suddenly came out from behind a tree and asked them what they were doing.

"We are going to hide out in the forest," Maria answered.

"Are you crazy? Haven't you been listening to the radio?" he shouted at them.

"Yes. That is why we are running to hide. Radio Strasbourgh is telling the people to hide out in the forests. By the way, who are you?" It suddenly occurred to Maria that they were alone in the woods with a strange man in a German uniform telling them that they were crazy.

"I am with the *Feld Polizie*. Don't you know that you shouldn't be out here alone?" he asked. "I can't believe that they are telling the people to do that. It must be a plot to kill as many Germans as they possibly can."

Maria and her mother had never heard of such a police corps, but he wore an unusual field green uniform, with an oval, metal badge large enough to cover his chest hanging on a chain around his neck with the words *Feld Polizie* (Field Police) on it.

He shouted, "Get back into town now. Gather the people together in large groups for protection. Listen. The artillery is getting closer! The French will be here within hours. Hurry! Go door to door and tell the people to gather at the Burgermeister's house. The larger the group, the safer you will all be. They are vicious animals, the French. I have heard that they are raping everything in their path. Not even men or children are safe!"

"My dear God in Heaven!" Anna said. " Let's hurry and get back now."

Just at that point, an artillery shell whistled by and exploded on the side of the mountain that rose from the meadow where they were standing. Simultaneously, they all threw themselves to the ground, assisted by the percussion of the explosion. Then they all sprang up like jackrabbits and started running into town.

"You two start knocking on the doors at this end of town and tell the people to form a large group at the Burgermeister's house. I will tell him that the people are coming," he shouted.

"You. Get back into town! Go to the Burgermeister's house! Now!" he yelled at a husband and wife who were running into the woods.

"Be sure to tell the people to gather in large groups. The larger the better. And most important of all, hang out a white flag, and be sure that no one has anything that looks like a weapon of any kind." Those were his parting words.

Artillery shells were exploding everywhere. One house disintegrated in a deafening explosion next to them.

Word quickly spread as the townspeople began to cram into the basement of the Burgermeister's house. It was not a large house, but it had a full basement. There were some shelves along the walls with nameless bottles and cans on them and other shelves that were wider with hay scattered on them. It was a small village of about five hundred people, so when his basement was full, the villagers went to another basement location down the street. Others more stubborn and brave than Maria and her mother decided to stay in their houses.

They were huddled there for two or three hours as the artillery shelling came closer; the blasts of the exploding shells made dust and plaster fall from the ceiling and the walls. The basement was filled with an excited din of voices that would rise and fall between the blasts outside. Maria heard someone say that they used artillery to soften up resistance before the occupying troops come in. The Bugermeister had brought a radio into the basement so the crowd could hear what was happening, even if some of the information was conflicting. The radio didn't last long because the electricity went out soon after they got there.

Suddenly, a deadly hush fell over the basement. Every man, woman, and child became still. Even the infants stopped crying. All of them perceived that something had changed. Maria and Anna grabbed hold of each other and hugged tightly. Families huddled together, embracing each other. Everyone tried to give support to everyone else. The artillery had stopped. The silence was almost alive. It was deafening. But somewhere in the bowels of this silence, Maria could hear a low hum, and minute by agonizing minute, it grew louder as the ground beneath their feet began to vibrate. The humming grew into an earth-shattering roar of confusing sounds that were to continue for at least an hour.

All of their faces lifted heavenward. It almost looked like they were praying all together. Their eyes were riveted on the tiny window of the basement that faced the main street. It was a small opening less than a meter long and a third of a meter wide. Then the unmistakable armor of the first tank rumbled past. Then more tanks rumbled by; metal clanked and brakes squeaked. There were the sounds of metal rubbing on metal, gunshots, and men barking orders. They could hear everything, but their view of the world was limited to what they could see through that small window. The tanks, vehicles, and soldiers must have gone by that window for an hour.

So many thoughts raced through Maria's mind. What kind of world would they emerge to? Would there still be a Germany? What would happen to her and her mother? Maria formulated a plan and then planned another plan over and over in her mind. She would tell them about how she had fought against the Nazis in her own way from the time she was just a little girl. They would have to know that she was a "good" German. She especially remembered how she had argued with her mother when she was eight or nine about attending the opening ceremony for the autobahn. Hitler was coming to Frankfurt to break ground for the autobahn. They were told in school how this would make Germany stronger by providing jobs and making one of the most modern transportation systems in the world. It would be an honor for them to be there for such a historic event. However, when they told the students that they all had to wear a tan suede jacket, she rebelled. She didn't want to wear a tan suede jacket; she wanted to wear a black suede jacket. Her mother had tried to explain the political reasons, but Maria didn't care if it was the Queen of England; she was going to wear black suede, not the tan required by Hitler. She thought to herself that if there were any pictures left of the sea of kids that were forced to be there, she would stand out among them in the black suede jacket she wore to the opening of the autobahn in front of Hitler. Hopefully, these invaders would believe her, understand that she was not a Nazi, and spare her.

Then she noticed with a start that it was suddenly, chillingly still. The tanks had stopped thundering past the little window. There were no gunshots, no soldiers shouting. . . nothing. Then the door crashed open, and ten soldiers burst through like an explosion. Some aimed machine-guns at them while some had a pistol in each hand. They stopped on the steps, as they looked over the gathering in the cellar. Terror filled the air in a tangible way. Maria could discern that the soldiers were scared too. They didn't know if any of the people in the basement had weapons or what they would do.

Then the soldiers started walking cautiously down the steps, machine-guns, pistols, and rifles aimed at the throng. They were speaking French. They did not know any German, and none of the villagers knew any French. The Bugermeister tried to communicate, but it didn't work. They pushed past him, knocking him down, and looked over the crowd for hidden weapons. They scanned the cramped space to determine if any German soldiers were hiding with the people.

The soldiers remained for several hours, searching each of the people in the room along with any belongings they had on them. They spoke only French, which only added to the fear of the townspeople since they didn't know what was going on. The troops must have been satisfied that they were a relatively harmless group because all of them cleared out of the cellar dimmed by twilight. After a few minutes, the Bugermeister went to the top of the steps and tried to open the door to look out. He was abruptly knocked in the face with the butt of a rifle and tumbled down the stairs. There were two guards posted outside the door. After that incident, they also posted one inside the door to guard them.

There they sat all night in the darkness wondering what would happen next. No one dared go up the steps to find out what was going on. There was no din, only hushed whispers. They could hear occasional artillery fire in the distance and smell smoke, but the worst element was listening to the trapped farm animals screaming all night when a shell would hit a barn and burn it.

The next morning, a farmer was permitted to enter the cellar. He reported that the troops were gone for the most part. He had seen their white flag outside the door, and he wanted to let them know that they could come out. The two guards still outside their door did not seem too concerned about them. There were guards stationed everywhere, but they left them alone. The farmer did warn them that the

French were raping people everywhere. The night before, the soldiers had been given twenty-four hours to do whatever they wanted. Some of those screams weren't only animals in the barns. During all that night of plunder, what saved Maria and her mother was that they were in a big group.

"One fifteen year old girl had jumped out of a window to escape being raped and died in the fall," he told them.

The troops were butchering the animals for food as well. As soon as he left, some of the people decided to go to their homes, but most decided that staying with the big group was still the safest thing to do.

Later in the day, some more people decided to leave. Maria took a little courage from this, so she decided against the wishes of her mother to go to their apartment to get some of their clothes out of the cellar there. She climbed the stairs and peeked out of the door. The guards at their door asked her some questions she could not understand, but they let her proceed. The only people she saw were the guards standing at each house, so she continued. However, when she walked around the corner of the house, she almost ran directly into two French guards. She could see the hate in their eyes as she tried talking with her hands. One of them raised his rifle and started to aim it at her, so she pointed to the cellar and gestured very slowly at her clothes. They must have understood because they let her go into the basement.

When she opened the door, she saw that the cellar was covered with about a foot of cider. There were several large casks down there. Her landlords, the farm couple they rented from, made apple wine. The French had shot holes in the casks, which had filled the cellar with the contents. Their suitcases were floating around in the cider. Maria's only pair of toe shoes, and a few ballet clothes were stained with cider. She grabbed the suitcase that was soaking wet and heavy and hurried back to the Burgermeister's cellar. The two guards just watched her with curiosity and contempt. She reflected on how dangerous it was for her to have gone out alone because the two guards at the house could have killed her or worse.

It was quiet for the rest of the day, but occasionally, a farmer would come by and report that there were Arab mercenaries and French troops wandering around in packs. Maria and her mother resolved to stay another night. The French had allowed some people to bring in food when they returned, so the group remained intact. Most of them felt that it was still the safest choice to remain where they were. That next night was much more quiet that the one before. There was no shelling, and the troops were quieter.

The next morning, Maria decided to go back to their apartment and pick up some more of their things. Anna wouldn't go out of the cellar and was extremely unhappy that Maria insisted on going there.

"It is only a few houses away," Maria protested.

"Are you insane? Alone. French packs everywhere. No! If you go, and are that stupid, you deserve what you get," Anna yelled.

"I went yesterday and nothing happened. I will be all right. You will see. Besides, I can get some food and other necessities."

"Ok. Go, you fool. But be careful." Anna would not let go of Maria's arm.

Maria pulled herself away from Anna and said, "I will be right back. Just stay calm."

Maria climbed the steps to the door and looked back to see her mother wiping the tears from her eyes. The guards practically ignored her as she walked toward her apartment. When she arrived there, the two French guards were gone. Everything was quiet. The sun was shining brightly. It was almost peaceful. She went upstairs to their apartment and gathered together some of their things. She threw shoes, blouses, underwear, and such stuff into a basket on the table. She filled a tote bag with the few cans of food in the kitchen along with the small rations she could scrounge up. She threw her purse with all of her important papers on top, picked up the basket, carrying the tote bag on her right arm, and started toward the door.

Suddenly, it burst open, and an Arab flew into the room making a screeching noise. It was a noise as if to say, "I found one." as he grabbed her left arm.

Maria was instantly filled with a horror she had never known. Her heart raced. Her mind churned. A million possible horrifying scenarios flashed through her mind. He was carrying a rifle, and he wore a turban and long robes. His face was pockmarked. His eyes were popping out of their sockets. A greasy beard covered his face. His robe was filthy, and he reeked so badly she wanted to gag. This was it. She desperately did not want to become the victim of this hideous creature.

She was wearing a suit jacket, and she slipped out of it as he grasped her arm tighter, all the while making weird guttural noises. She pushed past him to the stairway. As she dashed to her freedom, a deeper horror momentarily froze her in place. Two more Arabs were racing up the stairs, and they looked worse than the first one. There was a fourth one standing by the door at the bottom of the stairs. The one behind her was grasping for her, wielding a sword at the same time. She was utterly desperate beyond words. She knew she had to do something. She had only split seconds, so she used her ballet training and jumped over the railing at the top of the stairs to get away from the smelly Arab behind her in the room. Then she leaped as hard as she could and jumped over the heads of the two charging up the stairs at her.

She kept her knees bent so she could land softly and run. She thought to herself that she would rather break something and die than be raped by this gang of slimy smelly animals. Maria landed at the bottom of the stairs with such speed that she knocked the Arab guarding the door to the ground and ran.

The gamekeeper's house was just a block and a half away, so she would run there. She looked back over her shoulder as she was running, and she saw two of the hideous creatures kneel and aim their rifles at her, so she started to run zigzag. They shot several times, but missed her. The bullets bounced off the street next to her with a zing. She made it to the side door of the gamekeeper's house where no guards were posted and desperately pounded on the door with both fists, screaming to be let in.

The door opened, and when she looked up, she looked into the face of an ugly Arab in a French uniform. As she looked up into his eyes, her knees just gave out on her, and she fell limp. The gunshots ceased. He caught her in his arms as she sank to the ground, but the gamekeeper and his wife were standing right behind him. They grabbed her out of his arms and put her on a chair in the kitchen. Then they tried to calm her down and offered her something to drink.

The Arab that opened the door was the assigned guard for the gamekeeper, and he had some rank because he wore a French uniform rather than robes. Maria had barely caught her breath and was crying a bit because she had lost her purse with all her papers in it. After about fifteen or twenty minutes, when she had calmed down and regained her composure, the Arab said in German that there were five men out on the street with a mule they had stolen. He asked her to come to the window to identify them. She was afraid to go near him, but the gamekeeper's wife told her to look. Maria walked to the window shaking, wanting only to peek out, but the Arab threw back the curtain so they could see her and asked, "Is that them?"

"Yes," she stammered.

He said, "I can get your purse for you, but you will have to follow me out and identify it."

Maria said, "No! I don't need the papers that bad," she could not face the brutes who had just tried to rape and kill her a half an hour earlier.

The gamekeeper's wife assured her, "He is OK. He won't hurt you. And besides, you need your papers."

He opened the door, drew his pistol, and ordered them to stop.

He turned his head to Maria and said, "Stay right behind me."

She was trembling so violently, she could hardly walk. No performance or premier in the theater had made her this jittery.

He said something in Arabic, whereupon one of them produced her purse and handed it to him.

"Is this yours? "

Maria replied, "Yes," as she looked in it. Her papers were still in it, but nothing else." They had taken out anything that was shiny, her lipstick, pencils, and pens.

"Do you have everything you need?" he asked her.

"Yes," she said with a hesitant voice.

He then waved them on with his gun, and Maria and the Arab turned and walked back to the gamekeeper's house.

"I have to get back to the Burgermeister's house, to my mother."

"OK then. I will escort you there." He then walked her the short distance to the Burgermeister's cellar because she probably would never have been able to walk the short distance without being attacked.

Several hours later at dusk, another group of French soldiers burst into the Burgermeister's cellar, but they were much more hostile than the first bunch from the day before.

Maria caught the eye of one of them, who strutted over and started to make passes at her. He was an officer.

He wasn't fresh. He just took her one hand in his and kissed it. Then he took her other hand in his, fondled it for a while, and then kissed that one. She could barely breathe. She could feel the horror and revulsion rising inside of her. She tried to free her hand, but he gently yet firmly tightened his grip on it.

The tension in that small room was like static electricity. What should she do? He was speaking French, and she knew only about ten words of French other than ballet terms.

Then the gamekeeper sitting right across from them tried to speak a little French, but it did not work. So Maria tried some words - anything to get this French pest to go away. He didn't understand anything. She even tried some ballet terms, but he just kept stroking her hand. Why, she kept wondering, did he pick her out? She was plain. She did not have on any makeup. She wore plain cloths. She even had a scarf on her head so she would look like a peasant. She had taken every precaution to blend in with the villagers. She did everything she could not to draw attention to herself since she and her mother had come to the village.

Three of the soldiers hurried over to the gamekeeper. He apparently drew too much attention to himself by trying to help her. They grabbed him so roughly that they almost threw him up the stairs. They distrusted his green gamekeeper uniform, which he always wore. This was enough to draw away the attention of her tormentor. He dropped her hand in the confusion and helped the others remove the gamekeeper. He did, however, stop at the top of the stairs look down directly at her and said something.

The Arab who had been the gamekeeper's guard came in shortly after that, and told them in German that the soldiers who took the gamekeeper wanted to beat him up because they did not understand what his uniform meant. He went on, however, to say that he had explained the situation to the French troops before they beat him up. The gamekeeper was safe because they knew that he was not a military threat.

The Arab then looked directly at Maria from the stairs and said to her in his broken German, "The captain told you that he would be back for you at ten o'clock tonight."

He seemed to have some feelings for his captives. Maria decided that he felt sorry for them. She had the distinct feeling that he was especially worried about her fate. She determined also that he was a bit of a con man because he had watches up and down both arms. He walked to the bottom of the steps, and said that he was protecting the watches for people who would have otherwise had them torn off by the French. He claimed that he had the names and addresses of each person who owned each watch, and that after things settled down, he would send them back to their rightful owners for a fee. He then asked in his broken German if any of them had any jewelry they needed to have protected from the French? A few people gave him their watches, and then he left.

The Frenchman would be back at ten. There was no place to hide - no place to go. Everyone in the room was concerned about Maria's fate so they decided to hide her in one of the bins behind some hay. They were actually like two very deep shelves about four feet deep and four feet apart filled with hay, corn, and other miscellaneous items. So she crawled into one of the upper hay bins while the people piled straw and hay around her to hide her.

As ten o'clock arrived far too quickly, the people in the cellar sat in front of the bin in so as to make it difficult for anyone to move through that part of the room. They placed themselves in such a way to clutter up the room without drawing attention.

At ten, the officer walked through the door, speaking only French. The volume in his voice intensified as he strutted down the stairs and saw that his prize was gone. He then pulled his long knife out of its sheath, all the while talking calmly. The monotone of his voice was broken briefly when he stabbed into a bin of corn on the other side of the cellar.

He walked to the next bin. The anger in his voice did not need any translation as he stabbed the blade into a pile of straw repeatedly from one end of the pile to the other. As he stabbed it, he accented some words over others. They popped out in a staccato with each stab. He was in a fury. He approached closer and closer to the bin where Maria was hiding. She was curled up into a tight ball as far back in the corner as possible, and hoped that the sharp blade of his knife would not reach that far back.

He swung his knife at the people sitting in front of her, shouting loudly by now, and caused them to scurry to the other side of the room. He stabbed his knife into the stack of hay where she was. He stabbed once by her feet. She curled up into a tighter ball. He stabbed again and almost struck her left foot.

Maria thought to herself, this guy is now going to kill me. I might as well get out and perhaps live a little longer. Besides, he might start killing the old people and the kids if he can't find me. The Arab aide walked along behind him, translating what he said into German for the group. She figured it was better for her to die than to have all of those other innocent people die for her. What else could she do? Be stabbed to death in a dirty bin, or perhaps live a few more minutes and get out of this. So she pushed the straw aside with one hand.

"Ah ha," he said, with a look of faked surprise, as if he knew all along where she was and just wanted to torment her with the waiting. He picked his teeth with another shorter, more wicked-looking knife and stood there for a few seconds.

Maria jumped out of the bin and scurried over to sit by her mother. A sneer crept over his face as he twisted the knife in his right hand as if he were looking at the light reflect off of the blade. Suddenly, he snapped out of his reverie, strutted over, and forced himself between Maria and her mother almost slapping Anna onto the floor.

He grabbed the hair on the back of Maria's head with his left hand, pulled her head back over to his chest, and stuck the point of the knife into her throat. He was very rough, but very careful not to hurt her. The point of the knife lay lightly on her throat as he kept twisting it back and forth in his right hand. She was beyond terror at this point. She was just numb, and she kept hoping that she would die quickly and painlessly.

Abruptly, he let go of her hair and toyed with her. He gently let the tip of the knife drop to her chest. The point of it was now in the center of her chest between her breasts, and he continued to twist it back and forth in a menacing way. He talked. He never stopped talking. Then he took Maria's left hand in his and began fondling it. He kissed it tenderly, all the while twisting the point of his knife into her chest. Now the revulsion and horror of what she might have to live through before he killed her sank in.

He dropped to the floor, kneeling on his left knee, and kissed her hand up to her elbow.

My God! Maria screamed to herself inside her head. He is going to rape me right here in front of my mother and all these people.

She didn't know which thought was more revolting to her: being raped in front of these people or being killed in front of them. Worst of all, she thought to herself, he is good-looking.

As he knelt on the floor in front of her kissing her hand while twisting a knife into her chest, he suddenly started singing the aria from *La Boheme.* Since Maria knew the opera, her horror deepened. This was a death scene in which the character Mimi is sitting in the artist's atelier about to die.

The first two lines were enough to let her know what he was going to do: *"Wie eis kalt ist dein Händchen. Komm und lass es mich erwarmen...,"* "How cold is your dainty hand. Come here and let me warm you up...."

She knew that he was going to rape and murder her, and he was telling how her by picking this aria from this opera.

Maria thought to herself that he had a good voice. In fact, he had a trained voice. He also knew the words to an aria.

What a dumb thing to think. What a dumb thought. I am about to die, and I am analyzing his singing skills. This is like a surrealistic Stravinsky production, Maria pondered to herself. If she had to go through this, she might as well try to survive.

So she thought to herself, I know the whole damned opera. Try it.

She then began to hum it with him. He was stunned, surprised. He kept looking at her and continued to sing, but he pulled the knife away from her chest his eyes glistening. She could tell that she had taken him aback.

He rose to his feet, stared at her silently, kissed her hand one last time, and said something in French. He walked over to the steps clearly in love with her. He turned at the top of the steps, put two fingers to his lips and blew her a kiss. Maria had bought herself some time.

They could hear some commotion outside after the soldier and his Arab aide left. About a half an hour later, the Arab returned and told Maria that the Frenchman had said that she was his property and that he would be back to get her at ten o'clock in the morning.

The Arab said, "Do not worry. I will help you and your mother to a safe place." He seemed genuinely concerned for her safety. "I will be back later."

The night passed slowly, and at the same time more quickly than imaginable. Maria and her mother waited for the Arab to come back, but he didn't. Maria was consumed by anxiety. She kept seeing the anguished faces of women she had seen walking back from the hospital in the town further up the mountain. They had all been rape victims, and they had to walk up the mountain to the hospital in

Neuenbürg after their humiliation to be "cleaned." She could still see the blank, broken desolation in their faces. Some were even raped again returning home from the hospital, and they had to go back. Finally, the hospital ran out of supplies and couldn't help them anymore.

Maria did not sleep, nor did her mother. All she could say to Maria was, "Oh God, what a fate! If only we had died in the bombings, we would be free now."

Maria tried to comfort her. "Don't worry. The Arab said he would help us."

"Oh God. Oh God. He probably is going to rape and kill us in the woods."

"No. I don't think so. I think he is worried about us."

"It's five thirty where is he?" Anna asked.

Eventually, dawn began to light up the little window. It was six o'clock, and Maria's doom was only hours away. The Arab slipped silently through the door and motioned to Maria and her mother to follow him. He held his fingers up to his lips so no one would speak. He even carried their bags for them and escorted them to Gertrude's Inn. No one bothered them, but then there were no people on the street because of the curfew. Maria surmised that anyone who saw them would think that it was official business because the Arab was an officer. He walked with an air of confidence that must have averted suspicion.

When they arrived at Gertrude's Inn, they were greeted at the door by Gertrude, her daughter, and various other people that were there. Edith and her niece Helen were there too. It was good to see her safe and alive, and it was good to be among friends again.

That night, there was an informal search throughout the village. The captain was trying to find Maria and her mother. However, he could not throw the full weight of the French army into finding the object of his lust, so the search was thorough but not complete.

Gertrude showed the two of them to the entrance of a hidden fruit cellar under her kitchen floor. They pushed a heavy oak table a few feet across the room and exposed the old door. Maria and Anna went into the cold dampness. They could hear the heavy table being slid over the opening. Within a half an hour, they heard a muffled knock at the door. They held their breath in the darkness because they could hear the voices of French soldiers barking at Gertrude and the others. A short time later, the familiar screech of the oak table awoke the silence, and the door opened. Gertrude greeted them and told them that it was safe to come out.

Chapter 18

Once Maria and her mother had moved into the inn, life took on a new routine. All of them, Gertrude and her daughter, Edith and her niece, and Maria and her mother were relatively safe now since they had their own guard posted at the door. About three days after the two of them moved in, Edith brought out a picture album and showed it to all of them.

She said, "These are pictures of the last movie I made before I came here. It was called *Zwei Im Schnee.*" They were fascinating pictures of movie stars having fun behind the scenes. Some of the pictures she recognized as being scenes from various movies. Maria shared with them some of the few pictures of theater productions she had salvaged from the bombings.

"I'm surrounded by famous people," Gertrude said.

"Oh, don't be silly. We are all lucky to be alive. I don't think there is anything famous left in the world," Edith said.

"I don't either," Maria added.

"Here are some pictures of my clown number that got all those standing ovations." Maria told them the story of the incredible curtain calls. "Here is one of me in my Swan Lake costume."

Maria in classic arabesque pose

"That is astounding," Edith said.

"I knew all along that you two were different. You are too beautiful, even without makeup and the peasant scarves to hide your faces. I think people suspected all along what you were up to," Gertrude said.

"You know. Anna, Maria, and I suspected you were famous long ago." She explained. That was how they spent the days immediately after the French occupation of Waldrennach.

Life was a mixture of developing a routine and devising a plan to get out of that place. Nothing was normal. The only thing that was normal was that nothing was normal.

One day, they learned why they had a high-ranking white French guard at the Inn door when no other building in town except the Burgermeister's house had one. All the other guards were Arabs. That was the day the French brought special identification papers to Edith indicating that she was Jewish. It had taken some time since the occupation to process the paperwork. The guard was positioned there for her and her niece's protection as Jews more than for the protection of the rest of them.

Maria and her mother wanted to return to Frankfurt, and Edith and her niece wanted to get back to Berlin. They all wanted to get back to the life they had known before. The trains still weren't running, but things were improving a little at a time. The occupation had been in place for about three weeks, and it still wasn't safe to go out alone.

The French apparently had a bizarre sense of humor. A group of French soldiers had become completely drunk one day when they stole some paint from a store and painted all of the farm animals in the village to look like zoo animals. There were cows that looked like elephants, goats that looked like zebras and tigers, and animals that didn't look like anything. Some cows had polka dots painted on them. It was weird and funny to see all the animals in town painted in bright colors. The soldiers then went on "safaris" and hunted some of the animals.

The villagers so disliked the French and the Arabs that there was even gossip that they were raping the animals when they ran out of women, children, and men.

Late one night, just before they were all about to go to bed, there was a gentle tapping at the back window of the inn. Gertrude slid the window to the side and opened it a crack.

A voice whispered out of the darkness, "Please help me. I am a German soldier, a regular, not a Nazi. I am trying to get back home. Please. Do you have some food? I just need a little help to get home."

"If you wait, I can arrange to hide you in the fruit cellar. Just –"

"What are you whispering about out there?" the French guard snapped at Gertrude in the kitchen as he roamed freely through the inn part of the building.

"Nothing. I just dropped the salt in the sink, and I was cursing about it," Gertrude replied picking up a saltshaker.

The guard just glared at her momentarily and proceeded to wander through the inn.

"Come in. I can put you in the fruit cellar," Gertrude whispered.

"No. It is not safe, especially for you. I still have on my army uniform," he answered.

"Stay around, I will make you a sandwich." With that, Gertrude made him a sandwich and a bag full of food.

As she passed it to him through the window, Gertrude stopped and said, "Don't go yet. I have some of my husband's old clothes in the bedroom. He has been dead for a while, but it will be better for you to have them, even if they don't fit."

A few minutes later, she gave him a shirt, a pair of shoes, and a pair of pants.

"Thank you. Thank you so much. God bless you, kind woman."

"And God bless and protect you so you can get home to your wife and children, if, in God's will they are still alive for you," Gertrude said back to him.

With that, his shadow blended into the darkness of the pine forest on this moonless, forbidding night as he scurried into oblivion.

Maria and her mother sympathized with his feelings because they wanted to get back to Frankfurt for the same reason. All the family they had left in the world was there, if they were anywhere.

Gertrude told them all what had happened after the French guard settled himself outside the door. They all went into a depression. This incident brought down all of their spirits as they sat and wondered if they were all alone in the world. Tears filled their eyes as they pondered if their families were still alive. The mood was contagious. Maria and her mother started a self-pity session that affected everybody in the inn. They all cried and felt sorry for themselves.

A similar incident with a soldier occurred once again, and Gertrude fed him too. The guard never discovered these transgressions because no one of them ever talked about it afterward.

A few days after that incident, their guard was removed. Apparently, the French did not feel threatened by the villagers anymore. It was relatively safe to go out. So Maria, her mother, Edith, and her niece decided to leave. But first, they needed transportation to Neuenbürg, where the station for the local train was located. They all had one or two suitcases that were too heavy to tote down the mountain by hand. So they set out to find some form of transportation. Eventually, they found a farmer with a horse and wagon. Edith had the biggest trunk, and Maria had her cider-stained suitcase that smelled like apple wine.

They had a brief, tearful departure at the door of the inn when they said goodbye to Gertrude. Then the four of them piled on the wagon. They waved and wept as they moved further from the village. Gertrude stood in the doorway alternately waving a handkerchief and wiping tears from her eyes with it.

When they finally arrived at the train station, they just waited. They had been told that the trains were running again, but there was nothing like a schedule to keep them on time. So the four of them sat and waited, and waited some more. Finally, after about a half a day, the local came from Wildbad and took them to Pforzheim.

Their first glimpse of Pforzheim shocked them all. It had been a quaint town, but as they approached, they could see out of the window that there was not much left. The shells of burnt-out buildings lined the rubble-strewn streets as far as they could see. They disembarked into half of a train station. From there, all Maria could see in any direction were piles of rubble with cluttered streets running between them.

This was the beginning of the English Zone. It took some time to clear their papers, but the English were much nicer than the French. They actually felt safe for the first time in a long time. Maria was sure that if it had not been for Edith's special papers, it might have taken them a month longer to get out of the French zone.

There was a train leaving for Frankfurt. It couldn't travel all the way there because the tracks weren't repaired yet, but it would take them as far as Heidelberg. Edith was going to Frankfurt with Maria and Anna because that was the only train running. Nothing was running anywhere near Berlin yet.

"This train ride is a luxury," Maria said, shielding herself from the wind that was blowing into the windowless compartment through a hole in the side of the train.

"Are you finally cracking up on us, Maria?" Edith asked her.

"No, no. Ask my mother. The last time mama and I were on a train, it was bombed. And when I came from Berlin, I almost didn't make it here because we were bombed," Maria answered.

"That must have been horrible," Edith said as she leaned forward to look out the hole in the wall, scrutinizing it in a circle with her eyes as if to punctuate the irony of their "luxury."

"At least we're getting closer to home," Anna added.

"Yeah. I wonder if there's anyone left. Do you think we will find Karl, Mama?" Maria asked her mother.

"I'm sure everyone is doing just fine. They are probably more worried about us than we are about them right now sweetie. Just pray and hope to be together soon." Anna was clearly pretending to have confidence in the unknown to comfort the others.

When they arrived in Heidelberg, they discovered that there was no way to move any closer to Frankfurt by train. This forced them to look for a place to live for a while. Luckily, Edith and Maria had a lot of money between them, and they were able to purchase a tiny hotel room at an inn at black market prices. The inn was operational because it was too small to be a billet for the occupying troops. The room was too small for four people, but it was a place to live, and that was all that mattered. They realized that their lack of planning could have had them all sleeping on the street or in a tent shelter somewhere. They recognized their luck to be in relative luxury once again.

Heidelberg had some rubble, but it must have been spared because of its castle and the history surrounding it. Compared to Pforzheim, it looked like a city. Heidelberg castle was completely untouched, but it was difficult to discern what were ancient ruins and what were modern ones.

The four of them tried everything to get to Frankfurt. They attempted to hire a car, a truck, or anything that could move them there. They offered large sums of money, but there was no transportation to be found. Eventually, they became friends with some of the people they tried to hire, and they, in turn, attempted to help them find some transportation.

Not everything was routine. One morning they saw one of the most incredible incidents they had seen in this war yet. A German officer dressed to perfection in his uniform and wearing a Ritter Kreutz around his neck was strutting down the street as if he had won the war. No one could understand why he was wearing his uniform since the safest thing for a German to be at that time was anonymous. One would definitely not want to be identified as a Nazi officer. He strutted up to a contingent of American soldiers and demanded to see the highest-ranking officer in charge. He had come to surrender, and as an officer he would not surrender to common soldiers, but only to ranking officers. He was a renowned Nazi pilot, well known for shooting down enemy planes.

The four of them were stranded in Heidelberg. All they could do was take long walks, sightsee, and try to get information about Frankfurt. There was no telephone, no telegraph. Newspapers were not permitted to be printed yet. Then one day, one of their Heidelberg friends told them that he had heard of a delivery truck that was scheduled to go to Frankfurt the next day. The four of them tracked down the owner of the truck and asked him to take them with him. They offered him a substantial amount of money. He told them that he already had six people signed up. They told him that they didn't care how crowded it was. They just desperately wanted to get to Frankfurt. Then they offered him several hundred more marks, and he agreed to take them.

The next morning, a small van with no windows pulled up to their inn. The driver opened the back door. The truck was already full with the other six people and their belongings. Two of them were children. There were trunks and two bicycles. There was even a dog in there.

After he loaded their trunks on the van, he collected one hundred marks from each of them plus the several hundred more that Edith and Maria paid him. There was only enough room to stand up when they climbed into the van; however, none of the four of them cared nor did the other people. They were focused on getting to Frankfurt.

Twenty minutes later, he picked up two more people, but they did not have any bags. It was an uncomfortable ride, especially because it was one filled with anticipation and fear of what they might find, or not find.

Twenty minutes later, they arrived at the American Zone. The rickety van screeched to a halt, throwing all of them forward. The American soldiers made all of them pile out of the van. They did not realize how difficult it was to get anywhere in Germany since the war ended. This was like a boarder crossing to another country, only they were crossing from British-occupied Germany to American-occupied Germany. Maria wondered what had happened to her country.

The first thing they had to do was show their Kennkarte or identification papers. Then they had to explain where they were going and why. Germans were only permitted to travel to their homes at that time. Edith and Helen had to explain that they were with Maria and Anna, but on their way to Berlin. She had to convince the Americans that the only route to Berlin was through Frankfurt where, she might be able to book a train. The soldier handling her papers looked at her, then at her papers, and then back at her again. He walked away to consult with another soldier in front of the van. He returned to them, handed Edith her papers, and said, "OK, you can go through."

The last thing the Americans did was to check the all of their trunks. They were very courteous. Maria had been happy to see the English when they left the French Zone, but she was even happier to see the Americans. They seemed almost courteous. The Americans passed them through without any problems.

The driver dropped them off at the Hauptbahnhof, the main train station. The four of them took all of their belongings inside and put them in a big pile. Amazingly, the train station was still intact, but there were no trains running. Helen and Anna stayed behind and guarded the pile of suitcases, while Edith and Maria went off to reconnoiter.

There were many intact hotels around the train station. Mostly Americans were billeted there, but they were also used to house Jews. The hotels occupied by the Americans had no room for them, so the two of them were directed to the ones reserved for Jews.

Maria and Edith went across the street to the one the Americans had indicated. It was in remarkably good condition. In fact, the whole Bahnhof square was in good shape. It was like this part of the city was spared the heavy bombing.

The hotel was packed. They asked for two rooms, but there wasn't even one available. However, when Edith showed them her identification papers, they moved some people around and were able to procure one room for the four of them. Edith and Maria went back to the train station to bring Anna and Helen and their bags to the hotel. They tried walking a short distance when they realized that their luggage was too much for them to carry.

The station was strangely normal, with many people milling around, but the din of people's voices was the only sound that filled the huge building. The sounds of clacking wheels, screeching brakes, and the hiss of escaping steam were conspicuous because of their absence. They scanned the crowd carefully and finally asked a couple of safe-looking men who were milling around the area to help them carry their bags to the room. Edith gave them several marks, and the men thanked them graciously. Edith and Maria still had quite a bit of money between them, so they were able to pay for many things that other people could not afford.

The hotel room was small by any standard. The four of them and their belongings filled it up. Nevertheless, they were grateful to have a place to stay. Ironically, if it had not been for Edith's Jewish background, they would have been sleeping on the street or in the train station that night. Those papers came in handy.

They had no sooner settled in the room than both Maria and her mother became more agitated with anticipation. They had suppressed thinking about their family until this moment. Now they had to try to find her brothers. They needed to know who, if anyone, was still alive.

The four of them tentatively set out in an attempt to find any trace of their family. The city was too big for Anna to walk very far, but fortunately, Helen was a good companion for her. She was too young to be left alone, and Anna's knees were too weak to walk too far too fast. They were good company for each other. They stayed in a park by the Main River while Edith and Maria went on. They all decided that it would be best for Anna not to see it if Karl's or Heinrich's house was gone. It was better if Maria went alone with Edith.

It was difficult starting out. So many thoughts went through Maria's mind. She had no idea where Karl might be living. She didn't even know if he was alive. She did know where Heinrich's house was, but it was not easy to identify landmarks because so many of them were gone.

A block past the untouched square of the train station, the city turned into a grotesque nightmare of destruction and civilization. People were already busy cleaning up the debris, but there was so much of it. The air still had the muted smell of spent fire and damp ashes. As they walked past the standing shell of one building, Maria looked up through a gaping hole and was bewildered at the sight of soft, puffy clouds drifting across the deep, blue sunlit sky. Nature, unlike them, was oblivious to the reality of the horror they were walking through. Often, they had to detour around huge piles of rubble in the street. They walked past where Maria's house used to be. All that was left of her former home was a pile of unremarkable rubble around the ghosts of walls and the skeletons of consumed buildings. Enough rubble had been removed to get into the cellar from which Maria and Anna had run to the river during the firestorm. Everything was ruined. The china was brown and black. The stench of scorched melted items was overwhelming. Maria spotted the box that held pictures and all of her memorabilia of her career in the theater. She ran to it hoping to find a bright moment, but when she opened the lid it was filled with ashes. All of her precious pictures were destroyed. There were still some clothes hanging in a corner that looked untouched, but when she went to grab them, they weirdly just disintegrated into dust.

Edith stood there in disbelief and said, "That is so strange. I don't think you will save anything Maria."

"You're right. Let's get out of here. Everything is lost." Maria responded wiping tears from her eyes.

Maria was thrilled, however, to see that the Frankfurt Dom, the cathedral were she had had her confirmation, was still standing. Then she realized that she should not have been able to see it from that point in the city. Everything between where she was standing and the cathedral was destroyed.

In the direction they strolled, they would have to walk past the opera house. As they came around the corner and Maria saw the sun shining on its half-ruined shell, she felt herself weaken. She cried uncontrollably, and only Edith kept her from falling to her knees by quickly putting her arm around her waist to comfort her.

"That's where it all started," Maria sobbed as she wiped her eyes pointing to the ruins of the opera house as the two of them just kept walking on. Maria did not look back.

Finally, they came to the street where Heinrich had lived in a house across the street from a police station. Maria stopped before they rounded the corner and told Edith that she needed to catch her breath to build up her strength for the worst. Edith tried to assure her that everything would be all right. If the house was gone, they could go the authorities, who had set up location networks to try to reunite families.

As they rounded the corner, Maria could see that the police station was still standing. But only the half of it facing Heinrich's house remained. She breathed a sigh of relief.

"Oh God! The police station is still standing. The whole block looks like it was spared," she said to Edith.

They walked on. Maria held a handkerchief in front of her eyes to wipe away tears, but she was also using it as a shield in case his building was gone. But it was there.

"It is still there. It is still standing," Maria shouted as she ran up to the door and pounded on it. There was no answer. No one was home.

"Oh God! There's no one here," she yelled to Edith. "Where are they?" She shouted as she ran from window to window trying to see into the dark rooms. "The house is here. How come they aren't?"

"I'm sure everything will be fine," Edith said as she tried to calm her. "Let's just walk for a while and come back later. It will help relax you."

They sat on the curb for a while, and then they walked back and forth up and down the block for a while. Finally, they sat on the curb again and waited for someone to show up. However, it was getting dark, so they had to head back to the hotel to be off the street before the curfew started.

When they made their way back to the park, Helen and Anna were still there. Maria's mother just wept. She could barely hold on any hope after their long ordeal to get back to Frankfurt. They learned that it is more difficult not to know if a loved one is dead than it is to know. They had a fitful night of sleep. The damn curfew. They wanted to go back to Heinrich's house. They could not sleep because of their anxiety. In addition, the accommodations were not conducive to sleep. There was only room for two on the bed, so one of them slept on the sofa, and one on a chair or the floor. Furthermore, the hotel never quieted down. It was a mad house of people sobbing, laughing, and squealing with delight because they found a loved one. People were yelling and talking all night.

The next morning, immediately after the curfew was lifted, the four of them set out for Heinrich's house. Maria's mother talked endlessly with meaningless phrases to keep her anticipation at bay. She reacted much the same as Maria had the first time she walked through the ruins of Frankfurt. They tried to identify where landmarks used to stand. They cried, and then they laughed when they would remember some funny incident. Then they came to a familiar street, where suddenly, her mother's friend Hilda appeared in the doorway of her building.

"Oh, Hilda. You are there, here, alive. Oh how wonderful," Maria's mother shouted as she ran to her old friend.

"Oh Anna, it is so good to see you. And Maria, you are both OK. Thank God," she cried as she hugged them both at the same time.

"You have some friends with you?" Hilda asked, nodding toward Edith and Helen.

"Yes, this is Edith and her niece, Helen," Anna replied.

"Well, how do you do? You look good. You all look so good to these tired eyes. Do come in and have coffee with me," she offered.

"Have you seen Karl or Heinrich?" Was the first question out of Anna's mouth.

"No. I'm sorry, I haven't. Everything is still very unsettled," Hilda answered.

They all went in and sipped a very weak cup of coffee with her. She was happy to share her small ration of this precious brew with them. They told her that they needed a place to live, and they asked her if she had any apartments available. Hilda owned the six-story apartment building that she lived in, but she told them that the authorities required her to rent the single rooms of apartments as if they were apartments because of the housing shortage. Then each family had to share the kitchen and toilet facilities.

"Oh, how can that be?" Maria asked. "Here we are all together. We should all stay together."

Finally, Hilda said, "This building has an apartment on the sixth floor, but it was condemned, and the building inspector will not let anyone live in it. It would be in livable condition if my son and his friends would return from the front, but they are still in Russia."

Disappointed, they left after a while. Anna wanted to see Heinrich's house.

As fate would have it, just as they rounded the corner of the street where Heinrich lived, they practically crashed into Karl. Maria, Anna, and Karl all reacted the same way. They just looked at each other speechless in amazement for a few seconds. Their eyes widened, their mouths dropped open, and they jumped back a step. Then they started to cry and hug each other. For several minutes, no words were spoken. The mere act of holding each other said everything that could be said. Anna alternated between hugging Karl, taking his cheeks in both of her hands, and looking at his face and saying, "It's you! It's you. Thank you, Jesus, Mary, and all the saints."

Anna asked, "Where is Heinrich?"

Karl hesitated and replied, "No one has heard from him yet. But I am absolutely certain that he will be home soon." He was clearly putting on a front to give them courage. "No mail was moving yet, and troops would have an especially difficult time sending messages home even if they were prisoners of war. At this time, it's almost impossible to make a phone call or send a wire."

Maria responded, "I know. We almost went crazy in Heidelberg trying to get a message to you or find out anything about Frankfurt."

He told them, "Herta is not home today either. Her work sometimes keeps her away for long periods of time. She is such a good wife to Heinrich. I make a point of it to come by Heinrich's house as often as possible in the hopes that this would be a place for all of us to meet." Maria looked around and saw Edith and

Helen, both of whom she had forgotten in the reunion with Karl. She introduced them all to each other.

"Karl, Hilda has a small apartment that is condemned right now, but if we could all work on it, Mama and I could live close by."

He then went back to Hilda's apartment building with them to take a look at the place. He knew the building well since he had been a good friend with her son when they were in school, and they used to play there. It was across the street from the courthouse, which was damaged but already under repair.

Hilda was glad to show it to them. The stairwell that led up to it was damaged but passable. The outside wall of the stairwell had large holes in it where Maria could look out at the empty, bombed-out block beyond. When they arrived at the top of the stairs, the hall was in shambles. The door to the apartment was off its hinges. There was no plaster on the walls of the hall or in the apartment. It lay in neat piles on the floor next to the walls it was supposed to cover. The walls were made up of slats and open holes where the windows once were. The ceiling was almost nonexistent. The plaster was gone. There was one very large gaping hole in the ceiling that mirrored the same size hole in the floor where a bomb had passed through, but had failed to explode. Through the hole in the ceiling, they could see that the roof had been repaired. That was required by regulations before anyone could live in the building.

They could look into the apartment below them through the hole in the floor. The people, who were living there, looked up at them, smiled, waved and said hello. They all waved back and told them that they had a nice apartment with a good view of this one. They agreed, and all of them chuckled. There was no furniture, and the place had a musty, mildewed smell to it.

"I can fix this place up for you in a short time," Karl said. "First, that hole in the floor needs to be repaired. And it has to be done right because it will be inspected before people will be allowed to live in here."

Hilda was thrilled at the idea of having them live there, so she told Karl to go ahead with the work. Karl walked them all back to the hotel for the night.

The next day, they went back to Heinrich's apartment. Herta was there, finally. So they all spent some time together over thin coffee speculating about Heinrich. She told them that the last she had heard, Heinrich was in Italy somewhere.

Herta was positive that he would be coming home soon because he was in the regular army. She had been told that if soldiers were taken prisoner, that it was advantageous for the other army to send captured Germans home than hold them as prisoners of war for any length of time. This was especially true if they weren't Nazis. It was a great burden for an army to feed and house great numbers of prisoners. They all rationalized that the compassion of the Americans and the British would save him. Of course, all of them denied the fact that he could indeed be dead.

Herta did not have much room, but she could take in Maria and Anna. So they went back to the hotel, and Karl helped them pack their bags and carried them to Herta's house.

Later that day, they went back to the apartment. Karl had found some lumber to fix the floor. He worked on that project for several days before it passed inspection for habitation. They all worked day and night to clear the debris out of the apartment, and it slowly evolved into a livable environment.

This was actually the best therapy for the depression of the war-torn city. It kept them all focused on a major project that would provide them with one of the rare prizes in Germany at that time – a place to live. Maria's mother wasn't able to do much, so Edith, Helen, and Anna spent most of their time in the park by the river's edge or walking around Frankfurt.

Next, the apartment needed to be equipped with electrical wiring so it could pass inspection. Karl was able to procure the wire at some reconstruction center, but he was called away for a day, so he taught Maria how to do the wiring.

"Are you nuts?" Maria shouted at him. She would not even touch the wire at first because she was afraid of it. "You know I'm deathly afraid of electricity ever since I was almost electrocuted in Wuppertal at my makeup table in the theater there."

"Oh yes. That is the time you touched the metal frame with a hanger and got stuck to the frame while getting fried." Karl chuckled.

"Yes, that's right. Stop laughing. And you want me to wire a house. They never taught this to us in Catholic school," Maria chided him.

"Look. The wire is not connected to anything," he said, holding up the harmless spool of wire. "All you have to do is tack it into the walls and ceiling. I will draw you a diagram of where to put all of the switches and outlets. You just run the wire, and I will connect it when I get back. All you have to do is cut it at these places. You can expose the ends of the wires if you want to so my job will be a little easier. Like this." He showed her how to peel the wire off the ends. He also taught her how to splice the wire together if she became really brave.

He handed her the wire and said, "Here, try it."

Maria took the wire and tacked it along the wall by the door until she came to rest where the switch was supposed to be. "What do I do now?"

"Cut it."

As she cut the wire, Karl lunged at her, making a hissing sound like an electric spark. She screamed, dropped the cutter, and ran out of the room. Karl was laughing uncontrollably. It scared her to death. Maria knew the wire wasn't connected to anything, but she was sure she would get electrocuted anyway.

She did gradually manage to wire all of the walls, and when Karl returned, he told her that she had done a great job. She knew he was telling the truth because he did not redo any of her work. He just spliced in the outlets and switches where they were needed. The electricity passed inspection without incident. Maria was so proud because she was now a ballerina/electrician. They had light and water. It felt like they were reinventing civilization. Even though they could not move in quite yet, they celebrated with a beer that afternoon in the apartment.

Chapter 19

The trains finally started running, a few at first, perhaps one or two a day, but eventually, Edith was able to buy a ticket to Berlin. She and Helen wanted to return there as much as Maria and her mother had wanted to get back to Frankfurt earlier.

That evening, Edith, Maria, Anna, and Helen talked deep into the night. They reminisced about Mehrmund, Waldrennach, the war, and the future.

"Maria, you have to come to Berlin. I can introduce you to the people who can put you in the movies. You are a natural comedienne," Edith told her.

"You have been working on me since Waldrennach to go into acting, Edith," Maria answered.

"Your stories about the theater are so funny. I just know they would make a movie about your life, and it would be funnier than anything anybody could write."

"No. I simply cannot talk in front of a bunch of people, and a camera would make me freeze. I would keep posing and not move," Maria whined.

"I think you're wrong. You dance in front of thousands of people all of the time. You know, you will always have a place in my heart, and if you ever change your mind –"

Maria interrupted her. "I love dancing. But it is not like acting. I interact with the audience on an emotional level. We communicate, but we do not have to talk. I can express love, sorrow, and compassion. Why think of *Swan Lake.* I even cried the last time I danced the solo in that."

"Well, then come and dance in the movies," Edith prodded.

"I would be like one of those stars from the silent pictures who look so beautiful on screen, but the moment you hear the star's voice, it sounds like a soprano meat grinder with a flat tire." Maria said.

"Oh Maria, I love you," Edith laughed. "It is a loss to the German movie industry, but the theater is very lucky to have a gem like you."

"I promise, though, that I will come to Berlin as soon as I can to visit with you and little Helen," Maria vowed.

The four of them went to the train station accompanied by Herta and Karl to say goodbye. They all stood on the railroad platform and hugged and cried repeating all of their promises to each other. Then the engineer shouted, "All aboard," ending their good-byes. Edith and Helen scrambled onto the train and it slowly slid out of the station headed for their home in Berlin.

Karl was able to find some white cardboard that they nailed over the slats. Plaster was out of the question for a long time. They even put the cardboard over the windows and cut openings so they could open and close the flaps during the day. Maria and her mother moved in. The apartment was dilapidated. It was essentially a three-room cardboard box with a floor, electric and running water. To the two of them, it felt like a palace after the commotion of the hotel, and it was a palace indeed if the alternative was to live in the street. Karl had a knack for rummaging up furniture and other necessities, so the three room cardboard box on the sixth floor became a home.

Heat hadn't been a problem for them up to now because it was late summer. Yet one day, Karl showed up with an old-fashioned, potbellied, wood-burning stove for heat. The burner that they had been using for a stove wasn't safe for heating. He hooked up the stove, and they were prepared to heat the place if necessary. Life was good.

Later that month, the owner of a winery a couple of blocks away told the neighbors to spread the word that they should come and get the wine before the Americans took it away. He had heard that the Americans were going to confiscate the wine and did not want them to get it.

People came from all around the neighborhood carrying anything that would hold liquid. They brought empty beer bottles, buckets, and even empty dishpans. The owner of the winery gladly filled anything anyone held under the spigot. He did not want the occupation forces touching his precious German brew.

That night, the whole neighborhood got drunk. It was kind of like a celebration after all the tension of the war, and trying to put their lives back together again. People were singing and dancing in the streets. Strangers embraced strangers and sang drinking songs. Others sat on their windowsills with their legs dangling down, singing and shouting to the street below. It was a wonderful, festive summer afternoon, and for a few brief moments, life was good.

A week later, they received a notice from the authorities that they had to share their apartment with another family. The policy was that Germans had to house one family per room until more housing could be constructed. This was disconcerting to Maria and Anna because they had just settled in, but they were glad to help anyone they could. After all, Germany and its people had to survive.

Fortunately, their apartment had two doors. The main door from the hall opened into their room, and another one opened into the smaller bedroom in the back. A single woman moved in. She caused no problems. She turned the small hallway leading into her room into a small, makeshift kitchen. They rarely bothered each other because they kept the door between their rooms locked.

The woman whose name was Ruth appeared to have a lot of money. Her wealth seemed out of place since no one had much of anything at that time. However, she was an excellent resource. She worked for the Americans at the Bahnhof. She always had food. Lots of it. They often thought that she stole it. And she did. One day, she came home and told them that the Americans had dismissed her. It seems that she had stolen a whole slab of bacon by tying it around her waist under her coat, and she was apprehended. She had been stealing food all along and selling it on the black market. She was lucky that the Americans only fired her because people were still being shot for less than that.

Frau Kroenung's son never came home. Heinrich never came home either. The days were turning into weeks. Maria went to the railroad station every day to watch for him as the trains full of troops returned because many soldiers were simply sent home rather than being held as prisoners. Anna then started to go to the Haupt Bahnhof with Maria to look for Heinrich. They were little help to each other. As a matter of fact, they kept each other's spirits down. They would return every day from the train station crying, and they would depress everyone in the household. Anna and Frau Kroenung hoped that their sons would be among those returning soldiers.

Frau Kroenung had learned from some of her son's returned friends that he had probably been sent to work in the lead mines inside Siberia. After that, she was fallen. She told Maria and Anna to stop going to the train station because it was tearing them up inside. There was no news of Heinrich at all. All hope was fading because the troop trains were not coming in as often, and the war had been over for weeks.

One day, they were just sitting at Heinrich's house with his wife Herta sipping some diluted coffee when the door swung open. Heinrich staggered into the room and looked at them in disbelief. They could hardly recognize him. He was gaunt. Maria had never seen him so thin. He had no shoes on his feet, which were bound in rags. They were bloody and bruised. He smelled foul. He was unshaven. His hair was uncombed and long. He still had on his uniform, but it was torn and filthy under an overcoat a sympathetic soul had given him one night as he worked his way home from Italy under the cover of darkness.

After the shock wore off and the reality that this was the real, living Heinrich, not some apparition, set in, they all fell into each other's arms and embraced, cried, kissed and wiped tears from each other's eyes.

Maria had never been so happy, so sad, so full of elation, and so full of sorrow all at the same time in her life. She was happy that Heinrich was alive, and yet at the same time she felt so sorry for him. She knew instinctively that she could not show that. So she hoped he saw her tears as the happy ones not the tears of sadness.

Heinrich was exhausted. Maria and Anna left so that Herta could help him clean up and rest. A few days later, after he had regained some of his strength, he told them his story of how he escaped and returned home.

"Do you remember Eckert? We grew up together," he asked.

"Yes," Maria said.

"Well, he saved my life in Genoa, Italy. He was in the American army."

" Wasn't he Jewish? How did he get there?"

"He left Germany years ago and moved to America where they drafted him," Heinrich said. "When we were captured, he helped me escape."

"What a twist of fate."

"The hardest part of my trek was getting out of Italy. The partisans were everywhere so I had to travel at night, but when I got to Germany people helped me get home."

"Oh, God, Heinrich. We helped soldiers just like you when they came to Gertrude's place in Waldrennach. God has watched over all of us." Maria said.

Chapter 20

It seemed like Maria and her mother were always working on their apartment or helping someone else restore their home to make it habitable. It was becoming a terribly boring existence. The theaters were still not operating, and life seemed like a hopeless cycle of despair.

One day, there was a knock at the door. It was Mini, Maria's friend from the early years at the conservatory.

"Oh, Mini! My God. How are you?" She grabbed her and hugged her.

"I had heard that you were back, and I had to look you up. Gosh, you look so good. And you too, Anna." When she let go of Maria, she smiled and went over to hug Maria's mother.

They recounted what they each had gone through during the war.

"So that's how we got back to Frankfurt," Maria finished up.

"All that matters is that we are all alive and finding people we love again," Mini said. "I wonder when they are going to do anything about the theater. I'm starting to go stir crazy. I'm getting so out of shape."

"I know. I am too. All I do is carpenter work. I did a lot to make this place livable. Look at my elegant walls, and I even did the wiring," Maria told her in an ironic tone of voice as she ran her hand over the rippled cardboard walls.

"Yikes. I'm getting out of here. This is a dangerous place." Mini mocked Maria with a chuckle.

"Don't worry. Karl finished all the important stuff, so I think we're pretty safe." Maria mused. "Why don't we start working out together so we stay in shape?"

"I think that's a wonderful idea. It might cheer us up a bit. Have you checked with the theater yet?" Mini asked.

"Let's check things out tomorrow," Maria suggested.

The next morning, they went to the Frankfurt Opera House, but it was boarded up tight. They walked around the building several times, but there was no opening, and no place to get information.

"What do we do now?" Mini asked.

"Well. Let me think," Maria mused out loud. "The courthouse is right across the street from my apartment. They are reconstructing it, and half of it is open for business. Why don't we check there?"

"That's a great idea," Mini said.

The courthouse was filled with the noise of hammering, buzz saws and clanking lumber. They tried one office after another with no luck. No one had any information regarding theaters. By chance, they went into an office that granted permits for most of the activities that required licensing.

The official there told them that with Maria's credentials, she would be able to put together a show. There was a great need just then for entertainment.

"I can give you the papers to fill out now, and here is the address of a German booking agent," the short, bald man behind the counter said as he handed her the papers.

Maria and Mini decided to start their own floorshow with just the two of them. They began by contacting the German booking agent. It was not easy to start their enterprise. First, they had to go through a series of interviews to prove that they had the credentials to put on a show. Then they were required to swear that they were not Nazis before a board of Germans and Americans. Finally, they were granted the permit and were able to put their show together.

The German booking agency primarily did bookings for what was left of the German army. Of course, there were not many German engagements, so he gave her name to the U.S.O.

Within two days, there was a knock at Maria's apartment door. She opened the door to find a tall, blonde, handsome American soldier standing there with a big smile on his face. He spoke no German, and they spoke no English, but they managed to decipher what each was saying. While he and Maria were trying to communicate, Mini arrived at the apartment.

"Do you two dance?" he asked.

"I think he wants to dance," Mini said.

The soldier continued to gesture as they spoke.

"I think he wants to see some pictures too."

"No. He wants to know if we dance," Maria said.

They rummaged through Maria's photographs until they found a couple of suitable ballet pictures. Then they showed them to him.

He looked at the pictures and then looked up at them, and with his big smile and a chuckle, he said, "Oh, no no no no no no." He shook his head in a negative manner along with his right index finger.

Mini looked at Maria and asked, "What is he doing? What does he mean?"

Maria shrugged her shoulders. "I don't know. He wants us to dance, but then he says no. I don't get it," Maria replied.

"Like this," he interrupted as he got up and took off one sleeve of his coat, humming some unknown tune.

"Mini," Maria whispered, grabbing her arm. "Is he taking off his clothes?"

Just at that moment, Anna came from the other room in time to see him take off his coat and swing it in circles as he pranced around the room. "I don't know what you two are up to, but I don't want to know. What is this man doing wandering around our apartment humming and taking off all of his clothes?" Anna asked with a quizzical look on her face, putting her hands on her cheeks and covering her mouth that had dropped open.

"Like this, girls. This is how I want you to dance." The soldier smiled his big American smile.

"Mini, I think he wants us to take off our clothes. He thinks that we are strippers."

Maria stood up and said to him in the same manner he had said to her, "Oh, no no no no no no no no!" while she pushed his coat into his arms. "We do not dance like that."

The soldier then took a big wad of money out of his pocket, and held it out toward them, smiling and nodding. "This should help you make your decision."

"Oh, no no no no no no no." Mini was almost breathless.

Maria joined her as they both kept repeating in unison, "No no no no no no no no."

He mumbled something that they were probably better off not understanding and left the apartment.

"Can you believe that?" Maria blurted out.

"My God, strippers. What has the world come to?" Mini mused.

"Well, at least you would stay in shape for when the theaters reopen," Anna added, laughing at the absurdity of the whole incident.

After that, the two of them were wary of working for the Americans because they thought that was all they would want from them, so they told their agent to try to keep their contacts German.

Mini and Maria worked up a delightful floorshow. They developed a catchy polka number that involved the audience. They even made their own costumes from scraps.

Maria owned a couple of stained items that had floated in cider. She had salvaged a wide skirt that she could make smaller by cutting out the stains. Mini had a similar costume. The dress was made of taffeta. They bought some chiffon on the black market to make scarves, and they made them glittery with a few sequins. They developed a very polished professional look.

They practiced at Mini's house because she had a piano, and of course, she played it well. Maria choreographed while Mini played. Then, after she created a dance, they would both hum the melody so they could dance together and synchronize their moves as they practiced. Mini put together the music arrangements for a small band to play if there would be one at any of their engagements.

A few weeks later, the German agent called them and said that there was going to be some kind of an American party booked by the U.S.O. at an officers' club. They thought about it carefully and figured that if the U.S.O. and an officers' club were involved, they would be safer than with some private American strip party. So they accepted.

When they arrived there, they discovered that the Americans did not want any ballet dances, so Maria and Mini added more tap dances to the polkas and international dances. Their favorite tap number was to the American song, "Nickelodeon."

When they arrived at the officers' club, they gave the band their music. The bandleader could not understand them, nor could they understand him. The band seemed like they just wanted to hassle them because they were German. They claimed that they had consumed so much beer that they couldn't play their music. So Mini played the piano, and Maria danced. Some of their numbers required two people to act them out. Naturally then, when Maria did those by herself, they looked foolish. Between their "half act," the American's total drunkenness, and occasional catcalls of Nazis, Mini and Maria flopped that night.

Before they left, some of the more friendly Americans offered them beer and chili. They had never had chili, so they tried it. To them, it was not edible, but it was the hottest stuff they had ever eaten. By the time they decided to leave, the curfew had started, so they stayed the night in a hotel.

"These Americans are crazy," Mini said. "That was a disaster tonight. They ruined our program on purpose."

"I know. I think it is still too close to the fighting, and there is too much anger to go into groups of foreigners. Let's insist on German bookings from now on, Mini," Maria said.

"That is just fine with me," Mini added.

The German agency next booked them into a huge hall that held hundreds of people. He indicated that there would be an orchestra there, so they could use their music. All they knew about the engagement was that it was a large affair, and they knew they would be sharing the stage with some famous German singers and comedians.

By the time they arrived, the hall was filling up with people. The orchestra was warming up, and there seemed to be excitement in the air. Maria gave the music to the conductor, and she and Mini went backstage to change into their costumes. However, when they walked around behind the curtain, they saw the backdrop.

Maria's heart stopped, and panic struck her completely. There on the backdrop was the largest hammer and sickle on a bright red background she had ever seen. It hung from the ceiling to the floor and spanned the stage from side to side.

"Mini! Mini! Look at this," Maria whispered as she gestured for Mini to come over by her. "Look!" She pointed at the backdrop.

"Oh my God! It's a communist rally!" Mini blurted out.

"I'm not dancing for any communists," Maria added.

Mini said, "Me neither."

Maria asked, "How can they get away with something like this so soon after the war?"

"Let's get out of here now," Mini choked.

"We really can't leave because we signed a contract. This has to be legitimate. The occupation would not allow something this big without permission. Besides, they are allies right now."

They dutifully did their part of the show and quickly slipped out the back door hoping not to be seen. Maria never liked the communists before the war, and this was extremely alarming to her.

"I hope the Americans are smart enough to get the communists out of Germany. They're worse than the Nazis," Maria was still whispering to Mini several blocks away from the rally. "I've had enough of this. I'm going to start my own show with my own dancers, orchestra, and singers. and." Maria paused, "I will be in charge of my own bookings. This is ridiculous."

Maria returned to the courthouse and inquired about getting a permit to start her own entertainment troupe. After some investigating, the German authorities indicated that she was one of the few people who could do something like this because of her title ballet meister and choreographer, so they issued her a permit. She then had to work through the American bureaucracy to become completely legal. The only major restraint specified in her government contract was that she could not hire any Nazis or former Nazis. That was no problem because most entertainers were never in the Nazi party anyway.

Once the paperwork was done, Maria began work on her project. Luckily, she did not need any financial backing. She and Mini had enough money between them to get started. Her first order of business was to hire a small, five-piece band. She did not have to audition the band members. She knew most of them from the theater, so she had confidence in their abilities. She then hired the singer, who was a talented soprano. Next she looked for a comedian who it turned out was an older man who was blind, but he was one of the funniest acts in Frankfurt. She pulled the troupe together in about three weeks. All of them were happy at the prospect of working again and earning some badly needed money. Karl had a friend with contacts in the printing business, so he took care of printing tickets and programs.

The capital to start up this troupe was minimal because they were all glad to work. They rehearsed for free, which they used as an opportunity to practice. In fact, it served as practice for all of them and kept them in shape. The blind comedian was the most costly, but he was a big draw for the show.

The bookings started to come in since the German people needed and wanted the entertainment. The town halls and city halls around Frankfurt had nice facilities with stages. The troupe always sold out their two-hour show. They always had steady bookings because their reputation grew along with their success, and they started to bring in some good money. After a performance, Maria would pay each performer a percentage of the profits, which kept everyone in the troupe happy. Best of all, they controlled where they went, what they performed, and they were not called names.

Chapter 21

Diagonally across the street from Maria and Anna's building was an apartment building a little smaller than theirs, and it was also in much better condition than theirs. Margot lived there. She was about forty, a middle-aged dressmaker by profession. She was a plain woman with dark brown hair that fell over her shoulders. What distinguished her from most other people at the time was the crisp cut of her well-tailored clothes.

Everyone in the neighborhood knew each other somewhat. The wine spree made them all a bit closer, so they had become a rather tight-knit group of people who looked out for each other. The local people had very little work for Margot to do because most of them didn't have anything left to sew. Maria, Mini, and their mothers were about the only Frankfurters that gave her work, occasionally having her make or modify a costume. However, Margot always had plenty of work from the American soldiers. They constantly needed their pants shortened, jackets repaired, and buttons sewed. She had a good reputation as a seamstress among them, so she managed better than most Germans with her ability to earn good money.

One day, a civilian worker for the army brought her a jacket to repair and pants to shorten. His name was John and he was shorter than she was. This struck Maria because in her mind, all Americans were tall and handsome. Margot told him that his clothes would be ready in two days and that he could pick them up then. However, he asked her to deliver them to an apartment building in Hoechst. She didn't want to do it, but the offer of five America dollars was too great of an incentive. Besides, it was double what she would normally charge. It was a lot of money that she could not pass up.

Margot came dashing over to Maria's apartment to share the news of her windfall and her fear of going alone to an apartment inhabited by Americans outside of Frankfurt.

"Please come with me, Maria," she pleaded.

"I don't want to go to anybody's apartment," she said.

"Listen, we'll just drop the pants off very quickly and leave immediately. Besides, I'll make five dollars, American. Please. Please go with me."

Maria trusted her and wanted to help Margot; besides Margot genuinely did not want to go there alone, so Maria agreed to accompany her. It might be interesting, she thought to herself.

Two days later, Margot came to get Maria, and they left for Hoechst in the late afternoon. For some reason, John hadn't been able to explain to Margot exactly how to get to the apartment, so because of their lack of communication, she had agreed to meet him at the bus stop. They arrived at the bus stop at about six p.m., almost dusk. Margot had counted on the fact that he would pay her there so that she and Maria would get back on the bus and return before the curfew started. However, he said that he had forgotten his money and he would have to go back to the apartment to get it.

Both Margot and Maria assumed he was telling the truth. Besides, she needed the money, so they followed him back to the apartment. They felt a little uncomfortable, but they were confident that they would be safe. Also, the

Americans did not have a reputation like the French when it came to women. They just lacked tact and finesse.

They followed him through the billeted compound to a courtyard, and down a dimly lit, ornately decorated hall.

John went in first while Margot and Maria waited in the hall. "Come in. Come in. It's OK," he said as he waved them in with his arm. They timidly entered the room just inside the door, huddled close together.

The apartment was lavish. It was a billet headquarters for American officers located on the first floor of a four-story building with a beautiful cobblestone courtyard in the center. The rooms were large and decorated with expensive furniture. These had obviously been the homes of upper class Germans who could afford the finer things that life had to offer. Maria felt a little uneasy, but she was confident that if necessary, a loud scream would bring a rescue because it seemed like such a fine place. Somehow, the elegance of the place put her and Margot at ease.

John smiled, all the while chattering on in English. He convinced them to have a seat as he gestured for them to sit. "Have a seat, ladies." He smiled.

"Margot, let's go," Maria said to her in German.

"Would you ladies like a drink or something? Ein cognac, perhaps?" he asked in a feeble attempt to speak German as he held a glass and a bottle toward them with a lit cigarette between his fingers.

"What do you think, Maria?" Margot asked.

"He seems nice enough. I think he's just lonely and wants to be friendly. We could have one small sip," Maria told her.

"We have to watch the time though because we have to be home and off the street by the curfew."

John was pleasant. He offered then each a cigarette and lit if for them. They chatted and communicated through gestures about the apartment and speculated on who might have lived there, what they did, and so forth. It was light chitchat, and pleasant since this guy was so friendly and good looking.

Suddenly, the doorbell rang. John walked over and opened it. "Hey, Sonny. Come on in. I have someone I would like you to meet." He shook the officer's hand, put his arm around his shoulders, and guided him to where Maria and Margot were sitting.

Maria almost stopped breathing. At her very first glance, she thought Sonny was Peter, the doctor from the Black Forest, standing there. She blinked her eyes and shook her head, thinking that she could shake reality into it. John introduced them. Sonny bore such a striking resemblance to Peter that it was uncanny. He had the same sandy-colored hair and a mustache a shade darker than his hair; he was built the same, and he was the same height.

Another short American. The thought passed through Maria's mind. They may be short, but they are handsome.

He could have been Peter's brother if it were not for the fact that he was American. She was in love at first sight because of this resemblance. He noticed her rapt attention, and his face broke into a charming smile. It seemed that he could not take his eyes away from her.

He and John had met at the officers' club in Hoechst a few days before. John had told Sonny in the club that a German girl was coming to his place tonight, and that she might have a girlfriend with her. He had set it up so they could have some female companionship, and he invited Sonny there.

Maria couldn't take her eyes off of Sonny, and he was equally interested in her. They just stood there and looked at each other, and continued to look at each other. Maria finally had to look away, afraid that he would think the wrong thing about her. She had to maintain her dignity, but she had to look back just as quickly. Sonny looked away and just as quickly looked back at her.

John went over to the gramophone in one corner of the room and put on a record with a scratchy rendition of *Liebestraum.*

"Maria, do you think this is safe?" Margot asked her.

"I think we are perfectly safe," she answered as she stared at Sonny, lulled into a sense of security at her memory of Peter. "Besides, he is so handsome." They spoke in German. Sonny and John could not understand them.

"You get the dark-haired one. Wow, what a body. She looks like a model with that hat. I'll take the other one. Besides she seems to have a thing for you already. See how she keeps looking at you? You lucky dog," John said smiling, holding his glass up as if to make a toast to at Margo and Maria. They had no idea what he was saying in English.

"See, they are such gentlemen," Maria said.

They all had a good time trying to communicate since they all knew some very basic words in each other's language and peppered their conversation with grand arm gestures as if those would translate the words.

It softened the mood. As Margot and Maria's concerns melted away, John and Sonny convinced them to have another drink, and they all chattered on. Suddenly the two of them realized that it was a little past seven.

Maria looked at her watch, jumped up, and said, "We have to go. We have to get home because of the curfew."

"Oh my gosh, you are right," Margot added. They had been so involved with the conversation that they forgot all about the time. "I need to powder my nose before we go, though." She stood up to go to the bathroom.

John stood up to show Margot where it was. Sonny and Maria continued talking, enjoying their physical attraction to each other.

Their mood was instantly broken by a terrible scream from the bathroom. Sonny and Maria jumped up to see what had happened.

John had followed Margot into the bathroom and had locked the door behind him. She was screaming that he was trying to rape her. Maria tried to pull the door open, but it was locked.

"Help, Maria. He is trying to rape me," Margot screamed.

Sonny followed behind her and tried to force the door open. It wouldn't budge.

"Hey John, open the door! What the hell is going on in there? Open the god-damn door," Sonny yelled.

John yelled back, "Go away. Leave us alone. We'll be outa here in a minute."

Margot screamed again, and Sonny and Maria could hear glass crashing to the floor as they struggled.

"Hilfe!! Maria!! Hilfe!!" Margot screamed.

"Do something," Maria screamed at Sonny.

"Open the door, you son-of-a-bitch, or I'll kill you," Sonny boomed kicking the door violently. He then threw his body at the door, but it would not give.

A moment later, the door opened, and Margot rushed out, and John attacked Sonny, taking a wild swing at him with his right fist. They fell to the floor in a tangle.

Maria grabbed Margot's hand, ran over to the table, grabbed their purses, and headed for the door. The two men burst through the bedroom door behind them, falling over the sofa to the floor, where Sonny had John in a headlock.

"Let's get out of here," Margot sobbed hysterically, pushing the hair out of her face.

"You're right. And fast," Maria added.

An officer came in just then and glared at them hatefully. As they pushed past him, he growled at them, "German Swine!"

As they ran into the hallway, doors began to open up and down the corridor with curious American officers popping out in various degrees of dress. Some were only in their underwear. Unfortunately, the two of them were at the end of the hall away from the entrance door that led to the courtyard. They were too terrified to run past all of the men, so they ran up the stairs close by. They felt it was the only safe exit for them. Luckily, no one followed them, so they stopped at the exit to the roof and paused there, out of breath.

Margot was in a panic. Maria was trying to figure out a safe plan of escape. She determined that the only way out was the way they had come. After a little while, the commotion calmed down somewhat, so they decided to sneak back down the stairs and get to the first floor. The hall was empty, the doors were closed, and there was still a commotion in John's room. They could hear it build as they passed the door. Voices were rising again. They tried to sneak along the hall to the entrance, but hall doors started to open again, and the door to John's apartment opened too.

Maria and Margot ran through the hall for the main door as fast as they could, where it entered the cobblestone courtyard. It was only a few yards to the main exit, so they headed for it at a full gallop.

Suddenly, Maria felt a hand grab the hair on the back of her head as it knocked off her beautiful, expensive hat. She became so enraged at the thought of her hat being harmed that she didn't think about her own safety right away. Hats were always her special trademark in the theater. She screamed and struggled to get loose as she turned, and saw that is was John.

He yanked her backwards, throwing her down to the cobblestone on her butt. He yanked at her blouse. He dragged her across the ground by her collar to rape her in a secluded corner of the courtyard. Margot was hysterical, and of absolutely no help trembling, crying, and screaming.

Maria was kicking and fighting, twisting and turning, but she couldn't do anything because of how John controlled her by the back of the neck. She was screaming desperately for help. She couldn't understand why the American soldiers watched him drag her to the corner of the courtyard. Some had guns drawn. One even had a revolver in both hands, but no one helped.

Then John abruptly stopped dragging her, swung her around, threw himself on top of her, and tore open her blouse. One hand was tearing at her hair, and the other was tearing at her chest at the same time pulling up her skirt. It was hopeless. She felt the added terror of a possible gang rape by the on looking soldiers. All of a sudden, Sonny pushed his way through the crowd knocking some soldiers to the ground. He grabbed John by the collar, yanked him off Maria, and punched him to the ground. Maria broke loose and staggered to her feet. She lunged toward Margot, grabbed her arm, and ran pulling her along. None of the onlookers stopped them as the two of them pushed past them and made their way to the street.

Now she and Margot had two problems. The curfew was in effect. Nothing was running, including streetcars, and they could be shot for being on the street.

Maria quieted Margot down a little. Her legs were bleeding, and her stockings were torn from being dragged over the cobblestones. Her hat was crushed which still made her mad. Her blouse was torn, but that didn't make her as mad as she was about her expensive hat. Yet she was remarkably calm for some reason, perhaps because she was trying to come up with a plan to save their lives.

If they were caught on the street, they would be shot on sight; if they went back to the apartment... well, they couldn't do that. They would rather be shot on the street because they were now afraid of the Americans. They ran along the street, knocking on doors up and down the block to seek refuge from the Americans and the curfew patrols, but people were afraid to open their doors after curfew for fear that they would be shot. Margot could not calm down as she babbled on between hysterical sobs about dying.

"We are going to die. I just know we are going to die," Margot sobbed.

"No. Now think. We have to get off the street. Look for a place to hide," Maria encouraged her to distract her and calm her down.

Just then, they saw a door ajar. When they made their way to it, they could see that it led into a long, dark hallway. Maria pushed it open a little, but she could see nothing. It was too dark to distinguish anything.

She said to Margot, "We have got to go in. We have got to get off the street."

Margot just sobbed and nodded her head wiping, her eyes with her handkerchief. The two of them cautiously pushed the door open and slid around it into the hall, closing it behind them so that only the smallest crack was left.

The hall seemed to be empty with a few doors on either side. It also seemed like it was endlessly long. They tried very quietly to open each door, testing the knobs lightly to see if they would open because they did not want to disturb the silence. All of the doors were locked except one. They cautiously nudged it open and found steps leading down into a dark, black cellar. Neither of them would go there.

Finally, their eyes adjusted to the dark a little. There was enough light that came through the crack in the front door that they could make out the features of the corridor. It was a plain, dark hall about forty feet long with doors on either side of it. They huddled together, leaned against the back wall, slid against it to the floor and sat in the darkness.

Margot was completely hysterical, sobbing uncontrollably, and she could barely breathe. Maria finally calmed her a little by diverting her attention to her bloody legs.

"My legs are a bloody mess. Here, help me dab them with this handkerchief."

Margot calmed down with something to occupy her mind. They sat for some time in the darkness and complete silence.

Suddenly, they both became abruptly stiff. They heard a creak and saw the shaft of light at the door grow a fraction. They had no idea how long they had been there.

"Oh no. No. No. No." Margot whimpered, gulped, and inhaled at the same time as if she were taking her last breath. She tightened up into a ball and buried her head in Maria's arms.

The door creaked again, but steadily this time as it opened wide. They could see the black silhouette of a man standing there with his pistol drawn.

"It's him. It's that John. He is going to kill us," Margot sobbed. She was a tight, trembling ball.

Maria whispered, "Keep yourself together. Stop this. There are two of us and only one of him. Maybe we can get out of this. "

Maria surprised herself at her calmness and clear thinking. Her experiences with the French in the Black Forest were a training ground for survival in a situation like this.

"Sh!" Quiet," she said. "Maybe he won't see us and leave if we are quiet." So they sat there in silent terror.

The shadowy figure called out in a soft whisper, "Girls, girls, are you in here?"

Maria whispered to Margot, "It's him, not the bad one. She then asked with a shaky voice, "Sonny?"

"Yes. Are you all right?" he asked as he moved toward them in the dark. The two of them stumbled to their feet and moved hesitantly toward Sonny and the light behind the door. He put his pistol in its holster and then put his arms around both of them, speaking in a soothing tone to comfort them.

He held Maria in one arm and petted Margot's head with the other, saying, said "Don't worry. Everything will be OK."

After a while, he said, "I've got to get you girls out of here. I'll have to take you with me. You can't go anywhere on your own."

Meanwhile, they could see the jeeps and trucks of the curfew patrol outside through the crack in the door.

Sonny stepped out onto the street and motioned for the two of them to follow.

"No we will get arrested or shot." Maria said.

He could not understand her, but he knew what she meant. "Don't worry. You are with me. I am an officer. I will not be stopped. "

Just then, a truck covered with canvas came toward them. Sonny stepped onto the street in front of it and flagged it down. It screeched to a halt. The soldiers saluted, and he asked for a ride. They could not refuse him because he was a lieutenant, an officer.

When the driver and his companion saw him, they became very nervous. But when they saw Margot and Maria, they became a little relieved. The three of them started to get in the front, but the driver motioned for them to ride in the back, claiming that there was not enough room in the cab.

When Sonny opened the canvas flap, he saw that the truck was full of GIs and German girls, drinking and kissing. Margot, of course, went off and started to cry again. She wasn't so sure that they had really been rescued. The group suddenly became very somber when they saw an officer standing there. The men were trying to scramble to their feet, straighten their clothes, and salute at the same time.

Apparently, this was how this group of GIs and girls entertained themselves - a party in the back of the truck while it was allegedly enforcing the curfew.

Sonny said, "At ease men. Carry on as you were."

Their mood immediately shifted back when they saw that this officer had two girls with him.

"Wow, Sir. You officers really score well. "Two for one," one of the enlisted men chided as he wrapped his arm around a beautiful blonde girl with her hair up in typical Tyrolean braids. The rest chimed in a chorus, applauding and making catcalls to cheer Sonny on.

"Just carry on men. I will take care of my own business." Sonny diverted their attention away from himself.

He ordered the driver to drop them off at his billet. After a short ride that seemed endless to the Maria and Margot, the truck brakes squealed, and the three of them jumped out the back from under the cover of the canvas. They saw that Sonny's billet was a fenced-in mansion on the outskirts of Frankfurt.

Maria and Margot knew that they would have to spend the night with Sonny there. They were so exhausted by the time they entered his apartment that they could only look at each other, and laugh a bit. Maria was torn up and bloody. Sonny was also bloody, and his trim-fitting uniform was torn in several places.

Maria held up her hat in front of herself and said, "My hat. My beautiful hat is unrecognizable."

Margot was the only one who did not look bad, but her eyes were beady blue spots in puffy red sockets. Maria tried to calm her down more and teased that she would have a job forever, and get rich at it, with the Americans tearing each other's clothes up. They laughed nervously.

Sonny shared the apartment in the mansion with three other men who did not wake up when they came in. There was no place for the two of them to sleep but in his room.

"Come in here. You will be safe here," Sonny motioned them to his room.

"Oh no." Margot hesitated.

"Margot, be quiet. That is all we can do." Maria said.

They all took turns in the bathroom and cleaned up the best they could under the conditions.

Sonny directed the two of them to the bed and told them to sleep there. They climbed on the bed with their clothes on and lay down. He went over to the other side of the room, plunked into a large, overstuffed chair, and quickly drifted to sleep.

Maria and Margo slept fitfully and arose at dawn. Sonny was up with them immediately. He tried to offer them some coffee, but they just wanted to get out of there and return home as soon as possible. They freshened up a little and left with the first tram back to Frankfurt. Sonny was very understanding and asked for Maria's address. She hesitated but she trusted him. After all, he had rescued her, she thought to herself; so she wrote it down for him, expecting that she would never hear from him again. He was very reassuring and kind. However, as appreciative as she was, Maria just wanted to be away from there.

Anna was worried to tears. There had been no way for Maria to call her, to let her know that they were even alive.

"I'm so glad you are all right, sweetie," Anna said.

"Me too. You know, mama, I never seem to be able to settle down. I feel like I'm always being chased."

Another tearful reunion was added to the constant turmoil of Maria's life in those times.

Chapter 22

A few days later, an Opal drove up to the apartment. It was painted in with camouflage. An American officer was sitting in the back with a chauffeur in the front. The soldier driving the car jumped out and opened the door for the officer. Maria could see that it was Sonny. The memories of that terrible night flooded back into her consciousness, and she wondered if she should greet him or pretend that she wasn't home. Her mother was out. She was alone. He had been a perfect gentleman, though so she wasn't sure what should she do. Suddenly, the silence in the apartment was broken by a harsh knock at the door that resounded around the room. Maria slowly opened the door a crack. Sonny had a package in his hand, and when she opened the door, he held it out to her. With that, Maria opened the door completely and invited him in.

"Go ahead. Open it. It's OK," he said, motioning for Maria to open the package.

She knew that he wanted her to open it, but she coyly hesitated and said, "I really cannot take a gift from you," she shook her head.

"Oh, go ahead. Open it. I just want to be friends." Sonny motioned for her to open the package.

Maria unwrapped it and could scarcely believe her eyes. He had brought her two oranges. This was a treasure since it was impossible to find much food let alone fruit anywhere in the city.

Maria held them up to her cheeks and waltzed around the room. "Oh, this is so sweet. We haven't had oranges in years, since the war started. Wait until my mother sees these."

Sonny had no idea what she was saying, but he seemed to know that he had done the right thing.

"Would you like to go for a ride?" he asked.

Maria sat the oranges on the table, shrugged her shoulders and said, "ich do not spreche English. No verstehe."

"Go for a ride." He motioned like he held a steering wheel in his hands. "Du und me." He pointed at Maria and then to himself.

"Ach. Auto fahren. Mit you."

"Ja, yes auto furren."

They mutilated English and German as they tried to communicate.

Maria hesitated and looked around the room as if searching for a reason in the air not to go, but then she remembered how he had helped Margot and her. She thought that she could trust him, so she agreed to accompany him. Besides, his resemblance to Peter, the doctor kept intruding on her. They drove around Frankfurt to look at the city. Maria was shocked at the totality of the damage, the skeletons of buildings and the piles of rubble.

On the other hand, it was fun for Maria because Sonny knew a few words of German he had learned from his grandmother, and she knew a few words of English. They had a wonderful time trying to communicate through pantomime, gesture, and some weird form of German/English.

After a couple of hours, Sonny asked, "How would you like to see an American officers' club?"

"Ein Offizer Klub? Amerikanish?" she repeated.

I can't go to an officers' club, Maria thought to herself. What if they are like the ones from a few nights before.

"No. Ist not good," she said.

"Believe me, you will be safe with me. I will protect you. It is OK."

"OK?" She was having such a good time, and she really felt safe with Sonny.

The officers' club was in Hoechst on the outskirts of Frankfurt. It was lavish, elegantly furnished. It had obviously been some type of club before the Americans took it over because it had a kitchen and a bar.

"No schpeeken mit anyone," Sonny told Maria in pigeon German, holding his finger up to his mouth.

No Germans were permitted to be in there. However, there were a few German women who waited tables and served sandwiches. Maria didn't say anything, but if she spoke a little German to some of the workers, she was able to get away with it. The people thought that she could speak both languages. It was a very classy place, and the officers and the women had an air of sophistication. Maria did not feel uncomfortable because she thought that half the women there were just like her. A few of Sonny's buddies came over to the table.

"I see we have a lady friend, and a beauty at that. You dog you," a friend of his chided him.

"What is your name? Where are you from? How did you hook up with a derelict like this?" another buddy jokingly asked Maria as he raised his drink to his lips with a cigarette between his fingers.

"Aw, go on. Get out of here. We're just getting to know each other." Sonny waved his friend off.

"OK, but you let me know if he gets out of hand. And if you get tired of him, my name is Hawkins," he said to Maria.

With that, Hawkins and the other officer turned to walk away while he shook his hand in front of his chest, rolled his eyes, blew out a sigh, and whispered to his companion, "Hot tamale."

Maria just smiled and acted like she knew what they were saying.

Sonny put his hand on hers and said in a low voice, "Das vas good." After that they had a couple of drinks and danced a few dances. Then Sonny took her home.

"Can I see you tomorrow?" he asked Maria.

"What are you saying?" Maria shrugged her shoulders.

"Can I see you tomorrow?" Sonny repeated louder as if volume would help Maria understand.

Maria shrugged her shoulders.

"Let's see, tomorrow, tomorrow. What the hell is the German word for tomorrow?" he asked himself out loud. Then it came to him, "Morgen. Du and me. Morgen?" he said, pointing back and forth from Maria to himself.

"Ach. Yes," Maria responded in perfect drawn-out English. "Yes."

"Is six o'clock OK?" he asked holding up six fingers.

"Yes," Maria said again in perfect English. "Six o'clock."

The next day, he arrived at exactly six to pick her up. He had another package. Maria allowed him to come in as soon as he knocked at the door. Maria's mother was there this time, so she introduced the two of them.

"You were right. He is handsome," Anna said as she held out her hand to shake his. "How do you do?" She spoke each word slowly and deliberately.

Sonny, thinking very quickly, handed the package to her instead of Maria. "Here is a gift for a beautiful woman."

Anna opened it, and there before her unbelieving eyes were two oranges. "Oh my God. Two more oranges. He is handsome and thoughtful."

"Look what I brought for us," he said to Maria as he reached in his pocked and pulled out a German to English dictionary.

"*Ein Wörterbuch.*" she told Anna. "Dis ist good," Maria told Sonny.

The dictionary made it much easier for them to communicate after that. They returned to the same officers' club that night and danced most of the evening. During later dates, they went back to that officers' club often. Sonny's friends quickly figured out that Maria was German. It did not seem to bother anyone. Many of the officers danced with her and enjoyed trying to carry on a conversation. The two of them became friends with the officers and the American women. The Americans were all so friendly Maria thought..

One evening, Sonny took Maria to his apartment in the mansion. He had a table covered with a black velvet tablecloth and set with a candle in a silver holder, two glasses, and a bottle of champagne. The chamber was elegant.

They entered the room, and Sonny took her coat, hung it up, and went over to the record player. He had chosen Liszt's *Liebestraum* to play softly in the background. It was one of the most romantic settings Maria had ever seen.

Gazing at her through the candlelight, Sonny took her hand in his and said, "I have a gift for you." He took a very beautiful, very expensive Swiss watch out of his pocket and put it gently on her wrist. Then he walked around the table and caressed her. She fell into his arms, trusting him completely, and they kissed.

He then took her hand and asked, "Would you like to dance?"

They danced to *Liebestraum* in the candlelight. Then they sat at the table, sipped Champagne, and ate the delicious meal Sonny had prepared. She would hold the watch up in the candlelight so that it would glisten in the dancing light. Sonny would take her hand and say, "I love you." Maria was in love too. The hardship of the war seemed years away as she fell into his strong arms and felt safe and in love.

Sonny invariably had a present for Maria every time he saw her. Whenever he gave her a gift, he did something romantic. Sometimes it would be the gift itself. Once he gave her a Spanish doll dressed like a Flamenco dancer. Maria loved that, but the cutest gift of all was what he called the "rascal." It was a donkey being ridden by a Mexican in a big sombrero.

As time went on, their romance bloomed into a love affair, and they became more comfortable with each other. They both loved to take long car rides in the country. It was an escape for both of them.

When they would wander out deep into the countryside, Sonny taught Maria how to drive and then let her do most of the driving so she could get the practice. It was great fun. Maria loved driving, and Sonny enjoyed sitting in the back with his feet propped up, sipping wine from a bottle.

One day Sonny wanted to see the Rhine. It was not too far from where they were. They were not supposed to be out this far in the country, but they had grown bolder with each outing, taking them further from Frankfurt. One day, while Sonny was driving, they came to a bridge that went across the Rhine.

Sonny said, "Let's give it a try."

The American zone was on their side; the French zone was on the other.

Maria replied, "No, I don't want to go. I'm afraid of the French." They were becoming so good at communicating after seeing each other for a couple of months that they did not have to use gestures much any more. Although Sonny did not fully understand what Maria was saying, he did understand her trepidation.

Since Maria was dressed in a tan tailor-made suit, and could pass as an American woman, she agreed with him after much protesting. He was supposed to have a pass to cross into the French zone, but he didn't. The fact that he was out with a German could get him thrown in jail. The fact that she did not have a pass could have them both thrown in jail, but nobody checked for anything beyond Sonny's papers.

"Let me see your papers," the French guard barked at Sonny. He looked at the papers, at Sonny, and then at Maria.

"This is my secretary," Sonny said.

The French guard saluted Sonny and waved them through.

After they drove a few kilometers into the country away from the bridge, he said, "How about you drive?" Maria enjoyed driving because it was like an amusement park ride for her to be able to control a vehicle. She had ridden trains and trams all her life so this was great fun. Sonny placed himself in the back seat, propped his feet up, popped open a bottle of Champagne, and drank it from the bottle.

Suddenly, they came upon a roadblock. It was a checkpoint. The French soldier came up to the window and asked, "Pass Freulein?" He mumbled some jumbled German words, but Maria just ignored him. She said absolutely nothing. She couldn't even breathe. She so loathed and feared the French.

Sonny had straightened up in the back seat, took his papers out of his pocket, and said, "Here," as he handed them to Maria in the front seat. She took them and handed them to the French soldier. Maria figured that the soldier thought that she was American because she didn't react at all. She didn't flinch an eyelid. Their lives depended on it. The soldier handed the papers back to her and waved them on. It was frightening yet exhilarating at the same time.

They continued on because they thought that there were no more roadblocks. So they drove along the Rhine toward Bonn and stopped at every castle they could find along the way.

Later in the day, they saw a castle nestled at the top of a small mountain. Sonny wanted Maria to drive over to it. The road that led to it was difficult to locate, but after some driving around, she found the road. It was a narrow winding road with steep cliffs. Maria loved driving, but she refused to drive on this road so Sonny drove. She was nervous just being a passenger because the road was barely wide enough for one car, and there was a precipitous drop on her side. She didn't even look out the window.

When they neared the castle, a large iron gate blocked their way. They rang the bell on the gate. There was no response for a long time. They rang it two more times. Then slowly, the massive doors began to open, and a dark-haired man with a sneer on his face sauntered out to the gate.

"What do you want?" he growled in German.

Since he spoke German, Maria answered in German. "We are sightseeing, and we were wondering if you would be so kind as to let us see the inside of the castle."

He said, "Wait here," as he went back into the castle.

While he was gone, they speculated. The place looked completely abandoned, so there seemed to be no reason why this peculiar man was acting so privately. He returned in a few minutes and said, "OK, go in."

They left the car parked by the gate and followed him to the huge front doors. When they entered, there was a tall man wearing a German army uniform standing on the stairs a couple of steps up.

"How do you do?" he greeted them in impeccable, aristocratic German. He looked Maria up and down, and then he glared at Sonny in his American officers' uniform. His eyes narrowed, and he shot a hateful look at each of them. It was one of those cases where the phrase "If looks could kill" really meant what it says. It was probably made worse by the fact that Sonny was American and that she was German. They were like a mixed race couple to a man like this. Maria began to fear that they might never get of that place alive.

Both Maria and Sonny felt completely uneasy. Sonny started small talk about the armor and the swords on the wall. They didn't ask to see much. Maria told him that they only wanted to see the inside of the old castles along the Rhine - that they were sightseeing. He led them into a couple of rooms that were interesting because they looked like museum rooms.

Then he asked menacingly, "Would you like to see the weapons room upstairs?"

Sonny and Maria exchanged glances. They both understood, and neither of them wanted to go up there. However, since they had asked to see the place, they could hardly refuse. The stairs at the back of the hall were too narrow for them to walk side by side, so they climbed the stairs single file. The German officer led the way. Maria was in the middle. Sonny was in the back. They both had the feeling that something might happen. They followed the eerie man up the steps slowly. Maria could see out of the corner of her eye that Sonny had his hand near his pistol, but he did it in such a way that it was not obvious or threatening to their "host."

Maria babbled in German. She would ask questions about different weapons. When he would answer, his eyes narrowed, and the familiar hateful glare shot back at them. Maria began to speculate that this remote castle was a hideout for Nazis. If this was true, it could mean that they might never get out of there alive. There were no outward signs that it was a hideout, but it seemed obvious by the behavior of the inhabitants.

This damned French zone. I hate it here. Nothing good ever happens here, she thought to herself.

The dark man escorted them back down the stairs out to the camouflaged Opal parked by the gate. As soon as they rounded a curve out of sight of the castle, Sonny gunned the car, and they flew down the winding mountain road.

"Now I understand why these roads were built like this." Sonny said, gripping the steering wheel. Maria just held on to the sides of the seat for her life.

Once on the main highway, they started back to Frankfurt since the day was fading into late afternoon. They continued to look over their shoulders for a considerable distance. Later, they stopped at a winery owned by a jolly elderly couple. The little old man was like a cherub with ruddy cheeks. He was so proud of his wines that he encouraged the two of them to taste each vintage. They, of course, did not turn him down. Sonny was the first American they had ever encountered, and they were full of questions about America, Hollywood, and hamburgers. His chubby peasant wife asked Sonny all of the questions her husband forgot. They all sat on the huge barrels and tasted and tasted. His wife brought them all a snack of dark bread and cheese; it was a great time.

They took the same route to return to Frankfurt, but to their amazement, they never encountered the French roadblock on the way back. It must have been moved. However, when they neared the bridge to cross back into the American zone, Maria told Sonny, "Stop the car." She got out and walked to the back.

"What are you doing?" he asked.

"I'm hiding in the trunk. I don't want to get stuck in the French zone," she insisted.

She curled up in the trunk, and Sonny closed the lid. She felt the car lurch forward, and shortly later come to a halt. She could hear muffled voices as the soldiers asked for Sonny's papers. She could hear a few more words, and the car started to move forward again. They never checked out the car or the trunk. She was ever so glad to get out of the French Zone, again.

How could I have been so dumb to go there? She thought to herself. Something keeps pulling me back there. I will never get close to it again. I promise me. It was a place she dreaded the most, and a place where she was almost shot and raped.

Three weeks after their first drive across the Rhine, Sonny said he had a friend that he had to take to the airport in Mainz.

"Do you want to go with me Maria?" he asked.

"No! Absolutely not!" she answered.

"It's OK. I have all the proper papers."

"You have all the papers? Well, I have the time. I guess I'll go." Maria reluctantly agreed.

This time, Sonny was better prepared. He had procured a pass for Maria so that she wouldn't have to go into the French zone in the trunk of the car. They dropped Sonny's friend off and returned to Frankfurt. However, the flight was canceled. Much to Maria's chagrin, they had to go and pick him up and then take him back again. Each trip required her to be confronted by her favorite paper checkers, the French.

This is crazy. I keep going to the area that I still fear the most. If I didn't love Sonny so much, I would never go on these excursions, she thought to herself.

In April and May, whenever Sonny could get leave and Maria didn't have a show booked, they would take off and drive to the country. They had a favorite place that they called their own. It was the ruins of the castle Konegstein on the outskirts of Frankfurt. They would always go up there and put a blanket down at the top of the highest-standing turret. It was out of the wind because the wall that went around the top of it shielded them from the cool, spring, evening breezes. It was a wonderful place to have a picnic, drink a bottle of wine, and cuddle and make love. The air on those starlit evenings was like liquid crystal that magnified the beauty of the stars of the night sky.

They would sit up there for hours drinking champagne, snacking, and talking. Later in the evenings, they would make love inside the turret on a landing about halfway down the tower.

Sonny had a portable radio he would bring along to play music. One night, Maria became tipsy. A lively polka drifted from the radio. She suddenly became animated and jumped up to dance. She climbed up on top of the turret wall and did the polka around the top of the tower, twirling and singing.

Sonny, trying not to show his alarm, tried to coax her to come down, but when he would get close, she would dance away from him. He was sure that she was going to spin right off the wall. Finally, she twirled and fell into his arms, laughing. He did not say any more that night, but the next day, they rode back out to the castle in the daylight. Sonny took Maria by the hand and walked her around the bottom of the castle to show her how high the turret was and how reckless she had been. She almost fainted. She never danced on the wall again. In fact, she stayed back from the wall whenever they climbed up the tower. She felt safe for the first time in the years since the war had started. She loved Sonny, and he loved her.

One warm evening in May, they took their usual picnic gear to Konegstein. There was a gentle warm breeze that carried the aroma of spring flowers and fresh earth to the two of them up on the top of the tower. They stood there contemplating the mountain range in the distance as dusk drew the veil of night across the valley. Sonny had his arm around Maria, and she hugged him with her head on his shoulder.

"I love you so much." Maria said, comforted by the warmth of his body.

"I love you even more," Sonny answered.

"Guess what?" she asked.

"I don't know. What?" he answered.

"Well, I have a surprise for you. I'm pregnant." Maria was positive Sonny would be happy, but there was a lingering doubt in her mind,

"You're kidding," he said "Really?" He pushed her back with his hands and looked deeply into her eyes.

"Yes." Maria nodded and rubbed her stomach with both hands.

Sonny then grinned and burst into a smile as he pulled Maria to him and held her tightly. They stood there for a long time embracing, lost in the joy and love of the moment. They could feel each other's heartbeats.

Sonny pushed her back again, looked into her eyes, and said, "This means that I am going to be a father. Me. A father. And you, you are going to be a mother. We, you and me, are going to be a father and a mother."

Maria laughed. "I think that's how it works.

"Me, father. You, mother." Sonny mimicked an old Tarzan movie as he pointed to himself and then at Maria.

"Yes. You, father. Me, mother. This, baby." Maria pointed at Sonny, then at herself, and finally at her stomach. They embraced again and kissed.

They spent the rest of the evening planning for their new family and their future. Sonny drank to celebrate and paced around the top of the tower, overwhelmed at his good luck. Then he would sit next to Maria for a while until he had to pace again in his excitement.

"How did this happen?" Anna blurted out. "No. No. I know how it happened, but how did it happen?" The words were not flowing well for her.

"We have been seeing each other regularly. You saw that we were in love. It was bound to happen," Maria answered.

"I know, sweetie. I'm so happy for you. Sonny is such a nice man, and I am going to be an *Oma*. But." She lingered over the words, "you're not married."

"Oh, we are going to be married," Maria assured her.

"Thank God. When? We have to prepare for a wedding."

"It's not that easy. He is an American, and I am a German, and in these times, the Americans will not let the soldiers or officers marry here." Maria lied to her mother for the first time in her life.

"Then you are not getting married?" her mother asked.

"Yes, we are, but later," Maria, answered.

"Later? How much later?" Anna asked.

"After Sonny gets back to America. He will send for the baby and me, and eventually you. We will be married there." Maria tried to comfort her mother.

"But you are going to be walking around pregnant without a husband. Can't you have a civil ceremony?" she asked.

"It will be all right," Maria assured her. "Everything will work out."

Maria had never told her mother that Sonny was still married to another woman in America. That relationship had been over for more than a year. She had sent him a "Dear John" letter in which she brutally told him that she had found someone else. He was not even to come to the house when he returned. She would put his belongings on the lawn, and he could pick them up out there. Maria couldn't tell her mother that this gentleman, this father of her grandchild, was married, and that the child would be born out of wedlock.

Sonny would have to return to the United States and get a divorce before they could marry.

A week later, Sonny and Maria went to their favorite officers' club in Hoechst. Almost everyone knew Maria by then. They liked her immensely, and they were all good friends with Sonny. The small band was playing dance music, so the two of them danced and sipped drinks.

At about nine o'clock, a group of people came over to their table and announced that they were going to have a wedding that night.

Maria asked Sonny, "What are they doing?" She did not understand fully.

"I don't know. They are all crazy," he answered.

Sonny's close friend picked up a glass and a spoon and clinked it loudly. In a booming voice, he announced, "May I have your attention please." He clinked the glass again. "Your attention please. I would like to announce the wedding here tonight of Sonny Miller and..." He paused and leaned over to Maria and whispered, "What is your full name?"

"Rosa Maria Happersberger," she answered.

"...and Rosa Maria Happersberger. Boy, there's a mouthful."

There was a rumble in the crowd, and sighs came from the women.

"OK, well... not a real wedding, but it will be a good reason to celebrate." The crowd applauded and cheered him on.

"Everyone over here," the officer went on as he led the two of them to the bandstand.

"What is going on, Sonny?" Maria wondered out loud, bewildered.

He explained that it was a mock wedding for them. She loved the idea. She noticed that the place was filled with flowers. They were mostly geraniums that the guys had commandeered from the local people. They were scraggly, but they added authenticity to the setting.

Sonny's friends produced a genuine-looking marriage license and other paperwork. A genuine chaplain performed the ceremony. It was realistic down to every detail, and everyone got into the spirit of the occasion. The mock reception was just like a real reception. Sonny's friends had done a wonderful job.

Chapter 23

When Maria and her mother had left Waldrennach, they could not take all of their belongings with them. Maria told Sonny about it, and he agreed to take her there to pick up anything that might be left. He procured a pass for her, and they went back into the French zone once again.

They had no problems crossing into the French zone because her pass cleared her. The French occupation troops in Waldrennach did not give them any problems other than to check their passes. They had brought an open jeep so they could carry more of Maria's belongings.

"This is a palace compared to my apartment in Frankfurt, and beyond a few craters left by the artillery shells, nothing is bombed," Maria said.

"Maybe you should move back," Sonny added.

"Oh no. Not with the French here. Besides, I would be too far away from you." Maria ran her finger under Sonny's chin and quickly turned to pack some items. They understood each other well through a language they had invented that was half German, half English.

Remarkably, the apartment had not been looted or ransacked. The farmer who had been her landlord had protected her belongings. She and Sonny loaded the jeep with pots and pans. They picked up throw rugs, sheets, a broom and a bucket. One couldn't find a bucket or a broom anywhere in Germany.

"This place was a gold mine, and no one looted it," Maria kept repeating.

They loaded up the jeep until it looked like a Gypsy van. To Maria, it was a treasure chest, and to Sonny, it was a rescue vehicle to help his love and her mother.

It was a very cold day; the jeep didn't have sides on it, so Sonny took army blankets and wrapped them around it. They looked like some forlorn refugees. Maria was totally amazed that they exited the French zone without any incidents. That French zone was her nightmare. It simply kept pulling her back as if to taunt her. But this time was different; she and Sonny had salvaged everything she needed, and she would never have to return to the French zone again.

One night, there was a particularly violent storm in Frankfurt. Anna, out of wartime habit, jumped up, grabbed her valuable papers, and took off for the cellar. She ran down all the flights of stairs, Maria directly behind her, trying to find shelter from the bombs. It wasn't until they were at the foot of the stairwell that they stopped, looked at each other, and started to laugh hysterically. This was no bombing. It was a thunderstorm. The other people in the building apparently heard them running and then laughing.

One man opened his door to check on the commotion, and when he saw the two of them he said, "Don't you two know that the war is over?"

Anna sputtered matter-of-factly, while laughing, "Yes, but it could have started again." Everyone in the whole building got a good laugh out of it.

The next morning, when they woke up, the two of them were greeted by the sight of their cardboard-covered windows melted into a warped pile of wet paper. They patched them up as best they could. Since they had a large stockpile of cardboard, they double reinforced the windows and solved that problem.

When Sonny saw what had happened, he said, "Don't you have any windows?"

"No. You can see for yourself," Maria answered, pointing to the pile of ruined cardboard.

Sonny didn't have a tape measure, but he was very clever and cut pieces of string to the length of each side of the windows as he measured them. Then he put the cardboard back over the windows.

"I'll see what I can do," he said.

Maria figured that they would not see windows for years with all the other needs in Germany. Two days later, Sonny showed up and said he had a surprise for them. Maria and Anna followed him down to the jeep, and in the back were two windows. The two of them were totally unbelieving. In his position, Sonny was able to cut a deal with other officers to trade for the windows.

The windows were used, salvaged from a ruined building. Sonny worked a half a day to make the openings the right size, and when he slipped the windows in the openings, they fit perfectly. Maria and her mother were ecstatic. It felt like they lived in a mansion. Neither of them had ever realized how happy a window could make a human being.

"Look. It goes up and down," Maria said as she smiled and slid the window up and down.

"The best part is that it will keep out the wind and the rain." Sonny proudly tapped on the pain of glass and blew at it.

The weather was turning colder, and Sonny realized that Maria and her mother were going to need heat to make it through the winter. One day in October, he and another officer brought a jeep full of coal to their apartment. They had negotiated for it through an American camp that was set up to house the Polish until they could go home. The coal was in tall burlap sacks that weighed about a hundred pounds each. It took the two of them to carry each of the seven sacks to Maria's storage bin in the cellar. It was more than enough to make their small apartment livable. The stove was tiny, but it put off a lot of heat, and it hardly used any coal at all. They only had to heat the kitchen and the small bedroom/living room. They were much more fortunate than most other people because they had a stove, and even luckier that they could get a little fuel.

Throughout the winter of '45 to '46, Sonny became a member of the family. Whenever he could get off duty, he would drive Maria, Mini, and their mothers to the towns where they had booked their show. The reputation of Maria's troupe had spread, and they always played to full houses with standing room only. They were about the only entertainment in Germany at that time, and their production took people's minds off their problems, if only for a little while.

Sonny sat in on the shows in the beginning, but he encountered hostility because of his American uniform. So eventually, he stayed outside and kept himself busy with military paperwork.

The rest of the summer into autumn, Sonny and Maria just fell deeper in love. They loved to drive through the countryside and explore castles. However, they had another "hobby." Sonny loved to take Maria with him to different officers' clubs.

It had become a game to see how often she could pass as an American when they would meet new people. On one occasion a couple of weeks after the "wedding," they went to the club in Hoechst. Since the weather was warm, the whole club was open, including the outdoor terrace.

They sat outdoors off to the side where they would be somewhat alone and inconspicuous. Maria usually blended in fairly well. Her tailored suits looked almost like uniforms.

As usual, these excursions usually resulted in awkward situations, and this one was no exception. Sonny went to the bar to get some drinks. He no sooner left than three officers and a WAC walked over to her. They asked her if they could sit down and join her. Of course, she could not fully understand them, so she just sat there, smiled, and nodded. They sat down and made themselves comfortable. The WAC sat next to Maria and started talking. Just then, Sonny came back with the drinks. He introduced himself and Maria.

They gave each other a look like, "How are we going to get out of this?"

Everyone introduced themselves. The WAC continued talking to her, and talking, and talking. Maria just nodded and smiled, hoping that she would just clam up, but she didn't seem to mind that Maria wasn't saying anything back to her. Sonny did not know any of these people, so it was very important that they not learn Maria's secret.

Then Sonny handed the drink to Maria. She reached for it, and it "accidentally" slipped through her hand right into the lap of the WAC. Maria didn't even know how to say, "I'm sorry" in English. The WAC didn't seem to mind. She went to the restroom to clean up. When she returned to the table, Sonny apologized and offered to pay to have her uniform cleaned.

The woman seemed a bit angry. Her mood had changed in the ladies' room. She asked, "What is her nationality?"

Sonny looked at her, and his eyes widened. His mind raced. "Norwegian. She is Norwegian, working in Frankfurt," he blurted out very quickly. From then on, that was their mode of operation at all officers' clubs because no one would dare question the word of an officer out of military respect. The WAC's demeanor changed, and she still kept trying to talk to Maria. Maria knew what Sonny had said, but she continued nodding and smiling. She did not speak because she did not know one word of Norwegian and did not want to give her secret away.

Perhaps one of the most elegant and lavish officers' clubs was in Kronberg. It was an aristocratic hunting castle. The rooms were massive and opulent. When Sonny and Maria walked into the ballroom, it took their breath away. The Americans had taken the best places for themselves.

The ballroom had a high ceiling covered with crystal chandeliers. The floor was wood, polished to the point where one could see one's reflection in it. The far wall was made up of massive glass doors that had thick beveled French windows. The doors were set in walls that were made of beveled glass. It was difficult to distinguish the doors from the wall. Everything sparkled. The bevels bent the light into pleasant slivers of color that danced on the glass. These doors were open so that the ballroom extended out onto a terrace. The valley spread below the promenade like a magnificent painting in a museum. There was a fifteen-piece orchestra playing wonderful music: Viennese waltzes, classical music, and some popular songs.

It was almost dark out, so the two of them tried to find an inconspicuous table out of the way on the terrace. They had just sat down when Sonny said that he had to go to the restroom. Almost immediately, a captain came to the table taking advantage of the situation, and asked her to dance. Maria didn't know how to tell him that she didn't want to dance in English, so she danced with him.

He kept talking to her, and she kept smiling and nodding. It was her standard smile and nod for situations like this.

She did know enough English to understand him when he asked, "You're not American, are you?"

She shook her head again.

"Do you speak English?"

She shook her head no.

"Are you French?" he asked.

She nodded her head and said, "Oui." She kept looking in the direction of the restroom, but Sonny did not appear. Then the officer started speaking French to her. Luckily, he only knew a few words. At the same time, Sonny came back to the table and looked for her. She waved at him. He waved back. The officer realized they were together and took her back to the table. Sonny kept teasing her, asking her if she wanted to go back to the French zone now that she was French.

She was a nervous wreck after that, so Sonny ordered a drink called "Franco's Revenge." She was so worried in this beautiful place that she gulped it. It didn't help the situation that she liked the flavor of the drink.

A little later, the orchestra played *Hungarian Dance Number Five* by Brahms. She was quite tipsy, and did not feel any pain by then. The quality of the music stirred her theatrical blood. She strutted to the middle of the floor like a peacock and danced the whole piece. When it ended, the whole place gave her a spontaneous standing ovation. Even the orchestra members applauded.

Of course, this had drawn unwanted attention to them, and many people came over to praise Maria's dancing ability. She had become Norwegian again because no one spoke Norwegian.

Sonny and Maria stayed late. They danced, talked, and closed the place. When they went out to the car to leave, a group of drunken officers were singing, "You are My Lucky Star." Maria enjoyed their singing so much that she climbed up on the roof of one of the cars and tap-danced. A crowd gathered around and joined in the singing and clapping.

She did a great dance, and did not even fall off the car. In fact, she did a spectacular dance. After the crowd sang the song two times, she bowed, and the throng in the parking lot went wild with applause again. It was the first tap dance most of them had ever seen done on the roof of a car. She knew it was the first tap dance she had ever performed on the roof of a car. Not even Fred Astair had ever done that. After that night, that became one of their favorite clubs to visit.

One night in late autumn, Sonny decided to take a shortcut back to Frankfurt.

Maria said, "No. Let's just get back."

He said, "Awh come on. The road is headed in the same direction. I'm going to try it."

The road kept getting narrower with deeper ruts. It was a cold evening, and there was a light dusting of snow on the ground. Then, near a cornfield, they slid into a deep rut and got stuck. The car would not budge. There was no sign of a farmhouse anywhere, so they decided that the safest thing to do was stay in the car. It was cold enough that even snuggling did not warm them up, so they spent most of the night talking about their future plans. Sonny had to leave in November. Because his time in the army was about over, he tried to get a civilian job in Frankfurt, but that fell through. He was very concerned about Maria and the baby, but he promised that as soon as he returned to America, he would scrape up the money and send for them. Their kind deception to Anna was holding up. Maria never doubted Sonny because they were so much in love, and he was so excited about the baby. He always loved to pat her stomach and express his pride at being a father.

The next morning a burly man knocking on the car window awakened them. It was the farmer who owned the lane. Maria spoke German to him. He said that he would have to use his horses to help pull them out of the rut. He also asked them to follow him to his house, which was not more than a kilometer away. They could have walked there the previous night had they known that. The farmer and his wife fed them the best breakfast they had ever eaten. They were very curious about America, and they asked Sonny endless questions. He seemed to be a popular item with these rural people.

When they finished breakfast, the farmer used his horses to pull the car out. Sonny offered him twenty marks, but the farmer would not take the money, and he rode off on one of the horses.

November was drawing closer. Sonny had orders to leave about six weeks before Christmas. He and a friend brought Maria and her mother coal again, but this time, he filled the storage area and even put some in the apartment itself. He wanted to be sure that Maria, her mother, and the baby would be warm. They should be able to make it through most of the cold weather with what he brought in several trips.

The day of his departure crept up on them more quickly than they wanted it to. They had decided to say goodbye at the apartment rather than at the railroad station so that Maria would not have to walk back alone.

The two of them embraced in the doorway of the apartment. Sonny had said his farewells to Anna and Maria's brothers. They waited upstairs and left the two of them alone.

They didn't say much. Maria clung to Sonny and sobbed. Sonny hugged Maria as hard as he could. They were hoping that their bodies would become one and that they would not have to part.

"I love you, my little mouse-chen. Try not to cry. It will be a very short time before we will be back together." Sonny tried to comfort her. His eyes were moist too.

"I miss you so much already, and you're not even gone yet. What will I do when you really have to leave?" Maria wept.

"You know that I will send for you as soon as I get the money together," Sonny tried to reassure her. He gently pulled away from her firmly but lovingly, prying himself from her embrace.

Maria slid slowly from his arms. She felt like a drowning person letting go of a lifeline.

Sonny then became animated, jumped toward the jeep, and said, "Got to catch the train. So long, my darling." He kissed Maria one last time and jumped in the jeep. He sprang back out of the jeep, ran back, kissed her again, and bounded back into the Jeep for the last time. He revved the engine and began to pull away. Maria started to run after him, but she stopped and waved her handkerchief. The jeep disappeared around the corner, and she caught the last wave from Sonny as he disappeared.

Maria felt so alone and abandoned even though she knew he would send for her soon. She could not move. She just stood there alone in the doorway, sobbing. She looked around at the ruins of Frankfurt - forlorn.

Sonny went to an officers club close to the railroad station when he arrived there. He was scheduled to go to Bramerhaven. All of the troops scheduled to leave that day were milling around. The locomotive had broken down, and there would be no movement of troops until they could find another engine. So Sonny took advantage of the opportunity, jumped in the jeep and rushed back to say goodbye to Maria once more. It was two hours later, and when he drove up, she was still standing by the mailboxes crying. She was disbelieving, but so happy to see him. She ran into his arms and cried out of happiness. She was a crying mess. They said goodbye all over again. And as he drove off in the jeep, she stood there alone again, crying. Her mother came downstairs and finally persuaded Maria to go in the house and have a cup of coffee.

Chapter 24

Soon, the season slipped into winter. Maria was forced to steal lumber from the reconstruction sights to use as kindling to start the fire in the pot-bellied stove whenever it went out.

Maria did not show her pregnancy much, so she was spared many of the prying, embarrassing questions that were usually aimed at a single pregnant woman. One day, however, in the middle of January, she started to get some cramps. Maria didn't know what they were, but her mother, having given birth to twelve children, knew that they were labor pains.

"Honey. I think those are labor pains," her mother told her.

"They can't be. The baby isn't due for a couple of weeks yet. I have reserved a room at the children's hospital," Maria moaned.

"Well, reservations or not, I think you are going to have a baby." Anna tried to reassure her.

Their doctor had told them that if anything like this ever happened that they could wake him by throwing pebbles at his window. There was no phone service yet.

The contractions were coming closer together. Anna wanted to run to his house, but he lived many blocks from them, and she did not want to leave Maria alone. Maria's contractions were coming closer together. Anna did, however, know a midwife who lived just one block away.

"I'm going to get Lydia," Anna said.

"Oh no. Don't go." Maria continued to moan.

"I've got to. I'll have Frau Kroenig stay with you. It will only be a few minutes." Anna tried to sooth Maria.

Anna breathlessly explained what was happening with Maria. Lydia threw on her coat, grabbed a bag, and followed Anna back to her home.

When she came in the door and examined Maria, she said, "You need to get to the hospital."

"I know, but it's on the outskirts of Frankfurt. There are no taxies." Maria moaned with another spasm.

Lydia said, "Never mind. You're not going to make it to the hospital anyway." She helped Maria out of the bed and had her pace around the room for a while. Then she made Maria lay down for a time. Next, she made her stand up and put her hands on the table palms down.

Lydia told her, "Push down on the table as hard as you can."

Maria paced, she lay down, and then she pushed down on the table. Finally, Lydia made her lay down, and the baby came out very easily. It was a beautiful little baby boy. The birth was no problem for her because Maria's ballet training had put her in top condition. Her mother had boiled pots of water, and had laid out towels and sheets. Lydia cleaned the baby and finished up.

Maria never did have to go to the children's hospital. Besides there was no way she would be admitted for another two weeks because that was when the birth was expected. Although Bobby was a premature, and very tiny at four pounds, the doctor reassured Maria and her mother that he was one of the healthiest babies he had ever seen. She had named him Robert after his father.

The rest of that year was uneventful. Sonny sent boxes of baby clothes though, and when the word about this spectacular gift spread to the neighbors, people came to visit them in droves. Everyone was in awe of this shrine of baby clothes. The opulence of it was so out of place for a people who could not buy food even if they had the resources. The visitors would walk around inside their cardboard box of an apartment feeling the fabric and holding up little pants and shirts. Those who could afford it offered to buy anything and everything. The fact that the stuff came from America made the items even more mysterious. Not a thing was missing. Maria was the proud owner of a "baby clothes museum," and a baby clothes fashion show all in one. Because of the large boxes the clothes came in, she even had extra cardboard to cover the walls. These baby items were such a unique curiosity that Maria thought that she could have charged people to look at them. Best of all, she had the best-dressed baby in all of Germany.

Maria fantasized in her thoughts and dreams how wonderful America must be. If the baby items there were this spectacular, she visualized how grand everything else there had to be.

Winter blended into spring. Spring became summer. And summer cooled into autumn. Maria had stopped producing shows to devote her time to taking care of the baby.

Sonny wrote in March in one of his daily letters that his divorce was complete and that he had raised money to send for her and the baby to come to America. He had purchased boat tickets. Maria and the baby were supposed to leave in June. They were going to take a ship to New York.

However, the ship lines were shut down due to a ship workers' strike. Passenger service between the United States and Europe was stopped.

Each week, Sonny would attempt to buy new tickets, but the strike dragged on month after month. The strike would not end. Finally, in early October, Sonny decided to fly Maria and the baby to America. It was more expensive, but at least they would be reunited sooner. The earliest flight Sonny could book was sometime in December. He could only book a flight for sometime in the month. No specific flight or seats could be confirmed until December came.

For Maria, it seemed like an eternity waiting to be united with Sonny. She spent all of November packing and repacking her suitcases. She couldn't decide what to take and what to leave behind. One day, she would pack an item; the next it sat on the dresser only to be packed again the next day.

The first of December rolled around, and they still couldn't get seats. The flights to America were very popular, and they were always fully booked. However, they were finally able to buy tickets at the beginning of the second week. Maria was thankful because she feared that she might have to wait until sometime the following year to leave. The soonest available flight from Frankfurt to America was on Christmas Eve. She and the baby were scheduled to depart in the early evening hours. She decided with her family that it would probably be easier if they said goodbye at home rather than at the airport.

Maria, her mother, and the whole family gathered at her brother Karl's house for a going-away party. Since it was Christmas Eve, they would have all been together anyway. Furthermore, Christmas Eve was also Anna's birthday. There was much to be thankful for. The war was over, they had all survived it; and they were all together on this special night of love and reverence. However, this Christmas Eve, there was the sadness of a farewell party at the same time. Karl and Heinrich repeated several times that they already missed their baby sister. They might never see her again. They remembered the good times and how they made it through the bad times.

They talked about their father, whom they lost as small children. They hugged, and they drank apple wine. Anna was resigned to the fact that her lifelong daughter, companion, and friend was about to go out of her life. She wept and at the same time hoped and prayed for the best possible future for Maria and the baby. Anna was deeply sad, but she also had the instinct for the preservation of her two babies, Maria and her grandson, that only a mother can have. They all embraced each other, cried, and then laughed.

Maria assured her mother that this separation was only temporary. She promised to visit. She also promised her mother that she would send for her to come and live in America. Maria didn't drink more than two glasses of wine because she wanted to be alert. However, the rest of them became progressively more drunk and maudlin.

One minute, they would speculate about the mystery of America and what her life would be like there. The whole family would all fantasize and become excited. America was still completely intact; it had not been bombed. That fact was a grim reminder whenever they would look out of Karl's window at the rubble-filled lot next to his apartment. The next minute, they would all cry, feeling sorry for themselves.

Karl had found a small pine bough missing half of its needles, and this served as their Christmas tree. It was decorated with a half a dozen or so broken ornaments. There were only a few packages under it wrapped in butcher paper, which was all they could find.

They gathered around the tree. Heinrich handed Maria his gift. She slowly unwrapped it. She sobbed when she saw what it was. He had given her his Saint Christopher pin that he swore had saved his live in Italy and the Swiss Alps. He had vowed that he would never give part with it. Now he wanted her and the baby to be safe forever. She kissed him and thanked him. They both wept.

Next, she slowly pealed the wrapping from the gift hidden in the package that Karl handed her. She wiped her eyes constantly with her handkerchief. It was much larger than the box Heinrich gave her. When she saw it, she blithered even louder. It was an old, yellowed family photograph of all of them sitting with their father in the shiny new car he had bought a month before his death. Karl had made a frame for it from scraps of wood. Maria was weak as she beheld her father wave at her from the picture across those many years.

Then her mother reached under the makeshift Christmas tree and handed Maria a package. This one had a little ribbon around it to make it a little festive.

"I'm almost afraid to look," she cried. She also smiled and tried to laugh as she looked at this dispirited group.

Once again, the family became silent in anticipation. Maria unwrapped it, put the gift down in her lap, and embraced her mother.

"What is it already?" Everyone asked.

"It's mama's favorite pin." Maria wept. It was an exquisite solid gold violin about two inches long.

"Oh no," she was shaking with emotion, "and papa's watch." She held up the intricately hand-carved timepiece. Her mother had managed to save these all throughout the war.

"You have all given me something from your hearts and souls. I know that each of these gifts is precious to each one of you, and they will bring me your love every time I look at them, even when I am thousands of miles away."

"Let's all have some apple wine," Karl shouted as he raised the bottle to fill glasses. "What a dreary group." He turned on the radio and found some Christmas music.

Karl's wife cooked a wonderful dinner, but there was so much meat. Not one of them could figure out where she procured the extra ration stamps for it. It was a delicious feast. In fact, it was more than any of them could eat.

"Tell me Mama," Karl said to his wife, "Where did you get all this meat? Have you been buying from the black market?"

"Well. . .," she dragged the word out, "not exactly." She answered.

"What is it? Beef? Pork? It doesn't taste familiar," Karl said.

"If it is cooked well and tastes good, don't complain. Just eat and enjoy a nice Christmas meal." She tried to divert all the questions.

"No. Come on, tell me. What is it?" He stopped, and a strange expression came over his face. "Is this what I think it is, Mama?"

"What do you think it is?" she asked wiping, her hands on her apron.

"Did you feed us horse meat?" Karl gasped.

"Well. . .," She dragged the word out again. "Yes. You know the government is encouraging people to eat alternative meat because of the shortage of food. You can get a double ration of meat if you buy horse meat."

Maria thought that it tasted fairly good the way Karl's wife had prepared it. Heinrich became sick immediately. Maria thought to herself that it was probably more from the excessive alcohol than the dinner. Anna grabbed her throat and started to gag. She thought it was coarse for Karl's wife not to tell them before they ate. Karl's wife kept telling them how they were all nuts, that no one complained when they ate it. She claimed that it wasn't all that bad. Maria hadn't eaten more than a couple of bites because she was so excited and sad. She thought it tasted good, and she had no other reaction.

Finally, the time for Maria and the baby to leave pressed its way into the gathering. The whole family walked them to the tram stop. They all stood there, hugging and crying.

Karl said, "If you ever need anything, you let me know and we will take care of you."

Everyone was passing the baby around kissing him. Maria kissed each of them one by one as the tram came.

She held her mother at arm's length and said, "I love you most of all. You have been my best friend and my mother. I am so lucky." She pulled Anna to her.

Anna petted the back of Maria's head and cried, "You will be OK, sweetie. We will be together soon. I love you."

"I love you too. I love all of you." She turned to get on the tram.

"*Aufweidersehen,*" they all chimed in unison.

"*Aufweidershehn,*" Maria shouted back. She thought for a moment about the true meaning of the familiar salutation, "upon seeing you again. " She made up her mind that she would abide by the true meaning of the word.

Maria had a sinking feeling in her stomach. It was like the feeling one gets riding a roller coaster. She was full of doubt. Was she doing the right thing leaving her family? Then, in the same moment, she would think of Sonny and her new life in America.

Karl's wife accompanied her to the airport to help her carry her bags. She was elected because she was better at dealing with these matters than any of the rest of them. She was always able to keep her composure. As they rode through the lengthening early evening shadows of Frankfurt, they passed block after block of rubble.

They passed the opera house. The place where Maria had started her career as a little dancing flower lay in ruins. For a split second, she was back there on the stage. She could hear the applause. She saw the ghostly images of the crazy night of Wagner week when she had no idea what she was doing as a page in *Tannhauser.*

She smiled a little smile as she looked out the window and dabbed her eyes with her handkerchief. She wept as the tram passed it.

A few blocks from there, they passed the rubble of the building where her original apartment was. All she could see was the image of the firestorm that consumed most of her city as her feet sank into the pavement. As she looked out the window at her beautiful Germany, all she saw was a country in ruin. She felt as if she had spent most of her life running from hardship. Germany was like a precious antique smashed by some immense monster. She saw, too, a country without enough food to feed its people, people who didn't have a decent place to live or clothes to wear. She did not want to leave her family here, but she wanted a better life, a better place for her child to grow up.

Maria drifted to her moments in all the theaters, those that were so funny and so great. She was there at her curtain calls. As they passed a small Christmas display, she saw herself standing next to the huge Christmas tree in their living room holding her father's coat tails as he lit the candles on it, and she could feel him hugging her.

The tram pulled into the airport. Karl's wife helped Maria unload her bags from the tram. Once the bags were unloaded, she hugged Maria and the baby and boarded the tram to return home.

Maria's plane was supposed to leave at six thirty p.m., but it had a one-hour delay that turned into a two-hour delay because of some refueling delays. She had checked in her two large suitcases and wandered around the airport to pass the time. The terminal had a few paltry decorations that reminded her that this was Christmas Eve. When Maria looked at them, she cried. The harsh sound of a woman's voice over the loudspeaker announced her flight. This made her feel weak. As she walked out to the plane, she wanted to turn and run home to the comfort of her mother's loving arms and the family that cherished her. A choir of children was singing *Silent Night* in the departure terminal.

At the end of the long line, carrying her baby in one arm and a small bag of baby supplies under the other, Maria climbed up the steps to the plane bound for another world. At the platform outside the door, she paused for a moment, and turned to look back at Frankfurt in ruins. The strains of *Silent Night* drifted over the silhouette of the humbled city. A tear ran down her cheek. Then she looked up at the black, crisp, and clear Christmas sky and saw one star brighter than the others that seemed to wink at her. She took her last deep breath of German air and stepped through the airplane door with her baby in her arms and an ache in her heart. She would never have to run again.

ABOUT THE AUTHOR

Before becoming an author, R. H. Miller spent a rewarding career as a college Department Chair/Professor helping students achieve academic success. He enjoys life with his wife of 35 years at their home on the shores of Lake Erie where he draws many of his ideas.

Printed in the United States
105240LV00003B/163-168/A

9 781418 425166